T0179861

NORA ROBERTS

Cold Nights, Warm Hearts

Includes *All I Want for Christmas* & *Captivated*

Silhouette Books

SILHOUETTE™

Cold Nights, Warm Hearts

ISBN-13: 978-1-335-08065-3

Copyright © 2024 by Harlequin Enterprises ULC

All I Want for Christmas
First published in 1994. This edition published in 2024.
Copyright © 1994 by Nora Roberts

Captivated
First published in 1992. This edition published in 2024.
Copyright © 1992 by Nora Roberts

Silhouette
22 Adelaide St. West, 41st Floor
Toronto, Ontario M5H 4E3, Canada
www.Harlequin.com

Printed in U.S.A.

Recycling programs for this product may not exist in your area.

CONTENTS

ALL I WANT FOR CHRISTMAS

To Tom and Ky and Larry, for having the good sense to marry well.

Prologue

Zeke and Zack huddled in the tree house. Important business, any plots or plans, and all punishments for infractions of the rules, were discussed in the sturdy wooden hideaway tucked in the branches of the dignified old sycamore.

Today, a light rain tapped on the tin roof and dampened the dark green leaves. It was still warm enough in the first days of September that the boys wore T-shirts. Red for Zeke, blue for Zack.

They were twins, as identical as the sides of a two-headed coin. Their father had used the color code since their birth to avoid confusion.

When they switched colors—as they often did—they could fool anyone in Taylor's Grove. Except their father.

He was on their minds at the moment. They had already discussed, at length, the anticipated delights and terrors of their first day in real school. The first day in first grade.

They would ride the bus, as they had done the year before, in kindergarten. But this time they would stay in Taylor's Grove Elementary for a full day, just like the big kids. Their cousin Kim had told them that *real* school wasn't a playground.

Zack, the more introspective of the two, had thought over,

worried about and dissected this problem for weeks. There were terrible, daunting terms like *homework* and *class participation,* that Kim tossed around. They knew that she, a sophomore in high school, was often loaded down with books. Big, thick books with no pictures.

And sometimes, when she was babysitting for them, she had her nose stuck in them for hours. For as long a time as she would have the telephone stuck to her ear, and that was long.

It was pretty scary stuff for Zack, the champion worrier.

Their father would help them, of course. This was something Zeke, the eternal optimist, had pointed out. Didn't they both know how to read stuff like *Green Eggs and Ham* and *The Cat in the Hat* because their dad helped them sound out the words? And they both knew how to write the whole alphabet, and their names and short things, because he showed them.

The trouble was, he had to work and take care of the house and them, as well as Commander Zark, the big yellow dog they'd saved from the animal shelter two years before. Their dad had, as Zack pointed out, an awful lot to do. And now that they were going to go to school, and have assignments and projects and real report cards, he was going to need help.

"He's got Mrs. Hollis to come in once a week and do stuff." Zeke ran his miniature Corvette around the imaginary race-track on the tree-house floor.

"It's not enough." A frown puckered Zack's forehead and clouded his lake-blue eyes. He exhaled with a long-suffering sigh, ruffling the dark hair that fell over his forehead. "He needs the companionship of a good woman, and we need a mother's love. I heard Mrs. Hollis say so to Mr. Perkins at the post office."

"He hangs around with Aunt Mira sometimes. She's a good woman."

"But she doesn't live with us. And she doesn't have time to help us with science projects." Science projects were a particular terror for Zack. "We need to find a mom." When Zeke only snorted, Zack narrowed his eyes. "We're going to have to spell in first grade."

Zeke caught his lower lip between his teeth. Spelling was his personal nightmare. "How're we going to find one?"

Now Zack smiled. He had, in his slow, careful way, figured it all out. "We're going to ask Santa Claus."

"He doesn't bring moms," Zeke said with the deep disdain that can only be felt by one sibling for another. "He brings toys and stuff. And it's forever until Christmas, anyway."

"No, it's not. Mrs. Hollis was bragging to Mr. Perkins how she already had half her Christmas shopping done. She said how looking ahead meant you could enjoy the holiday."

"Everybody enjoys Christmas. It's the best."

"Uh-uh. Lots of people get mad. Remember how we went to the mall last year with Aunt Mira and she complained and complained about the crowds and the prices and how there weren't any parking spaces?"

Zeke merely shrugged. He didn't look back as often, or as clearly, as his twin, but he took Zack at his word. "I guess."

"So, if we ask now, Santa'll have plenty of time to find the right mom."

"I still say he doesn't bring moms."

"Why not? If we really need one, and we don't ask for too much else?"

"We were going to ask for two-wheelers," Zeke reminded him.

"We could still ask for them," Zack decided. "But not a bunch of other things. Just a mom and the bikes."

It was Zeke's turn to sigh. He didn't care for the idea of giving up his big, long list. But the idea of a mother was beginning to appeal. They'd never had one, and the mystery of it attracted. "So what kind do we ask for?"

"We got to write it down."

Zack took a notebook and a stubby pencil from the table pushed against the wall. They sat on the floor and, with much argument and discussion, composed.

Dear Santa,
We have been good.

Zeke wanted to put in *very good,* but Zack, the conscience, rejected the idea.

We feed Zark and help Dad. We want a mom for Criss-mas. A nice one who smells good and is not meen. She can smile a lot and have yello hair. She has to like little boys and big dogs. She wont mind dirt and bakes cookys. We want a pretty one who is smart and helps us with homework. We will take good care of her. We want biks a red one and a bloo one. You have lots of time to find the mom and make the biks so you can enjoi the hollidays. Thank you. Love, Zeke and Zack.

Chapter One

Taylor's Grove, population two thousand three hundred and forty. No, forty-one, Nell thought smugly, as she strolled into the high school auditorium. She'd only been in town for two months, but already she was feeling territorial. She loved the slow pace, the tidy yards and little shops. She loved the easy gossip of neighbors, the front-porch swings, the frost-heaved sidewalks.

If anyone had told her, even a year before, that she would be trading in Manhattan for a dot on the map in western Maryland, she would have thought them mad. But here she was, Taylor's Grove High's new music teacher, as snug and settled in as an old hound in front of a fire.

She'd needed the change, that was certain. In the past year she'd lost her roommate to marriage and inherited a staggering rent she simply wasn't able to manage on her own. The replacement roommate, whom Nell had carefully interviewed, had moved out, as well. Taking everything of value out of the apartment. That nasty little adventure had led to the final, even nastier showdown with her almost-fiancé. When Bob berated her, called her stupid, naive and careless, Nell had decided it was time to cut her losses.

She'd hardly given Bob his walking papers when she received her own. The school where she had taught for three years was downsizing, as they had euphemistically put it. The position of music teacher had been eliminated, and so had Nell.

An apartment she could no longer afford, all but empty, a fiancé who had considered her optimistic nature a liability and the prospect of the unemployment line had taken the sheen off New York.

Once Nell decided to move, she'd decided to move big. The idea of teaching in a small town had sprung up fully rooted. An inspiration, she thought now, for she already felt as if she'd lived here for years.

Her rent was low enough that she could live alone and like it. Her apartment, the entire top floor of a remodeled old house, was a short, enjoyable walk from a campus that included elementary, middle and high schools.

Only two weeks after that first nervous day of school, she was feeling proprietary about her students and was looking forward to her first after-school session with her chorus.

She was determined to create a holiday program that would knock the town's socks off.

The battered piano was center stage. She walked to it and sat. Her students would be filing in shortly, but she had a moment.

She limbered up her mind and her fingers with the blues, an old Muddy Waters tune. Old, scarred pianos were meant to play the blues, she thought, and enjoyed herself.

"Man, she's so cool," Holly Linstrom murmured to Kim as they slipped into the rear of the auditorium.

"Yeah." Kim had a hand on the shoulder of each of her twin cousins, a firm grip that ordered quiet and promised reprisals. "Old Mr. Striker never played anything like that."

"And her clothes are so, like, now." Admiration and envy mixed as Holly scanned the pipe-stem pants, long overshirt and short striped vest Nell wore. "I don't know why anybody from New York would come here. Did you see her earrings today? I bet she got them at some hot place on Fifth Avenue."

Nell's jewelry had already become legendary among the female students. She wore the unique and the unusual. Her taste in clothes, her dark gold hair, which fell just short of her shoulders and always seemed miraculously and expertly tousled, her quick, throaty laugh and her lack of formality had already gone a long way toward endearing her to her students.

"She's got style, all right." But, just then, Kim was more intrigued by the music than by the musician's wardrobe. "Man, I wish I could play like that."

"Man, I wish I could look like that," Holly returned, and giggled.

Sensing an audience, Nell glanced back and grinned. "Come on in, girls. Free concert."

"It sounds great, Miss Davis." With her grip firm on her two charges, Kim started down the sloping aisle toward the stage. "What is it?"

"Muddy Waters. We'll have to shoehorn a little blues education into the curriculum." Sitting back, she studied the two sweet-faced boys on either side of Kim. There was a quick, odd surge of recognition that she didn't understand. "Well, hi, guys."

When they smiled back, identical dimples popped out on the left side of their mouths. "Can you play 'Chopsticks'?" Zeke wanted to know.

Before Kim could express her humiliation at the question, Nell spun into a rousing rendition.

"How's that?" she asked when she'd finished.

"That's neat."

"I'm sorry, Miss Davis. I'm kind of stuck with them for an hour. They're my cousins. Zeke and Zack Taylor."

"The Taylors of Taylor's Grove." Nell swiveled away from the piano. "I bet you're brothers. I see a slight family resemblance."

Both boys grinned and giggled. "We're twins," Zack informed her.

"Really? Now I bet I'm supposed to guess who's who." She came to the edge of the stage, sat and eyed the boys narrowly. They grinned back. Each had recently lost a left front tooth. "Zeke," she said, pointing a finger. "And Zack."

Pleased and impressed, they nodded. "How'd you know?"

It was pointless, and hardly fun, to mention that she'd had a fifty-fifty shot. "Magic. Do you guys like to sing?"

"Sort of. A little."

"Well, today you can listen. You can sit right in the front row and be our test audience."

"Thanks, Miss Davis," Kim murmured, and gave the boys a friendly shove toward the seats. "They're pretty good most of the time. Stay," she ordered, with an older cousin's absolute authority.

Nell winked at the boys as she stood, then gestured to the other students filing in. "Come on up. Let's get started."

A lot of the business onstage seemed boring to the twins. There was just talking at first, and confusion as sheet music was passed out and boys and girls were assigned positions.

But Zack was watching Nell. She had pretty hair and nice big brown eyes. Like Zark's, he thought with deep affection. Her voice was kind of funny, sort of scratchy and deep, but nice. Now and again she looked back toward him and smiled. When she did, his heart acted strange, kind of beating hard, like he'd been running.

She turned to a group of girls and sang. It was a Christmas song, which made Zack's eyes widen. He wasn't sure of the name, something about a midnight clear, but he recognized it from the records his dad played around the holiday.

A Christmas song. A Christmas wish.

"It's her." He hissed it to his brother, rapping Zeke hard in the ribs.

"Who?"

"It's the mom."

Zeke stopped playing with the action figure he'd had stuck in his pocket and looked up onstage, where Nell was now directing the alto section. "Kim's teacher is the mom?"

"She has to be." Deadly excited, Zeke kept his voice in a conspiratorial whisper. "Santa's had enough time to get the letter. She was singing a Christmas song, and she's got yellow hair and a nice smile. She likes little boys, too. I can tell."

"Maybe." Not quite convinced, Zeke studied Nell. She was pretty, he thought. And she laughed a lot, even when some of the big kids made mistakes. But that didn't mean she liked dogs or baked cookies. "We can't know for sure yet."

Zack huffed out an impatient breath. "She knew us. She knew which was which. Magic." His eyes were solemn as he looked at his brother. "It's the mom."

"Magic," Zeke repeated, and stared, goggle-eyed, at Nell. "Do we have to wait till Christmas to get her?"

"I guess so. Probably." That was a puzzle Zack would have to work on.

When Mac Taylor pulled his pickup truck in front of the high school, his mind was on a dozen varied problems. What to fix the kids for dinner. How to deal with the flooring on his Meadow Street project. When to find a couple hours to drive to the mall and pick up new underwear for the boys. The last time he folded laundry, he'd noticed that most of what they had was doomed for the rag pile. He had to deal with a lumber delivery first thing in the morning and a pile of paperwork that night.

And Zeke was nervous about his first spelling test, which was coming up in a few days.

Pocketing his keys, Mac rolled his shoulders. He'd been

swinging a hammer for the better part of eight hours. He didn't mind the aches. It was a good kind of fatigue, a kind that meant he'd accomplished something. His renovation of the house on Meadow Street was on schedule and on budget. Once it was done, he would have to decide whether to put it on the market or rent it.

His accountant would try to decide for him, but Mac knew the final choice would remain in his own hands. That was the way he preferred it.

As he strode from the parking lot to the high school, he looked around. His great-great-grandfather had founded the town—hardly more than a village back then, settled along Taylor's Creek and stretching over the rolling hills to Taylor's Meadow.

There'd been no lack of ego in old Macauley Taylor.

But Mac had lived in D.C. for more than twelve years. It had been six years since he returned to Taylor's Grove, but he hadn't lost his pleasure or his pride in it, the simple appreciation for the hills and the trees and the shadows of mountains in the distance.

He didn't think he ever would.

There was the faintest of chills in the air now, and a good strong breeze from the west. But they had yet to have a frost, and the leaves were still a deep summer green. The good weather made his life easier on a couple of levels. As long as it held, he'd be able to finish the outside work on his project in comfort. And the boys could enjoy the afternoons and evenings in the yard.

There was a quick twinge of guilt as he pulled open the heavy doors and stepped into the school. His work had kept them stuck inside this afternoon. The coming of fall meant that his sister was diving headfirst into several of her community projects. He couldn't impose on her by asking her to watch the twins. Kim's after-school schedule was filling up, and he simply couldn't accept the idea of having his children becoming latchkey kids.

Still, the solution had suited everyone. Kim would take the kids to her rehearsals, and he would save his sister a trip to school by picking them all up and driving them home.

Kim would have a driver's license in a few more months. A fact she was reminding everyone about constantly. But he doubted he'd plunk his boys down in the car with his sixteen-year-old niece at the wheel, no matter how much he loved and trusted her.

You coddle them. Mac rolled his eyes as his sister's voice played in his head. *You can't always be mother and father to them, Mac. If you're not interested in finding a wife, then you'll have to learn to let go a little.*

Like hell he would, Mac thought.

As he neared the auditorium, he heard the sound of young voices raised in song. Subtle harmony. A good, emotional sound that made him smile even before he recognized the tune. A Christmas hymn. It was odd to hear it now, with the sweat from his day just drying on his back.

He pulled open the auditorium doors, and was flooded with it. Charmed, he stood at the back and looked out on the singers. One of the students played the piano. A pretty little thing, Mac mused, who looked up now and then, gesturing, as if to urge her classmates to give more.

He wondered where the music teacher was, then spotted his boys sitting in the front row. He walked quietly down the aisle, raising a hand when he saw Kim's eyes shift to his. He settled behind the boys and leaned forward.

"Pretty good show, huh?"

"Dad!" Zack nearly squealed, then remembered just in time to speak in a hissing whisper. "It's Christmas."

"Sure sounds like it. How's Kim doing?"

"She's real good." Zeke now considered himself an expert on choral arrangements. "She's going to have a solo."

"No kidding?"

"She got red in the face when Miss Davis asked her to sing by herself, but she did okay." Zeke was much more interested in Nell right then. "She's pretty, isn't she?"

A little amazed at this announcement—the twins were fond of Kim, but rarely complimentary—he nodded. "Yeah. The prettiest girl in school."

"We could have her over for dinner sometime," Zack said slyly. "Couldn't we?"

Baffled now, Mac ruffled his son's hair. "You know Kim can come over whenever she wants."

"Not her." In a gesture that mimicked his father, Zack rolled his eyes. "Jeez, Dad. Miss Davis."

"Who's Miss Davis?"

"The m—" Zeke's announcement was cut off by his twin's elbow.

"The teacher," Zack finished with a snarling look at his brother. "The pretty one." He pointed, and his father followed the direction to the piano.

"She's the teacher?" Before Mac could reevaluate, the music flowed to a stop and Nell rose.

"That was great, really. A very solid first run-through." She pushed her tousled hair back. "But we need a lot of work. I'd like to schedule the next rehearsal for Monday after school. Three forty-five."

There was already a great deal of movement and mumbling, so Nell pitched her voice to carry the rest of her instructions over the noise. Satisfied, she turned to smile at the twins and found herself grinning at an older, and much more disturbing version, of the Taylor twins.

No doubt he was the father, Nell thought. The same thick dark hair curled down over the collar of a grimy T-shirt. The same lake-water eyes framed in long, dark lashes stared back at her. His face might lack the soft, slightly rounded appeal of his sons', but the more rugged version was just as attractive. He was long, rangy, with the kind of arms that looked tough without being obviously muscled. He was tanned and more than a little dirty. She wondered if he had a dimple at the left corner of his mouth when he smiled.

"Mr. Taylor." Rather than bother with the stairs, she hopped off the stage, as agile as any of her students. She held out a hand decorated with rings.

"Miss Davis." He covered her hand with his callused one, remembering too late that it was far from clean. "I appreciate you letting the kids hang out while Kim rehearsed."

"No problem. I work better with an audience." Tilting her head, she looked down at the twins. "Well, guys, how'd we do?"

"It was really neat." This from Zeke. "We like Christmas songs the best."

"Me, too."

Still flustered and flattered by the idea of having a solo, Kim joined them. "Hi, Uncle Mac. I guess you met Miss Davis."

"Yeah." There wasn't much more to say. He still thought she looked too young to be a teacher. Not the teenager he'd taken her for, he realized. But that creamy, flawless skin and that tidy little frame were deceiving. And very attractive.

"Your niece is very talented." In a natural movement, Nell wrapped an arm around Kim's shoulders. "She has a wonderful voice and a quick understanding of what the music means. I'm delighted to have her."

"We like her, too," Mac said as Kim flushed.

Zack shifted from foot to foot. They weren't supposed to be talking about dumb old Kim. "Maybe you could come visit us sometime, Miss Davis," he piped up. "We live in the big brown house out on Mountain View Road."

"That'd be nice." But Nell noted that Zack's father didn't second the invitation, or look particularly pleased by it. "And you guys are welcome to be our audience anytime. You work on that solo, Kim."

"I will, Miss Davis. Thanks."

"Nice to have met you, Mr. Taylor." As he mumbled a response, Nell hopped back onstage to gather her sheet music.

It was too bad, she thought, that the father lacked the outgoing charm and friendliness of his sons.

Chapter Two

It didn't get much better than a drive in the country on a balmy fall afternoon. Nell remembered how she used to spend a free Saturday in New York. A little shopping—she supposed if she missed anything about Manhattan, it was the shopping—maybe a walk in the park. Never a jog. Nell didn't believe in running if walking would get you to the same place.

And driving, well, that was even better. She hadn't realized what a pleasure it was to not only own a car but be able to zip it along winding country roads with the windows open and the radio blaring.

The leaves were beginning to turn now as September hit its stride. Blushes of color competed with the green. On one particular road that she turned down out of impulse, the big trees arched over the asphalt, a spectacular canopy that let light flicker and flit through as the road followed the snaking trail of a rushing creek.

It wasn't until she glanced up at a road sign that she realized she was on Mountain View.

The big brown house, Zack had said, she remembered. There weren't a lot of houses here, two miles outside of town, but she caught glimpses of some through the shading trees. Brown ones, white ones, blue ones—some close to the creek bed, others high atop narrow, pitted lanes that served as driveways.

A lovely place to live, she thought. And to raise children. However taciturn and stiff Mac Taylor might have been, he'd done a wonderful job with his sons.

She already knew he'd done the job alone. It hadn't taken long for Nell to understand the rhythm of small towns. A comment here, a casual question there, and she'd had what amounted to a full biography of the Taylor men.

Mac had lived in Washington, D.C., since his family moved out of town when he was a young teenager. Six years ago, twin infants in tow, he'd moved back. His older sister had gone to a local college and married a town boy and settled in Taylor's Grove years before. It was she, the consensus was, who had urged him to come back and raise his children there when his wife took off.

Left the poor little infants high and dry, Mrs. Hollis had told Nell over the bread rack at the general store. Run off with barely a word, and hadn't said a peep since. And young Macauley Taylor had been mother and father both to his twins ever since.

Maybe, Nell thought cynically, just maybe, if he'd actually talked to his wife now and again, she'd have stayed with him.

Not fair, she thought. There was no decent excuse she could think of for a mother deserting her infant children, then not contacting them for six years. Whatever kind of husband Mac Taylor had been, the children deserved better.

She thought of them now, those impish mirror images. She'd always been fond of children, and the Taylor twins were a double dose of enjoyment. She'd gotten quite a kick out of having them in the audience once or twice a week during rehearsals. Zeke had even shown her his very first spelling test—with its big silver star. If he hadn't missed just one word, he'd told her, he'd have gotten a gold one.

Nor had she missed the shy looks Zack sent her, or the quick smiles before he flushed and lowered his eyes. It was very sweet to be responsible for his first case of puppy love.

She sighed with pleasure as the car burst out from under the canopy of trees and into the light. Here were the mountains that gave the road its name, streaking suddenly into the vivid blue sky. The road curved and snaked, but they were always there, dark, distant and dramatic.

The land rose on either side of the road, in rolling hills and rocky outcroppings. She slowed when she spotted a house on the crest of a hill. Brown. Probably cedar, she thought, with a stone foundation and what seemed like acres of sparkling glass. There was a deck stretched across the second story, and there were trees that shaded and sheltered. A tire swing hung from one.

She wondered if this was indeed the Taylor house. She hoped her new little friends lived in such a solid, well-planned home. Then she passed the mailbox planted at the side of the road just at the edge of the long lane.

M. Taylor and sons.

It made her smile. Pleased, she punched the gas pedal and was baffled when the car bucked and stuttered.

"What's the problem here?" she muttered, easing off on the pedal and punching it again. This time the car shuddered and stopped dead. "For heaven's sake." Only mildly annoyed, she started to turn the key to start it again, and glanced at the dash. The little gas pump beside the gauge was brightly lit.

"Stupid," she said aloud, berating herself. "Stupid, stupid. Weren't you supposed to get gas *before* you left town?" She sat back, sighed. She'd meant to, really. Just as she'd meant to stop and fill up the day before, right after class.

Now she was two miles out of town without even fumes to ride on. Blowing the hair out of her eyes, she looked out at the home of M. Taylor and sons. A quarter-mile hike, she estimated. Which made it a lot better than two miles. And she had, more or less, been invited.

She grabbed her keys and started up the lane.

She was no more than halfway when the boys spotted her. They came racing down the rocky, pitted lane at a speed that stopped her heart. Surefooted as young goats, they streaked toward her. Coming up behind was a huge yellow dog.

"Miss Davis! Hi, Miss Davis! Did you come to see us?"

"Sort of." Laughing, she crouched down to give them both a hug and caught the faint scent of chocolate. Before she could comment, the dog decided he wanted in on the action. He was restrained enough to plant his huge paws on her thighs, rather than her shoulders.

Zack held his breath, then let it out when she chuckled and bent down to rub Zark on head and shoulders. "You're a big one, aren't you? A big beauty."

Zark lapped her hand in perfect agreement. Nell caught a look exchanged quickly between the twins. One that seemed both smug and excited.

"You like dogs?" Zeke asked.

"Sure I do. Maybe I'll get one now. I never had the heart to lock one up in a New York apartment." She only laughed again when Zark sat and politely lifted a paw. "Too late for formalities now, buddy," she told him, but shook it anyway. "I was out driving, and I ran out of gas right smack at the bottom of your lane. Isn't that funny?"

Zack's grin nearly split his face. She liked dogs. She'd stopped right at their house. It was more magic, he was sure of it. "Dad'll fix it. He can fix anything." Confident now that he had her on his own ground, Zack took her hand. Not to be outdone, Zeke clasped the other.

"Dad's out back in the shop, building a 'rondak chair."

"A rocking chair?" Nell suggested.

"Nuh-uh. A 'rondak chair. Come see."

They hauled her around the house, passed a curving sun-room that caught the southern light. There was another deck in the back, with steps leading down to a flagstone patio. The shop in the backyard—the same cedar as the house—looked big enough to hold a family of four. Nell heard the thwack of a hammer on wood.

Bursting with excitement, Zeke raced through the shop door. "Dad! Dad! Guess what?"

"I guess you've taken another five years off my life."

Nell heard Mac's voice, deep and amused and tolerant, and found herself hesitating. "I hate to bother him when he's busy," she said to Zeke. "Maybe I can just call the station in town."

"It's okay, come on." Zack dragged her a few more feet into the doorway.

"See?" Zeke said importantly. "She came!"

"Yeah, I see." Caught off balance by the unexpected visit, Mac set his hammer down on his workbench. He pushed up the brim of his cap and frowned without really meaning to. "Miss Davis."

"I'm sorry to bother you, Mr. Taylor," she began, then saw the project he was working on. "An Adirondack chair," she murmured, and grinned. "A 'rondak chair. It's nice."

"Will be." Was he supposed to offer her coffee? he wondered. A tour of the house? What? She shouldn't be pretty, he thought irrelevantly. There was nothing particularly striking about her. Well, maybe the eyes. They were so big and brown. But the rest really was ordinary. It must be the way it was put together, he decided, that made it extraordinary.

Not certain whether she was amused or uncomfortable at the way he was staring at her, Nell launched into her explanation. "I was out driving. Partly for the pleasure of it, and partly to try to familiarize myself with the area. I've only lived here a couple months."

"Is that right?"

"Miss Davis is from New York City, Dad," Zack reminded him. "Kim told you."

"Yeah, she did." He picked up his hammer again, set it down. "Nice day for a drive."

"I thought so. So nice I forgot to get gas before I left town. I ran out at the bottom of your lane."

A flicker of suspicion darkened his eyes. "That's handy."

"Not especially." Her voice, though still friendly, had cooled. "If I could use your phone to call the station in town, I'd appreciate it."

"I've got gas," he muttered.

"See, I told you Dad could fix it," Zack said proudly. "We've got brownies," he added, struggling madly for a way to get her to stay longer. "Dad made them. You can have one."

"I thought I smelled chocolate." She scooped Zack up and sniffed at his face. "I've got a real nose for it."

Moving on instinct, Mac plucked Zack out of her arms. "You guys go get some brownies. We'll get the gas."

"Okay!" They raced off together.

"I wasn't going to abduct him, Mr. Taylor."

"Didn't say you were." He walked to the doorway, glanced back. "The gas is in the shed."

Lips pursed, she followed him out. "Were you traumatized by a teacher at an impressionable age, Mr. Taylor?"

"Mac. Just Mac. No, why?"

"I wondered if we have a personal or a professional problem here."

"I don't have a problem." He stopped at the small shed where he kept his lawn mower and garden tools, then said, "Funny how the kids told you where we lived, and you ran out of gas right here."

She took a long breath, studying him as he bent over to pick up a can, straighten and turn. "Look, I'm no happier about it than you, and after this reception, probably a lot less happy. It happens that this is the first car I've ever owned, and I'm still a little rough on the finer points. I ran out of gas last month in front of the general store. You're welcome to check."

He shrugged, feeling stupid and unnecessarily prickly. "Sorry."

"Forget it. If you'll give me the can, I'll use what I need to get back to town, then I'll have it filled and returned."

"I'll take care of it," he muttered.

"I don't want to put you out." She reached for the can and that started a quick tug-of-war. After a moment, the dimple at the corner of his mouth winked.

"I'm bigger than you."

She stepped back and blew the hair out of her eyes. "Fine. Go be a man, then." Scowling, she followed him around the house, then tried to fight off her foul mood as the twins came racing up. They each held a paper towel loaded with brownies.

"Dad makes the best brownies in the whole world," Zack told her, holding up his offering.

Nell took one and bit in. "You may be right," she was forced to admit, her mouth full. "And I know my brownies."

"Can you make cookies?" Zeke wanted to know.

"I happened to be known far and wide for my chocolate-chip." Her smile became puzzled as the boys eyed each other and nodded. "You come visit me sometime, and we'll whip some up."

"Where do you live?" Since his father wasn't paying close attention, Zeke stuffed an entire brownie in his mouth.

"On Market Street, right off the square. The old brick house with the three porches. I rent the top floor."

"Dad owns that," Zack told her. "He bought it and fixed it all up and now he rents it out. We're in real estate."

"Oh." She let out a long breath. "Really." Her rent checks were mailed to Taylor Management…on Mountain View Road.

"So you live in our house," Zack finished up.

"In a manner of speaking."

"The place okay with you?" Mac asked.

"Yes, it's fine. I'm very comfortable there. It's convenient to school."

"Dad buys houses and fixes them up all the time." Zeke wondered if he could get away with another brownie. "He likes to fix stuff."

It was obvious from the tidy and thoughtful renovation of the old house she now lived in that their father fixed them very well. "You're a carpenter, then?" she asked, reluctantly addressing Mac.

"Sometimes." They'd reached her car. Mac merely jerked his thumb to signal the boys and dog to keep off the road. He unscrewed the gas cap and spoke without looking around. "If you eat another one of those, Zeke, I'm going to have to have your stomach pumped."

Sheepishly Zeke replaced the brownie on the paper towel.

"Excellent radar," Nell commented, leaning on the car as Mac added the gas.

"Goes with the territory." He looked at her then. Her hair was windblown and gilded by the sun. Her face was rosy from the walk and the breeze. He didn't like what looking at her did to his pulse rate. "Why Taylor's Grove? It's a long way from New York."

"That's why. I wanted a change." She breathed deep as she looked around, at rock and tree and hill. "I got one."

"Pretty slow, compared to what you'd be used to."

"Slow's something I do very well."

He only shrugged. He suspected she'd be bored senseless in six months and heading out. "Kim's pretty excited about your class. She talks about it almost as much as she does getting her driver's license."

"That's quite a compliment. It's a good school. Not all of my students are as cooperative as Kim, but I like a challenge. I'm going to recommend her for all-state."

Mac tipped the can farther up. "She's really that good?"

"You sound surprised."

He shrugged again. "She always sounded good to me, but the old music teacher never singled her out."

"Rumor is he never took much interest in any of his students individually, or in extra work."

"You got that right. Striker was an old—" He caught himself, glanced back at his kids, who were standing close by, all ears. "He was old," Mac repeated. "And set in his ways. Always the same Christmas program, the same spring program."

"Yes, I've looked over his class notes. I'd say everyone should be in for a surprise this year. I'm told no student from Taylor's Grove ever went to all-state."

"Not that I heard."

"Well, we're going to change that." Satisfied now that they had managed a reasonable conversation, she tossed back her hair. "Do you sing?"

"In the shower." His dimple flickered again as his sons giggled. "No comments from the brats."

"He sings really, really loud," Zeke said, without fear of reprisal. "And he gets Zark howling."

"I'm sure that would be quite a show." Nell scratched the grinning dog between the ears. He thumped his tail, and then some internal clock struck and had him pivoting and racing up the hill.

"Here you go, Miss Davis. Here." Both boys stuffed the loaded paper towels into her hands and barreled off after the dog.

"I guess they don't keep still very long," she murmured, watching them chase the dog up the rise.

"That was nearly a record. They like you."

"I'm a likable person." She smiled, glancing back at him, only to find him staring at her again with that not-quite-pleased look in his eyes. "At least in most cases. If you'd just put that on the backseat, I'll have it filled up for you."

"It's not a problem." Mac replaced her gas cap and kept the empty can. "We're friendly in Taylor's Grove. In most cases."

"Let me know when I'm off probation." She leaned into her car to set the brownies on the passenger seat. Mac had a tantalizing and uncomfortable view of her jean-clad bottom. He could smell her, too, something light and spicy that spun in his head a lot more potently than the gas fumes.

"I didn't mean it like that."

Her head popped back out of the car. She licked a smear of brownie from her finger as she straightened. "Maybe not. In any case, I appreciate the help." Her grin flashed as she opened the car door. "And the chocolate."

"Anytime," he heard himself say, and wanted to regret it.

She settled behind the steering wheel, tossed him a quick, saucy smile. "Like hell." Then she laughed and turned the ignition, revving the engine in a way that made Mac wince. "You should drop in on rehearsals now and again, Mac, instead of waiting out in the parking lot. You might learn something."

He wasn't certain he wanted to. "Put on your seat belt," he ordered.

"Oh, yeah." Obligingly, she buckled up. "Just not used to it yet. Say bye to the twins." She zoomed off at a speed just this side of reckless, waving a careless and glittering hand out the window.

Mac watched her until she rounded the bend, then slowly rubbed his stomach where the muscles were knotted. Something about that woman, he thought. Something about the way she was put together made him feel like he was defrosting after a very long freeze.

Chapter Three

Another half hour, Mac figured, and he could finish taping the drywall in the master bedroom. Maybe get the first coat of mud on. He glanced at his watch, calculated that the kids were home from school. But it was Mrs. Hollis's day, and she'd stay until five. That would give him plenty of time to hit the drywall, clean up and get home.

Maybe he'd give himself and the kids a treat and pick up pizza.

He'd learned not to mind cooking, but he still resented the time it took—the thinking, the preparation, the cleaning up afterward. Six years as a single parent had given him a whole new perspective on how hard his mother—that rare and old-fashioned homemaker—had worked.

Pausing a moment, he took a look around the master suite. He'd taken walls out, built others, replaced the old single-pane windows with double glazed. Twin skylights let in the fading sunlight of early October.

Now there were three spacious bedrooms on the second floor of the old house, rather than the four choppy rooms and over-size hallway he'd started with. The master suite would boast a bathroom large enough for tub and separate shower stall. He was toying with using glass block for that. He'd been wanting to work with it for some time.

If he stayed on schedule, the place would be put together by Christmas, and on the sale or rental market by the first of the year.

He really should sell it, Mac thought, running a hand over the drywall he'd nailed up that afternoon. He had to get over this sense of possession whenever he worked on a house.

In the blood, he supposed. His father had made a good living buying up damaged or depressed property, rehabing and renting. Mac had discovered just how satisfying it was to own something you'd made fine with your own hands.

Like the old brick house Nell lived in now. He wondered if she knew it was more than a hundred and fifty years old, that she was living in a piece of history.

He wondered if she'd run out of gas again.

He wondered quite a bit about Nell Davis.

And he shouldn't, Mac reminded himself, and turned away for his tools and tape. Women were trouble. One way or the other, they were trouble. One look at Nell and a smart man could see she was no exception.

He hadn't taken her up on her suggestion that he drop by the auditorium and catch part of a rehearsal. He'd started to a couple of times, but good sense had stopped him. She was the first woman in a very, very long time who had stirred him up. He didn't want to be stirred up, Mac thought with a scowl as he taped a seam. Couldn't afford to be, he reminded himself. He had too many obligations, too little free time, and, most important, two sons who were the focus of his life.

Daydreaming about a woman was bad enough. It made a man sloppy in his work, forgetful and…itchy. But doing something about it was worse. Doing something meant you had to find conversation and ways to entertain. A woman expected to be taken places, and pampered. And once you started to

fall for her—really fall for her—she had the power to cut out
your heart.

Mac wasn't willing to risk his heart again, and he certainly
wasn't willing to risk his sons.

He didn't subscribe to that nonsense about children need-
ing a woman's touch, a mother's love. The twins' mother had
felt less connection with the children she'd borne than a cat
felt toward a litter of kittens. Being female didn't give you a
leg up on maternal feelings. It meant you were physically able
to carry a child inside you, but it didn't mean that you'd care
once that child was in your arms.

Mac stopped taping and swore. He hadn't thought about
Angie in years. Not deeply. When he did, he realized the spot
was still sore, like an old wound that had healed poorly. That
was what he got, he supposed, for letting some little blonde stir
him up.

Annoyed with himself, he stripped the last piece of tape
off the roll. He needed to concentrate on his work, not on a
woman. Determined to finish what he'd started, he marched
down the stairs. He had more drywall tape in his truck.

The light outside was softening with the approach of dusk.
Shorter days, he thought. Less time.

He was down the steps and onto the walk before he saw her.
She was standing just at the edge of the yard, looking up at the
house, smiling a little. She wore a suede jacket in a deep bur-
nished orange over faded jeans. Some glittery stones dangled
from her ears. Over her shoulder hung a soft-sided briefcase
that looked well used.

"Oh. Hi." Surprise lit her eyes when she glanced over, and
that immediately made him suspicious. "Is this one of your
places?"

"That's right." He moved past her toward the truck and
wished he'd held his breath. That scent she wore was subtle
and sneaky.

"I was just admiring it. Beautiful stonework. It looks so sturdy and safe, tucked in with all the trees." She took a deep breath. There was the slap of fall in the air. "It's going to be a beautiful night."

"I guess." He found his tape, then stood, running the roll around in his hands. "Did you run out of gas again?"

"No." She laughed, obviously amused at herself. "I like walking around town this time of day. As a matter of fact, I was heading down to your sister's. She's a few doors down, right?"

His eyes narrowed. He didn't like the idea of the woman he was spending too much time thinking about hanging out with his sister. "Yeah, that's right. Why?"

"Why?" Her attention had been focused on his hands. There was something about them. Hard, callused. Big. She felt a quick and very pleasant flutter in the pit of her stomach. "Why what?"

"Why are you going to Mira's?"

"Oh. I have some sheet music I thought Kim would like."

"Is that right?" He leaned on the truck, measuring her. Her smile was entirely too friendly, he decided. Entirely too attractive. "Is it part of your job description to make house calls with sheet music?"

"It's part of the fun." Her hair ruffled in the light breeze. She scooped it back. "No job's worth the effort or the headaches if you don't have some fun." She looked back at the house. "You have fun, don't you? Taking something and making it yours?"

He started to say something snide, then realized she'd put her finger right on the heart of it. "Yeah. It doesn't always seem like fun when you're tearing out ceilings and having insulation raining down on your head." He smiled a little. "But it is."

"Are you going to let me see?" She tilted her head. "Or are you like a temperamental artist, not willing to show his work until the final brushstroke?"

"There's not much to see." Then he shrugged. "Sure, you can come in if you want."

"Thanks." She started up the walk, glanced over her shoulder when he stayed by the truck. "Aren't you going to give me a tour?"

He moved his shoulders again, and joined her.

"Did you do the trim on my apartment?"

"Yeah."

"It's beautiful work. Looks like cherry."

He frowned, surprised. "It is cherry."

"I like the rounded edges. They soften everything. Do you get a decorator in for the colors or pick them out yourself?"

"I pick them." He opened the door for her. "Is there a problem?"

"No. I really love the color scheme in the kitchen, the slate blue counters, the mauve floor. Oh, what fabulous stairs." She hurried across the unfinished living area to the staircase.

Mac had worked hard and long on it, tearing out the old and replacing it with dark chestnut, curving and widening the landing at the bottom so that it flowed out into the living space.

It was, undeniably, his current pride and joy.

"Did you build these?" she murmured, running a hand over the curve of the railing.

"The old ones were broken, dry-rotted. Had to go."

"I have to try them." She dashed up, turning back at the top to grin at him. "No creaks. Good workmanship, but not very sentimental."

"Sentimental?"

"You know, the way you look back on home, how you snuck downstairs as a kid and knew just which steps to avoid because they'd creak and wake up Mom."

All at once he was having trouble with his breathing. "They're chestnut," he said, because he could think of nothing else.

"Whatever, they're beautiful. Whoever lives here has to have kids."

His mouth was dry, unbearably. "Why?"

"Because." On impulse, she planted her butt on the railing and pushed off. Mac's arms came out of their own volition to catch her as she flew off the end. "It was made for sliding," she said breathlessly. She was laughing as she tilted her head up to his.

Something clicked inside her when their eyes met. And the fluttering, not so pleasant this time, came again. Disconcerted, she cleared her throat and searched for something to say.

"You keep popping up," Mac muttered. He had yet to release her, couldn't seem to make his hands obey his head.

"It's a small town."

He only shook his head. His hands were at her waist now, and they seemed determined to slide around and stroke up her back. He thought he felt her tremble—but it might have been him.

"I don't have time for women," he told her, trying to convince himself.

"Well." She tried to swallow, but there was something hard and hot lodged in her throat. "I'm pretty busy myself." She let out a slow breath. Those hands stroking up and down her back were making her weak. "And I'm not really interested. I had a really bad year, as far as relationships go. I think…"

It was very hard to think. His eyes were such a beautiful shade of blue, and so intensely focused on hers. She wasn't sure what he saw, or what he was looking for, but she knew her knees were about to give out.

"I think," she began again, "we'd both be better off if you decide fairly quickly if you're going to kiss me or not. I can't handle this much longer."

Neither could he. Still, he took his time. He was, in all things, a thorough and thoughtful man. His eyes were open and on hers as he lowered his head, as his mouth hovered a breath from hers, as a small, whimpering moan sounded in her throat.

Her vision dimmed as his lips brushed hers. His were soft, firm, terrifyingly patient. The whisper of contact slammed a punch into her stomach. He lingered over her like a gourmet sampling delicacies, deepening the kiss degree by staggering degree until she was clinging to him.

No one had ever kissed her like this. She hadn't known anyone could. Slow and deep and dreamy. The floor seemed to tilt under her feet as he gently sucked her lower lip into his mouth.

She shuddered, groaned, and let herself drown.

She was very potent. The scent and feel and taste of her was overwhelming. He knew he could lose himself here, for a moment, for a lifetime. Her small, tight body was all but plastered to his. Her hands clutched his hair. In contrast to that aggressive gesture, her head fell limply back in a kind of sighing surrender that had his blood bubbling.

He wanted to touch her. His hands were aching with the need to peel off layer after layer and find the pale, smooth skin beneath. To test himself, and her, he slipped his fingers under her sweater, along the soft, hot flesh of her back, while his mouth continued its long, lazy assault on hers.

He imagined laying her down on the floor, on a tarp, on the grass. He imagined watching her face as he pleasured them both, of feeling her arch toward him, open, accepting.

It had been too long, he told himself as his muscles began to coil and his lungs to labor. It had just been too long.

But he didn't believe it. And it frightened him.

Unsteady, he lifted his head, drew back. Even as he began the retreat, she leaned against him, letting her head fall onto his chest. Unable to resist, he combed his fingers through her hair and cradled her there.

"My head's spinning," she murmured. "What was that?"

"It was a kiss, that's all." He needed to believe that. It would help to ease the tightness around his heart and his loins.

"I think I saw stars." Still staggered, she shifted so that she could look up at him. Her lips curved, but her eyes didn't echo the smile. "That's a first for me."

If he didn't do something fast, he was going to kiss her again. He set her firmly on her feet. "It doesn't change anything."

"Was there something to change?"

The light was nearly gone now. It helped that he couldn't see her clearly in the gloom. "I don't have time for women. And I'm just not interested in starting anything."

"Oh." Where had that pain come from? she wondered, and had to fight to keep from rubbing a hand over her heart. "That was quite a kiss, for a disinterested man." Reaching down, she scooped up the briefcase she'd dropped before she'd run up the stairs. "I'll get out of your way. I wouldn't want to waste any more of your valuable time."

"You don't have to get huffy about it."

"Huffy." Her teeth snapped together. She jabbed a finger into his chest. "I'm well beyond huffy, pal, and working my way past steamed. You've got some ego, Mac. What, do you think I came around here to seduce you?"

"I don't know why you came around."

"Well, I won't be around again." She settled her briefcase strap on her shoulder, jerked her chin up. "Nobody twisted your arm."

He was dealing with an uncomfortable combination of desire and guilt. "Yours, either."

"I'm not the one making excuses. You know, I can't figure out how such an insensitive clod could raise two charming and adorable kids."

"Leave my boys out of this."

The edge to the order had her eyes narrowing to slits. "Oh, so I have designs on them now, too? You idiot!" She stormed for the door, whirling at the last moment for a parting shot. "I hope they don't inherit your warped view of the female species!"

She slammed the door hard enough to have the bad-tempered sound echoing through the house. Mac scowled and jammed his hands in his pockets. He didn't have a warped view, damn it. And his kids were his business.

Chapter Four

Nell stood center stage and lifted her hands. She waited until she was sure every student's eyes were on her, then let it rip.

There was very little that delighted her more than the sound of young voices raised in song. She let the sound fill her, keeping her ears and eyes sharp as she moved around the stage directing. She couldn't hold back the grin. The kids were into this one. Doing Bruce Springsteen and the E Street Band's version of "Santa Claus is Coming to Town" was a departure from the standard carols and hymns their former choral director had arranged year after year.

She could see their eyes light up as they got into the rhythm. *Now punch it,* she thought, pulling more from the bass section as they hit the chorus. *Have fun with it.* Now the soprano section, high and bright… And the altos… Tenors… Bass…

She flashed a smile to signal her approval as the chorus flowered again.

"Good job," she announced. "Tenors, a little more next time. You guys don't want the bass section drowning you out. Holly, you're dropping your chin again. Now we have time for one more run-through of 'I'll Be Home for Christmas.' Kim?"

Kim tried to ignore the little flutter around her heart and the elbow nudge from Holly. She stepped down from her position in the second row and stood in front of the solo mike as though she were facing a firing squad.

"It's okay to smile, you know," Nell told her gently. "And remember your breathing. Sing to the last row, and don't forget to feel the words. Tracy." She held out a finger toward the pianist she'd dragooned from her second-period music class.

The intro started quietly. Using her hands, her face, her eyes, Nell signaled the beginning of the soft, harmonious, background humming. Then Kim began to sing. Too tentatively at first. Nell knew they would have to work on those initial nerves.

But the girl had talent, and emotion. Three bars in, Kim was too caught up in the song to be nervous. She was pacing it well, Nell thought, pleased. Kim had learned quite a bit in the past few weeks about style. The sentimental song suited her, her range, her looks.

Nell brought the chorus in, holding them back. They were background now for Kim's rich, romantic voice. Feeling her own eyes stinging, Nell thought that if they did it this well on the night of the concert, there wouldn't be a dry eye in the house.

"Lovely," Nell said when the last notes had died away. "Really lovely. You guys have come a long way in a very short time. I'm awfully proud of you. Now scram, and have a great weekend."

While Nell moved to the piano to gather up music, the chatter began behind her.

"You sounded really good," Holly told Kim.

"Honest?"

"Honest. Brad thought so, too." Holly shifted her eyes cagily to the school heartthrob, who was shrugging into his school jacket.

"He doesn't even know I'm alive."

"He does now. He was watching you the whole time. I know, because I was watching him." Holly sighed. "If I looked like Miss Davis, *he'd* be watching *me*."

Kim laughed, but shot a quick glance toward Brad under her lashes. "She's really fabulous. Just the way she talks to us and stuff. Mr. Striker always crabbed."

"Mr. Striker *was* a crab. See you later, huh?"

"Yeah." It was all Kim could manage, because it looked, it really looked, as though Brad were coming toward her. And he *was* looking at her.

"Hi." He flashed a grin, all white teeth, with a crooked incisor that made her heart flop around in her chest. "You did real good."

"Thanks." Her tongue tied itself into knots. This was Brad, she kept thinking. A senior. Captain of the football team. Student council president. All blond hair and green eyes.

"Miss Davis sure is cool, isn't she?"

"Yeah." *Say something,* she ordered herself. "She's coming to a party at my house tonight. My mom's having some people over."

"Adults only, huh?"

"No, Holly's coming by and a couple other people." Her heart thundered in her ears as she screwed up her courage. "You could drop by if you wanted."

"That'd be cool. What time?"

She managed to close her mouth and swallow. "Oh, about eight," she said, struggling for the casual touch. "I live on—"

"I know where you live." He grinned at her again, and all but stopped her thundering heart. "Hey, you're not going with Chuck anymore, are you?"

"Chuck?" Who was Chuck? "Oh, no. We hung out for a while, but we sort of broke up over the summer."

"Great. See you later."

He strolled off to join a group of boys who were trooping offstage.

"That's a very cute guy," Nell commented from behind Kim.

"Yeah." The word was a sigh. Kim had stars in her eyes.

"Kimmy has a boyfriend," Zeke sang, in the high-pitched, annoying voice that was reserved for addressing younger siblings—or female cousins.

"Shut up, brat."

He only giggled and began to dance around the stage, sing-songing the refrain. Nell saw murder shoot into Kim's eyes and created a diversion.

"Well, I guess you guys don't want to practice 'Jingle Bells' today."

"Yes, we do." Zack stopped twirling around the stage with his brother and dashed to the piano. "I know which one it is," he said, attacking Nell's neat pile of sheet music. "I can find it."

"I'll find it," Zeke said, but his brother was already holding the music up triumphantly.

"Good going." Nell settled on the bench with a boy on either side of her. She played a dramatic opening chord that made them both giggle. "Please, music is a serious business. And one, and two, and…"

They actually sang it now, instead of screaming it, as they had the first time she invited them to try. What they lacked in style, they made up for in enthusiasm. In spades.

Even Kim was grinning by the time they'd finished.

"Now you do one, Miss Davis." Zack gave her his soulful look. "Please."

"Your dad's probably waiting."

"Just one."

"Just one," Zeke echoed.

In a few short weeks, it had become impossible for her to resist them. "Just one," Nell agreed, and reached into the nowmessy pile of music. "I picked up something you might like at the mall. I bet you've seen *The Little Mermaid*."

"Lots of times," Zeke boasted. "We've got the tape and everything."

"Then you'll recognize this." She played the opening of "Part of Your World."

Mac hunched his shoulders against the wind as he headed into the school. He was damn sick and tired of waiting out in the parking lot. He'd seen the other kids filing out more than ten minutes before.

He had things to do, damn it. Especially since he was stuck going over to Mira's for a party.

He hated parties.

He stomped down the hall. And he heard her. Not the words. He couldn't make out the words, because they were muffled by the auditorium doors. But the sound of her voice, rich and deep. A Scotch-and-soda voice, he'd thought more than once. Sensual, seductive. Sexy.

He opened the door. He had to. And the lush flow of it rolled over him.

A kid's song. He recognized it now from the mermaid movie the boys were still crazy about. He told himself no sane man would get tied up in knots when a woman sang a kid's song.

But he wasn't feeling very sane. Hadn't been since he made the enormous mistake of kissing her.

And he knew that if she'd been alone he would have marched right over to the piano and kissed her again.

But she wasn't alone. Kim was standing behind her, and his children flanked her. Now and again she glanced down at them as she sang, and smiled. Zack was leaning toward her, his head tilting in the way it did just before he climbed into your lap.

Something shifted inside him as he watched. Something painful and frightening. And very, very sweet.

Shaken, Mac stuffed his hands into his pockets, curled those hands into fists. It had to stop. Whatever was happening to him had to stop.

He took a long breath when the music ended. He thought—foolishly, he was sure—that there was something magical humming in the instant of silence that followed.

"We're running late," he called out, determined to break the spell.

Four heads turned his way. The twins began to bounce on the bench.

"Dad! Hey, Dad! We can sing 'Jingle Bells' really good! Want to hear us?"

"I can't." He tried to smile, softening the blow, when Zack's lip poked out. "I'm really running late, kids."

"Sorry, Uncle Mac." Kim scooped up her coat. "We kind of lost track."

While Mac shifted uncomfortably, Nell leaned over and murmured something to his sons. Something, Mac noted, that put a smile back on Zack's face and took the mutinous look off Zeke's. Then both of them threw arms around her and kissed her before they raced offstage for their coats.

"Bye, Miss Davis! Bye!"

"Thanks, Miss Davis," Kim added. "See you later."

Nell made a humming sound and rose to straighten her music.

Mac felt the punch of her cold shoulder all the way in the back of the auditorium. "Ah, thanks for entertaining them," he called out.

Nell lifted her head. He could see her clearly in the stage lights. Clearly enough that he caught the lift of her brow, the coolness of her unsmiling mouth, before she lowered her head again.

Fine, he told himself as he caught both boys on the fly. He didn't want to talk to her anyway.

Chapter Five

She didn't have to ignore him so completely. Mac sipped the cup of hard cider his brother-in-law had pressed on him and resentfully studied Nell's back.

She'd had it turned in his direction for an hour.

A hell of a back, too, he thought, half listening as the mayor rattled on in his ear. Smooth and straight, topped off by the fluid curve of her shoulders. It looked very seductive in the thin plum-colored jacket she wore over a short matching dress.

She had terrific legs. He didn't think he'd ever actually seen them before. He would have remembered. Every other time he'd run into her she'd had them covered up.

She'd probably worn a dress tonight to torment him.

Mac cut the mayor off in midstream and strode over to her. "Look, this is stupid."

Nell glanced up. She'd been having a pleasant conversation with a group of Mira's friends—and thoroughly enjoying the simple act of ignoring Mira's brother.

"Excuse me?"

"It's just stupid," he repeated.

"The need to raise more money for the arts in public school

is stupid?" she asked, well aware he wasn't referring to the topic she'd been discussing.

"What? No. Damn it, you know what I mean."

"I'm sorry." She started to turn back to the circle of very interested faces, but he took her arm and pulled her aside. "Do you want me to cause a scene in your sister's house?" Nell said between her teeth.

"No." He weaved his way through the minglers, around the dining room table and through the kitchen door. His sister was busy replenishing a tray of canapés. "Give us a minute," he ordered Mira.

"Mac, I'm busy here." Distracted, Mira smoothed a hand over her short brunette hair. "Would you find Dave and tell him we're running low on cider?" She sent Nell a frazzled smile. "I thought I was organized."

"Give us a minute," Mac repeated.

Mira let out an impatient breath, but then her eyebrows shot up, drew in. "Well, well," she murmured, amused and clearly delighted. "I'll just get out of your way. I want a closer look at that boy Kim's so excited about." She picked up the tray of finger food and swung through the kitchen door.

Silence fell like a hammer.

"So." Casually, Nell plucked a carrot stick from a bowl. "Something on your mind, Macauley?"

"I don't see why you have to be so…"

"So?" She crunched into the carrot. "What?"

"You're making a point of not talking to me."

She smiled. "Yes, I am."

"It's stupid."

She located an open bottle of white wine, poured some into a glass. After a sip, she smiled again. "I don't think so. It seems to me that, for no discernible reason, I annoy you. Since I'm quite fond of your family, it seems logical and courteous to stay as far out of your way as I possibly can." She sipped again. "Now, is that all? I've been enjoying myself so far this evening."

"You don't annoy me. Exactly." He couldn't find anything to do with his hands, so he settled on taking a carrot stick and breaking it in half. "I'm sorry...for before."

"You're sorry for kissing me, or for behaving like a jerk afterward?"

He tossed the pieces of carrot down. "You're a hard one, Nell."

"Wait." Eyes wide, she pressed a hand to her ear. "I think something's wrong with my hearing. I thought, for just a minute, you actually said my name."

"Cut it out," he said. Then, deliberately: "Nell."

"This is a moment," she declared, and toasted him. "Macauley Taylor has actually initiated a conversation with me, *and* used my name. I'm all aflutter."

"Look." Temper had him rounding the counter. He'd nearly grabbed her before he pushed his anger back. "I just want to clear the air."

Fascinated, she studied his now-impassive face. "That's quite a control button you've got there, Mac. It's admirable. Still, I wonder what would happen if you didn't push it so often."

"A man raising two kids on his own needs control."

"I suppose," she murmured. "Now, if that's all—"

"I'm sorry," he said again.

This time she softened. She was simply no good at holding a grudge. "Okay. Let's just forget it. Friends," she offered, and held out a hand.

He took it. It was so soft, so small, he couldn't make himself give it up again. Her eyes were soft, too, just now. Big, liquid eyes you'd have expected to see on a fawn. "You...look nice."

"Thanks. You, too."

"You like the party?"

"I like the people." Her pulse was starting to jump. Damn him. "Your sister's wonderful. So full of energy and ideas."

"You have to watch her." His lips curved slowly. "She'll rope you into one of her projects."

"Too late. She's got me on the arts committee already. And I've been volunteered to help with the recycling campaign."

"The trick is to duck."

"I don't mind, really. I think I'm going to enjoy it." His thumb was brushing over her wrist now, lightly. "Mac, don't start something you don't intend to finish."

Brow creased, he looked down at their joined hands. "I think about you. I don't have time to think about you. I don't want to have time."

It was happening again. The flutters and quivers she seemed to have no control over. "What do you want?"

His gaze lifted, locked with hers. "I'm having some trouble with that."

The kitchen door burst open, and a horde of teenagers piled in, only to be brought up short as Kim, in the lead, stopped on a dime.

Her eyes widened as she watched her uncle drop her teacher's hand, and the two of them jumped apart like a couple of teenagers caught necking on the living room sofa.

"Sorry. Ah, sorry," she repeated, goggling. "We were just…" She turned on her heel and shoved back at her friends. They scooted out, chuckling.

"That ought to add some juice to the grapevine," Nell said wryly. She'd been in town long enough to know that everyone would be speculating about Mac Taylor and Nell Davis by morning. Steadier now, she turned back to him. "Listen, why don't we try this in nice easy stages? You want to go out to dinner tomorrow? See a movie or something?"

Now it was his turn to stare. "A date? Are you asking me out on a date?"

Impatience flickered back. "Yes, a date. It doesn't mean I'm asking to bear you more children. On second thought, let's just quit while we're ahead."

"I want to get my hands on you." Mac heard himself say the words, knew it was too late to take them back.

Nell reached for her wine in self-defense. "Well, that's simple."

"No, it's not."

She braced herself and looked up at him again. "No," she agreed quietly. Just how many times, she wondered, had his face popped into her mind in the past few weeks? She couldn't count them. "It's not simple."

But something had to be done, he decided. A move forward, a move back. Take a step, he ordered himself. See what happens. "I haven't been to a movie without the kids... I can't remember. I could probably line up a sitter."

"All right." She was watching him now almost as carefully as he watched her. "Give me a call if it works out. I'll be home most of tomorrow, correcting papers."

It wasn't the easiest thing, stepping back into the dating pool—however small the pool and however warm the water. It irritated him that he was nervous, almost as much as his niece's grins and questions had irritated when she agreed to babysit.

Now, as he climbed the sturdy outside steps to Nell's third-floor apartment, Mac wondered if it would be better all around if they forgot the whole thing.

As he stepped onto her deck, he noted that she'd flanked the door with pots of mums. It was a nice touch, he thought. He always appreciated it when someone who rented one of his homes cared enough to bother with those nice touches.

It was just a movie, he reminded himself, and rapped on the door. When she opened it, he was relieved that she'd dressed casually—a hip-grazing sweater over a pair of those snug leggings Kim liked so much.

Then she smiled and had his mouth going dry.

"Hi. You're right on time. Do you want to come in and see what I've done to your place?"

"It's your place—as long as you pay the rent," he told her, but she was reaching out, taking his hand, drawing him in.

Mac had dispensed with the walls that had made stingy little rooms and had created one flowing space of living, dining and kitchen area. And she'd known what to do with it.

There was a huge L-shaped couch in a bold floral print that should have been shocking, but was, instead, perfect. A small table under the window held a pot of dried autumn leaves. Shelves along one wall held books, a stereo and a small TV, and the sort of knickknacks he knew women liked.

She'd turned the dining area into a combination music room and office, with her desk and a small spinet. A flute lay on a music stand.

"I didn't bring a lot with me from New York," she said as she shrugged into her jacket. "Only what I really cared about. I'm filling in with things from antique shops and flea markets."

"We got a million of them," he murmured. "It looks good." And it did—the old, faded rug on the floor, the fussy priscillas at the windows. "Comfortable."

"Comfortable's very important to me. Ready?"

"Sure."

And it wasn't so hard after all.

He'd asked her to pick the movie, and she'd gone for comedy. It was surprisingly relaxing to sit in the darkened theater and share popcorn and laughter.

He only thought about her as a woman, a very attractive woman, a couple of dozen times.

Going for pizza afterward seemed such a natural progression, he suggested it himself. They competed for a table in the crowded pizzeria with teenagers out on date night.

"So…" Nell stretched out in the booth. "How's Zeke's career in spelling coming along?"

"It's a struggle. He really works at it. It's funny, Zack can spell almost anything you toss at him first time around, but Zeke has to study the word like a scholar with the Dead Sea Scrolls."

"He's good at his arithmetic."

"Yeah." Mac wasn't sure how he felt about her knowing so much about his kids. "They're both taken with you."

"It's mutual." She skimmed a hand through her hair. "It's going to sound odd, but…" She hesitated, not quite sure how to word it. "But that first day at rehearsal, when I looked around and saw them? I had this feeling, this— I don't know, it was like, 'Oh, there you are. I was wondering when you'd show up.' It sounds strange, but it was as if I was expecting them. Now, when Kim comes without them, I feel let down."

"I guess they kind of grow on you."

It was more than that, but she didn't know how to explain. And she wasn't entirely sure Mac would accept the fact that she'd very simply fallen for them. "I get a kick out of them telling me about their school day, showing me their papers."

"First report cards are almost here." His grin flashed. "I'm more nervous than they are."

"People put too much emphasis on grades."

His brows shot up at the comment. "This from a teacher?"

"Individual ability, application, effort, retention. Those things are a lot more important than *A, B* or *C.* But I can tell you, in confidence, that Kim's aceing advanced chorus and music history."

"No kidding?" He felt a quick surge of pride. "She never did that well before. *B*s mostly."

"Mr. Striker and I have markedly different approaches."

"You're telling me. Word around town is that the chorus is dynamite this year. How'd you pull it off?"

"The kids pull it off," she told him, sitting up when their

pizza was served. "My job is to make them think and sing like a team. Not to slam Mr. Striker," she added, taking a generous bite. "But I get the impression he was just putting in time, counting the days until he could retire. If you're going to teach kids, you have to like them, and respect them. There's a lot of talent there, some of it extremely rough." When she laughed, the roses in her cheek bloomed deeper. "And some of those kids will do nothing more than sing in the shower for the rest of their lives—for which the world can be grateful."

"Got some clinkers, huh?"

"Well…" She laughed again. "Yes, I have a few. But they're enjoying themselves. That's what counts. And there are a few, like Kim, who are really something special. I'm sending her and two others for auditions to all-state next week. And after the holiday concert I'm going to hold auditions for the spring musical."

"We haven't had a musical at the high school in three years."

"We're going to have one this year, Buster. And it's going to be terrific."

"It's a lot of work for you."

"I like it. And it's what I'm paid for."

Mac toyed with a second slice. "You really do like it, don't you? The school, the town, the whole bit?"

"Why shouldn't I? It's a fine school, a fine town."

"It ain't Manhattan."

"Exactly."

"Why'd you leave?" He winced. "Sorry, none of my business."

"It's all right. I had a bad year. I guess I was getting restless before that, but the last year was just the pits. They eliminated my job at the school. Economic cutbacks. Downsizing. The arts are always the first to suffer." She shrugged. "Anyway, my roommate got married. I couldn't afford the rent on my own—not if I wanted to eat with any regularity—so I adver-

tised for another one. Took references, gauged personalities."
With a sigh, she propped her chin on her elbow. "I thought I
was careful. But about three weeks after she moved in, I came
home and found that she'd cleaned me out."

Mac stopped eating. "She robbed you?"

"She skinned me. TV, stereo, whatever good jewelry I had,
cash, the collection of Limoges boxes I'd started in college. I
was really steamed, and then I was shaken. I just wasn't comfortable living there after it happened. Then the guy I'd been
seeing for about a year started giving me lectures on my stupidity, my naïveté. As far as he was concerned, I'd gotten exactly what I'd deserved."

"Nice guy," Mac muttered. "Very supportive."

"You bet. In any case, I took a good look at him and our
relationship and figured he was right on one level. As long as I
was in that rut, with him, I was getting what I deserved. So I
decided to climb out of the rut, and leave him in it."

"Good choice."

"I thought so." And so was he, she thought, studying Mac's
face. A very good choice. "Why don't you tell me what your
plans are with the house you're renovating."

"I don't guess you'd know a lot about plumbing."

She only smiled. "I'm a quick learner."

It was nearly midnight when he pulled up in front of her
apartment. He hadn't intended to stay out so late. He certainly
hadn't expected to spend more than an hour talking to her
about wiring and plumbing and load-bearing walls. Or drawing little blueprints on napkins.

But somehow he'd managed to get through the evening
without feeling foolish, or pinned down or out of step. Only
one thing worried him. He wanted to see her again.

"I think this was a good first step." She laid a hand over his,
kissed his cheek. "Thanks."

"I'll walk you up."

Her hand was already on the door handle. Safer, she'd decided for both of them, if she just hurried along. "You don't have to. I know the way."

"I'll walk you up," he repeated. He stepped out, rounded the hood. They started up the stairs together. The tenant on the first floor was still awake. The mutter of a television, and its ghost gray light, filtered through the window.

Since the breeze had died, it was the only sound. And overhead countless stars wheeled in a clear black sky.

"If we do this again," Mac began, "people in town are going to start talking about us, making out that we're…" He wasn't quite sure of the right phrase.

"An item?" Nell supplied. "That bothers you."

"I don't want the kids to get any ideas, or worry, or…whatever." As they reached the landing, he looked down at her and was caught again. "It must be the way you look," he murmured.

"What must?"

"That makes me think about you." It was a reasonable explanation, he decided. Physical attraction. After all, he wasn't a dead man. He was just a careful one. "That makes me think about doing this."

He cupped her face in his hands—a gesture so sweet, so tender, it had every muscle in her body going lax. It was just as slow, as stunning, as sumptuous, as the first time. The touch of his mouth on hers, the shuddering patience, the simple wonder of it.

Could it be this? she wondered. Could it be this that she'd been waiting for? Could it be him?

He heard her soft, breathy sigh as he eased his mouth from hers. Lingering, he knew, would be a mistake, and he let his hands fall away before they could reach for more.

As if to capture one final taste, Nell ran her tongue over her lips. "You're awfully good at that, Macauley. Awfully good."

"You could say I've been saving up." But he didn't think it

was that at all. He was very much worried it wasn't that. "I'll see you."

She nodded weakly as he headed down the steps. She was still leaning dreamily against the door when she heard his car start and drive away.

For a moment, she would have sworn the air rang with the distant music of sleigh bells.

Chapter Six

The end of October meant parent-teacher conferences, and a much-anticipated holiday for students. It also meant a headache for Mac. He had to juggle the twins from his sister to Kim to Mrs. Hollis, fitting in a trip to order materials and an electrical inspection.

When he turned his truck into the educational complex, he was jumpy with nerves. Lord knew what he was about to be told about his children, how they behaved when they were out of his sight and his control. He worried that he hadn't made enough time to help them with their schoolwork and somehow missed a parental step in preparing them for the social, educational and emotional demands of first grade.

Because of his failure, his boys would become antisocial, illiterate neurotics.

He knew he was being ridiculous, but he couldn't stop his fears from playing over and over like an endless loop in his brain.

"Mac!" The car horn and the sound of his name had him turning and focusing, finally, on his sister's car. She leaned out the window, shaking her head at him. "Where were you? I called you three times."

"Bailing my kids out of jail," he muttered, and changed course to walk to her car. "I've got a conference in a minute."

"I know. I've just come from a meeting at the high school. Remember, we compared schedules."

"Right. I shouldn't be late."

"You don't get demerits. My meeting was about raising funds for new chorus uniforms. Those kids have been wearing the same old choir robes for twelve years. We're hoping to raise enough to put them in something a little snazzier."

"Fine, I'll give you a donation, but I shouldn't be late." Already he was imagining the young, fresh-faced first grade teacher marking him tardy, just another item on a growing list of negatives about Taylor males.

"I just wanted to say that Nell seemed upset about something."

"What?"

"Upset," Mira repeated, pleased that she finally had his full attention. "She came up with a couple of nice ideas for fundraisers, but she was obviously distracted." Mira lifted a brow, eyeing her brother slyly. "You haven't done anything to annoy her, have you?"

"No." Mac caught himself before he shifted guiltily from foot to foot. "Why should I?"

"Couldn't say. But since you've been seeing her—"

"We went to the movies."

"And for pizza," Mira added. "A couple of Kim's friends spotted you."

The curse of small towns, Mac thought, and stuffed his hands in his pockets. "So?"

"So nothing. Good for you. I like her a lot. Kim's crazy about her. I suppose I'm feeling a bit protective. She was definitely upset, Mac, and trying not to show it. Maybe she'd talk to you about it."

"I'm not going to go poking around in her personal life."

"The way I see it, you're part of her personal life. See you later." She pulled off without giving him a chance for a parting shot.

Muttering to himself, Mac marched up to the elementary school. When he marched out twenty minutes later, he was in a much lighter mood. His children had not been declared social misfits with homicidal tendencies after all. In fact, their teacher had praised them.

Of course, he'd known all along.

Maybe Zeke forgot the rules now and then and talked to his neighbor. And maybe Zack was a little shy about raising his hand when he knew an answer. But they were settling in.

With the weight of first grade off his shoulders, Mac headed out. Impulse had him swinging toward the high school. He knew his conference had been one of the last of the day. He wasn't sure how teachers' meetings worked at the high school, but the lot was nearly empty. He spotted Nell's car, however, and decided it wouldn't hurt just to drop in.

It wasn't until he was inside that he realized he didn't have a clue as to where to find her.

Mac poked his head into the auditorium, but it was empty. Since he'd come that far, he backtracked to the main office and caught one of the secretaries as she was leaving for the day. Following her directions, he turned down a corridor, headed up a ramp and turned right.

Nell's classroom door was open. Not like any classroom he'd done time in, he thought. This one had a piano, music stands, instruments, a tape recorder. There was the usual blackboard, wiped clean, and a desk where Nell was currently working.

He watched her for a long moment, the way her hair fell, the way her fingers held the pen, the way her sweater draped at the neck. It occurred to him that if he'd ever had a teacher who looked like that, he would have been a great deal more interested in music.

"Hi."

Her head snapped up. There was a martial light in her eyes that surprised him, a stubborn set to her jaw. Even as he watched, she took a long breath and worked up a smile.

"Hello, Mac. Welcome to bedlam."

"Looks like a lot of work." He stepped inside, up to the desk. It was covered with papers, books, computer printouts and sheet music, all in what appeared to be ordered piles.

"Finishing up the first marking period, grades, class planning, fund-raising strategy, fine-tuning the holiday concert— and trying to make the budget stretch to producing the spring musical." Trying to keep her foul mood to herself, she sat back. "So, how was your day?"

"Pretty good. I just had a conference with the twins' teacher. They're doing fine. I can stop sweating report cards."

"They're great kids. You've got nothing to worry about."

"Worry comes with the territory. What are you worried about?" he asked before he could remind himself he wasn't going to pry.

"How much time have you got?" she shot back.

"Enough." Curious, he eased a hip onto the edge of her desk. He wanted to soothe, he discovered, to stroke away that faint line between her brows. "Rough day?"

She jerked her shoulders, then pushed away from her desk. Temper always forced her to move. "I've had better. Do you know how much school and community support the football team gets? All the sports teams." She began to slap cassette tapes into a box—anything to keep her hands busy. "Even the band. But the chorus, we have to go begging for every dollar."

"You're ticked off about the budget?"

"Why shouldn't I be?" She whirled back, eyes hot. "No problem getting equipment for the football team so a bunch of boys can go out on the field and tackle each other, but I have to spend an hour on my knees if I want eighty bucks to get a piano tuned." She caught herself, sighed. "I don't have anything against football. I like it. High school sports are important."

"I know a guy who tunes pianos," Mac said. "He'd probably donate his time."

Nell rubbed a hand over her face, slid it around to soothe the tension at the back of her neck. *Dad can fix anything,* she thought, just as the twins had claimed. Have a problem? Call Mac.

"That would be great," she said, and managed a real smile. "If I can beat my way through the paperwork and get approval. You can't even take freebies without going through the board." It irritated her, as always. "One of the worst aspects of teaching is the bureaucracy. Maybe I should have stuck with performing in clubs."

"You performed in clubs?"

"In another life," she muttered, waving it away. "A little singing to pay my way through college. It was better than waiting tables. Anyway, it's not the budget, not really. Or even the lack of interest from the community. I'm used to that."

"Do you want to tell me what it is, or do you want to stew about it?"

"I was having a pretty good time stewing about it." She sighed again, and looked up at him. He seemed so solid, so dependable. "Maybe I'm too much of an urbanite after all. I've had my first run-in with old-fashioned rural attitude, and I'm stumped. Do you know Hank Rohrer?"

"Sure. He has a dairy farm out on Old Oak Road. I think his oldest kid is in the same class as Kim."

"Hank, Jr. Yes. Junior's one of my students—a very strong baritone. He has a real interest in music. He even writes it."

"No kidding? That's great."

"You'd think so, wouldn't you?" Nell tossed her hair back and went to her desk again to tidy her already tidy papers. "Well, I asked Mr. and Mrs. Rohrer to come in this morning because Junior backed out of going to all-state auditions this weekend. I knew he had a very good chance of making it, and I wanted to discuss the possibility with his parents of a music scholarship. When I told them how talented Junior was and how I hoped they'd encourage him to change his mind about the auditions, Hank Senior acted as though I'd just insulted him. He was appalled." There was bitterness in her voice now, as well as anger. "'No son of his was going to waste his time on singing and writing music like some…'"

She trailed off, too furious to repeat the man's opinion of musicians. "They didn't even know Junior was in my class. Thought he was taking shop as his elective this year. I tried to smooth it over, said that Junior needed a fine-art credit to graduate. I didn't do much good. Mr. Rohrer could barely swallow the idea of Junior staying in my class. He went on about how Junior didn't need singing lessons to run a farm. And he certainly wasn't going to allow him to take a Saturday and go audition when the boy had chores. And I'm to stop putting any fancy ideas about college in the boy's head."

"They've got four kids," Mac said slowly. "Tuition might be a problem."

"If that were the only obstacle, they should be grateful for the possibility of scholarship." She slapped her grade book closed. "What we have is a bright, talented boy who has dreams, dreams he'll never be able to explore because his parents won't permit it. Or his father won't," she added. "His mother didn't say two words the entire time they were here."

"Could be she'll work on Hank once she has him alone."

"Could be he'll take out his annoyance with me on both of them."

"Hank's not like that. He's set in his ways and thinks he knows all the answers, but he isn't mean."

"It's a little tough for me to see his virtues after he called me—" she had to take a deep breath "—a slick-handed flat-lander who's wasting his hard-earned tax dollars. I could have made a difference with that boy," Nell murmured as she sat again. "I know it."

"So maybe you won't be able to make a difference with Junior. You'll make a difference with someone else. You've already made one with Kim."

"Thanks." Nell's smile was brief. "That helps a little."

"I mean it." He hated to see her this way, all that brilliant energy and optimism dimmed. "She's gained a lot of confidence in herself. She's always been shy about her singing, about a lot of things. Now she's really opening up."

It did help to hear it. This time Nell's smile came easier. "So I should stop brooding."

"It doesn't suit you." He surprised himself, and her, by reaching down to run his knuckles over her cheek. "Smiling does."

"I've never been able to hold on to temperament for long. Bob used to say it was because I was shallow."

"Who the hell's Bob?"

"The one who's still in the rut."

"Clearly where he belongs."

She laughed. "I'm glad you dropped by. I'd have probably sat here for another hour clenching my jaw."

"It's a pretty jaw," Mac murmured, then shifted away. "I've got to get going. I've got Halloween costumes to put together."

"Need any help?"

"I…" It was tempting, too tempting, and far too dangerous, he thought, to start sharing family traditions with her. "No, I've got it covered."

Nell accepted the disappointment, nearly masked it. "You'll bring them by Saturday night, won't you? To trick-or-treat?"

"Sure. I'll see you." He started out but stopped at the doorway and turned back. "Nell?"

"Yes?"

"Some things take a while to change. Change makes some people nervous."

She tilted her head. "Are you talking about the Rohrers, Mac?"

"Among others. I'll see you Saturday night."

Nell studied the empty doorway as his footsteps echoed away. Did he think she was trying to change him? Was she? She sat back, pushing away from the paperwork. She'd never be able to concentrate on it now.

Whenever she was around Macauley Taylor, it was hard to concentrate. When had she become so susceptible to the slow, thorough, quiet type? From the moment he'd walked into the auditorium to pick up Kim and the twins, she admitted.

Love at first sight? Surely she was too sophisticated, too smart, to believe in such a thing. And surely, she added, she was too smart to put herself in the vulnerable position of falling in love with a man who didn't return her feelings.

Or didn't want to, she thought. And that was even worse.

It couldn't matter that he was sweet and kind and devoted to his children. It shouldn't matter that he was handsome and strong and sexy. She wouldn't let it matter that being with him, thinking of him, had her longing for things. For home, for family, for laughter in the kitchen and passion in bed.

She let out a long breath, because it did matter. It mattered very much when a woman was teetering right on the edge of falling in love.

Chapter Seven

Mid-November had stripped the leaves from the trees. There was a beauty even in this, Nell had decided. Beauty in the dark, denuded branches, in the papery rustle of dried leaves along the curbs, in the frost that shimmered like diamond dust on the grass in the mornings.

She caught herself staring out of the window too often, wishing for snow like a child hoping for a school holiday.

It felt wonderful. Wonderful to anticipate the winter, to remember the fall. She often thought about Halloween night, and all the children who had come knocking on her door dressed as pirates and princesses. She remembered the way Zeke and Zack had giggled when she pretended not to recognize them in the elaborate astronaut costumes Mac had fashioned for them.

She found herself reminiscing about the bluegrass concert Mac had taken her to. Or the fun they'd had when she ran into him and the boys at the mall just last week, all of them on a mission to complete their Christmas lists early.

Now, strolling past the house Mac was remodeling, she thought of him again. It had been so sweet, the way he'd struggled over choosing just the right outfit for Kim's present. No thoughtless gifts from Macauley Taylor for those he cared about. It had to be the right color, the right style.

She'd come to believe everything about him was right.

She passed the house, drawing in the chilly air of evening, her mood buoyant. That afternoon she'd been proud to announce that two of her students would participate in all-state chorus.

She had made a difference, Nell thought, shutting her eyes on the pleasure of it. Not just the prestige, certainly not simply the delight of having the principal congratulate her. The difference, the important one, had been the look on her students' faces. The pride, not just on Kim's face and that of the tenor who would go to all-state with her. But on the faces of the entire chorus. They all shared in the triumph, because over the past few weeks they had become a team.

Her team. Her kids.

"It's cold for walking."

Nell jolted, tensed, then laughed at herself when she saw Mac step away from the shadow of a tree in his sister's yard. "Lord, you gave me a start. I nearly went into my repel-the-mugger stance."

"Taylor's Grove's a little sparse when it comes to muggers. Are you going to see Mira?"

"No, actually, I was just out walking. Too much energy to stay in." The smile lit her face. "You've heard the good news?"

"Congratulations."

"It's not me—"

"Yeah, it is. A lot of it." It was the only way he knew to tell her how proud he was of what she'd done. He glanced back toward the house, where lights gleamed. "Mira and Kim are in there crying."

"Crying? But—"

"Not that kind of crying." Female tears always embarrassed him. He shrugged. "You know, the other kind."

"Oh." In response, Nell felt her own eyes sting. "That's nice."

"Dave's going around with a big fat grin on his face. He was talking to his parents when I ducked out. Mira's already called ours, as well as every other friend and relative in the country."

"Well, it's a big deal."

"I know it is." His teeth flashed. "I've made a few calls myself. You must be feeling pretty pleased with yourself."

"You bet I am. Seeing the kids today when I made the announcement...well, it was the best. And it's a hell of a kickoff for our fund-raiser." She shivered as the wind shuddered through the trees.

"You're getting cold. I'll drive you home."

"That'd be nice. I keep waiting for snow."

In the way of every countryman since Adam, he sniffed the air, checked out the sky. "You won't have to wait much longer." He opened the truck door for her. "The kids have already gotten their sleds out."

"I might buy one for myself." She settled back, relaxed. "Where are the boys?"

"There's a sleepover at one of their friends'." He gestured toward the house across the street from Mira's. "I just dropped them off."

"They must be thinking a lot about Christmas now, with snow in the air."

"It's funny. Usually right after Halloween they start barraging me with lists and pictures of toys from catalogs, stuff they see on TV." He turned the truck and headed for the square. "This year they told me Santa's taking care of it. I know they want bikes." His brow creased. "That's all I've heard. They've been whispering together about something else, but they clam up when I come around."

"That's Christmas," Nell said easily. "It's the best time for whispers and secrets. What about you?" She turned to smile at him. "What do you want for Christmas?"

"More than the two hours' sleep I usually get."

"You can do better than that."

"When the kids come downstairs in the morning, and their faces light up, I've got all I want." He stopped in front of her apartment. "Are you going back to New York for the holiday?"

"No, there's nothing there."

"Your family?"

"I'm an only child. My parents usually spend the holiday in the Caribbean. Do you want to come in, have some coffee?"

It was a much more appealing idea than going home to an empty house. "Yeah, thanks." When they started up the stairs, he tried to swing tactfully back to the holidays and her family. "Is that where you spent Christmas as a kid? In the Caribbean?"

"No. We had a fairly traditional setting in Philadelphia. Then I went to school in New York, and they moved to Florida." She opened the door and took off her coat. "We aren't very close, really. They weren't terribly happy with my decision to study music."

"Oh." He tossed his jacket over hers while she moved into the kitchen to put on the coffee. "I guess that's why you got so steamed about Junior."

"Maybe. They didn't really disapprove so much as they were baffled. We get along much better long-distance." She glanced over her shoulder. "I think that's why I admire you."

He stopped studying the rosewood music box on a table and stared at her. "Me?"

"Your interest and involvement with your children, your whole family. It's so solid, so natural." Tossing back her hair, she reached into the cookie jar and began to spread cookies on a plate. "Not everyone is as willing, or as able, to put in so much time and attention. Not everyone loves as well, or as thoroughly." She smiled. "Now I've embarrassed you."

"No. Yes," he admitted, and took one of the cookies. "You haven't asked about their mother." When she said nothing, Mac found himself talking. "I was just out of college when I met her. She was a secretary in my father's real estate office. She was beautiful. I mean eye-popping beautiful, the kind that bowls you over. We went out a couple of times, we went to bed, she got pregnant."

The flat-voiced recitation had Nell looking up. Mac bit into the cookie, tasting bitterness. "I know that sounds like she did it on her own. I was young, but I was old enough to know what I was doing, old enough to be responsible."

He had always taken his responsibilities seriously, Nell thought, and he always would. You only had to look at him to see the dependability.

"You didn't say anything about love."

"No, I didn't." It was something he didn't take lightly. "I was attracted, so was she. Or I thought she was. What I didn't know was that she'd lied about using birth control. It wasn't until after I'd married her that I found out she'd set out to 'snag the boss's son.' Her words," he added. "Angie saw an opportunity to improve her standard of living."

It surprised him that even now, after all this time, it hurt both pride and heart to know he'd been so carelessly used.

"To make a long story short," he continued, in that same expressionless tone, "she hadn't counted on twins, or the hassle of motherhood. So, about a month after the boys were born, she cleaned out my bank account and split."

"I'm so sorry, Mac," Nell murmured. She wished she knew the words, the gesture, that would erase that cool dispassion from his eyes. "It must have been horrible for you."

"It could have been worse." His eyes met Nell's briefly before he shrugged it off. "I could have loved her. She contacted me once, telling me she wanted me to foot the bill for the divorce. In exchange for that, I could have the kids free and clear. Free and clear," he repeated. "As if they were stocks and bonds instead of children. I took her up on it. End of story."

"Is it?" Nell moved to him, took his hands in hers. "Even if you didn't love her, she hurt you."

She rose on her toes to kiss his cheek, to soothe, to comfort. She saw the change in his eyes—and, yes, the hurt in them. It explained a great deal, she thought, to hear him tell the story. To see his face as he did. He'd been disillusioned, devastated. Instead of giving in to it, or leaning on his parents for help with the burden, he'd taken his sons and started a life with them. A life for them.

"She didn't deserve you, or the boys."

"It wasn't a hardship." He couldn't take his eyes off hers now. It wasn't the sympathy so much as the simple, unquestioning understanding that pulled at him. "They're the best part of me. I didn't mean it to sound like it was a sacrifice."

"You didn't. You don't." Her heart melted as she slid her arms around him. She'd meant that, too, as a comfort. But something more, something deeper, was stirring inside her. "You made it sound as if you love them. It's very appealing to hear a man say that he thinks of his children as a gift. And to know he means it."

He was holding her, and he wasn't quite sure how it had happened. It seemed so easy, so natural, to have her settled in his arms. "When you're given a gift, an important one, you have to be careful with it." His voice thickened with a mix of emotions. His children. Her. Something about the way she was looking up at him, the way her lips curved. He lifted a hand to stroke her hair, lingered over it a moment before he remembered to back away. "I should go."

"Stay." It was so easy, she discovered, to ask him. So easy, after all, to need him. "You know I want you to stay. You know I want you."

He couldn't take his eyes off her face, and the need was so much bigger, so much sweeter, than he'd ever imagined. "It could complicate things, Nell. I've got a lot of baggage. Most of it's in storage, but—"

"I don't care." Her breath trembled out. "I don't even have any pride at the moment. Make love with me, Mac." On a sigh, she pulled his head down and pressed her lips to his. "Just love me tonight."

He couldn't resist. It was a fantasy that had begun to wind through him, body and mind, the moment he first met her. She was all softness, all warmth. He'd done without both of those miraculous female gifts for so long.

Now, with her mouth on his and her arms twined around him, she was all he could want.

He'd never considered himself romantic. He wondered if a woman like Nell would prefer candlelight, soft music, perfumed air. But the scene was already set. He could do nothing more than lift her into his arms and carry her to the bedroom.

He turned on a lamp, surprised at how suddenly his nerves vanished when he saw hers reflected in her eyes.

"I've thought about this a long time," he told her. "I want to see you, every minute I'm touching you. I want to see you."

"Good." She looked up at him and his smile soothed away some of her tension. "I want to see you."

He carried her to the bed and lay down beside her, stroking a hand through her hair, over her shoulders. Then he dipped his head to kiss her.

It was so easy, as if they had shared nights and intimacy for years. It was so thrilling, as if each of them had come to the bed as innocent as a babe.

A touch, a taste, patient and lingering. A murmur, a sigh, soft and quiet. His hands never rushed, only pleasured, stroking over her, unfastening buttons, pausing to explore.

Her skin quivered under his caress even as it heated. A hundred pulse points thrummed, speeding at the brush of a fingertip, the flick of a tongue. Her own hands trembled, pulling a laughing groan from her that ended on a broken whimper when she at last found flesh.

Making love. The phrase had never been truer to her. For here was an exquisite tenderness mixed with a lustful curiosity that overpowered the senses, tangled in the system like silken knots. Each time his mouth returned to hers, it went deeper, wider, higher, so that he was all that existed for her. All that needed to.

She gave with a depthless generosity that staggered him. She fit, body to body, with him, with a perfection that thrilled. Each time he thought his control would slip, he found himself sliding easily back into the rhythm they set.

Slow, subtle, savoring.

She was small, delicately built. The fragility he sensed made his hands all the more tender. Even as she arched and cried out the first time, he didn't hurry. It was gloriously arousing for him simply to watch her face, that incredibly expressive face, as every emotion played over it.

He fought back the need to bury himself inside her, clung to control long enough to protect them both. Their eyes locked when at last he slipped into her. Her breath caught and released, and then her lips curved.

Outside, the wind played against the windows, making a music like sleigh bells. And the first snow of the season began to fall as quietly as a wish.

Chapter Eight

He couldn't get enough of her. Mac figured at worst it was a kind of insanity, at best a temporary obsession. No matter how many demands there were on his time, his brain, his emotions, he still found odd moments, day and night, to think about Nell.

Though he knew it was cynical, he wished it could have been just sex. If it was only sex, he could put it down to hormones and get back to business. But he didn't just imagine her in bed, or fantasize about finding an hour to lose himself in that trim little body.

Sometimes, when she slipped into his head, she was standing in front of a group of children, directing their voices with her hands, her arms, her whole self. Or she'd be seated at the piano, with his boys on either side of her, laughing with them. Or she'd just be walking through town, with her hands in her pockets and her face lifted toward the sky.

She scared him right down to the bone.

And she, he thought as he measured his baseboard trim, she was so easy about the whole thing. That was a woman for you, he decided. They didn't have to worry about making the right moves, saying the right thing. They just had to…to be, he thought. That was enough to drive a man crazy.

He couldn't afford to be crazy. He had kids to raise, a business to run. Hell, he had laundry to do if he ever got home. And damn it, he'd forgotten to take the chicken out of the freezer again.

They'd catch burgers on the way to the concert, he told himself. He had enough on his mind without having to fix dinner. Christmas was barreling toward him, and the kids were acting strange.

Just the bikes, Dad, they told him. *Santa's making them, and he's taking care of the big present.*

What big present? Mac wondered. No interrogation, no tricks, had pulled out that particular answer. For once his kids were closed up tight. That was an idea that disturbed him. He knew that in another year, two if he was lucky, they'd begin to question and doubt the existence of Santa and magic. The end of innocence. Whatever it was they were counting on for Christmas morning, he wanted to see that they found it under the tree.

But they just grinned at him when he prodded and told him it was a surprise for all three of them.

He'd have to work on it. Mac hammered the trim into place. At least they'd gotten the tree up and baked some cookies, strung the popcorn. He felt a little twinge of guilt over the fact that he'd evaded Nell's offer to help with the decorating. And ignored the kids when they asked if she could come over and trim the tree with them.

Was he the only one who could see what a mistake it would be to have his children become too attached? She'd only been in town for a few months. She could leave at any time. Nell might find them cute, attractive kids, but she didn't have any investment in them.

Damn it, now *he* was making them sound like stocks and bonds.

It wasn't what he meant, Mac assured himself. He simply wasn't going to allow anyone to walk out on his sons again.

He wouldn't risk it, not for anything in heaven or on earth.

After nailing the last piece of baseboard in place, he nodded in approval. The house was coming together just fine. He knew what he was doing there. Just as he knew what he was doing with the boys.

He only wished he had a better idea of what to do with Nell.

"Maybe it'll happen tonight." Zeke watched his breath puff out like smoke as he and his twin sat in the tree house, wrapped against the December chill in coats and scarves.

"It's not Christmas yet."

"But it's the Christmas concert," Zeke said stubbornly. He was tired of waiting for the mom. "That's where we saw her first. And they'll have the music and the tree and stuff, so it'll be like Christmas."

"I don't know." Zack liked the idea, a lot, but was more cautious. "Maybe, but we don't get any presents until Christmas."

"We do, too. When Mr. Perkins pretends to be Santa at the party at the firehouse. That's whole weeks before Christmas, and he gives all the kids presents."

"Not *real* presents. Not stuff you ask for." But Zack set his mind to it. "Maybe if we wish real hard. Dad likes her a lot. Aunt Mira was telling Uncle Dave that Dad's found the right woman even if he doesn't know it." Zack's brow creased. "How could he not know it if he found her?"

"Aunt Mira's always saying stuff that doesn't make sense," Zeke said, with the easy disdain of the young. "Dad's going to marry her, and she's going to come live with us and be the mom. She has to be. We've been good, haven't we?"

"Uh-huh." Zack played with the toe of his boot. "Do you think she'll love us and all that?"

"Probably." Zeke shot his twin a look. "I love her already."

"Me, too." Zack smiled in relief. Everything was going to be okay after all.

"All right, people." Nell pitched her voice above the din in the chorus room. It doubled as backstage on concert nights, and students were swarming around, checking clothes, makeup and hair and working off preperformance jitters by talking at the top of their lungs. "Settle down."

One of her students had his head between his knees, fighting off acute stage fright. Nell sent him a sympathetic smile as her group began to quiet.

"You've all worked really hard for tonight. I know a lot of you are jumpy because you have friends and family out in the audience. Use the nerves to sharpen your performance. Please try to remember to go out onstage in the organized, dignified manner we've practiced."

There were some snickers at that. Nell merely lifted a brow. "I should have said remember to be more dignified and more orderly than you've managed at practice. Diaphragms," she said. "Projection. Posture. Smiles." She paused, lifted a hand. "And above all, I expect you to remember the most vital ingredient in tonight's performance. Enjoy it," she said, and grinned. "It's Christmas. Now let's go knock 'em dead."

Her heart was doing some pretty fancy pumping of its own as she directed the children onstage, watched them take their positions on the risers as the murmurs from the audience rose and ebbed. For many, Nell knew, this concert would be her first test. Decisions from the community would be made tonight as to whether the school board had made a good or a bad choice in their new music teacher.

She took a deep breath, tugged at the hem of her velvet jacket and stepped onstage.

There was polite applause as she approached the solo mike.

"Welcome to Taylor's Grove High School's holiday concert," she began.

"Gosh, Dad, doesn't Miss Davis look pretty?"

"Yeah, Zack, she does." *Lovely* was more the word, he thought, in that soft-looking deep forest-green suit, with holly berries in her hair and a quick, nervous smile on her face.

She looked terrific in the spotlight. He wondered if she knew it.

At the moment, all Nell knew was nerves. She wished she could see faces clearly. She'd always preferred seeing her audience when she was performing. It made it more intimate, more fun. After her announcement, she turned, saw every student's eyes on hers, then smiled in reassurance.

"Okay, kids," she murmured, in an undertone only they could hear. "Let's rock."

She started them off with a bang, the Springsteen number, and it had eyes popping wide in the audience. This was not the usual yawn-inspiring program most had been expecting.

When the applause hit, Nell felt the tension dissolve. They'd crossed the first hurdle. She segued from the fun to the traditional, thrilled when the auditorium filled with the harmony on "Cantate Domine," delighted when her sopranos soared on "Adeste Fideles," grinning when they bounced into "Jingle Bell Rock," complete with the little stage business of swaying and hand clapping they'd worked on.

And her heart swelled when Kim approached the mike and the first pure notes of her solo flowed into the air.

"Oh, Dave." Sniffling, Mira clutched her husband's hand, then Mac's. "Our baby."

Nell's prediction had been on target. When Kim stepped back in position, there were damp eyes in every row. They closed the concert with "Silent Night," only voices, no piano. The way it was meant to be sung, Nell had told her students. The way it was written to be sung.

When the last note died and she turned to gesture to her chorus, the audience was already on its feet. The kick of it jolted through her as she turned her head, saw the slack jaws, wide eyes and foolish grins of her students.

Nell swallowed tears, waiting until the noise abated slightly before crossing to the mike again. She knew how to play it.

"They were terrific, weren't they?"

As she'd hoped, that started the cheers and applause all over again. She waited it out.

"I'd like to thank you all for coming, for supporting the chorus. I owe a special thanks to the parents of the singers onstage tonight for their patience, their understanding and their willingness to let me share their children for a few hours every day. Every student onstage has worked tremendously hard for tonight, and I'm delighted that you appreciate their talent, and their effort. I'd like to add that the poinsettias you see onstage were donated by Hill Florists and are for sale at three dollars a pot. Proceeds to go to the fund for new choir uniforms. Merry Christmas, and come back."

Before she could step away from the mike, Kim and Brad were standing on either side of her.

"There's just one more thing." Brad cleared his throat until the rustling in the audience died down. "The chorus would like to present a token of appreciation to Miss Davis for all her work and encouragement. Ah..." Kim had written the speech out, but Brad had been designated to say it. He fumbled a little, grinned self-consciously at Kim. "This is Miss Davis's first concert at Taylor High. Ah..." He just couldn't remember all the nice words Kim had written, so he said what he felt. "She's the best. Thanks, Miss Davis."

"We hope you like it," Kim murmured under the applause as she handed Nell a brightly wrapped box. "All the kids chipped in."

"I'm..." She didn't know what to say, was afraid to try. When she opened the box, she stared, misty-eyed, down at a pin shaped like a treble clef.

"We know you like jewelry," Kim began. "So we thought—"

"It's beautiful. It's perfect." Taking a steadying breath, she turned to the chorus. "Thanks. It means almost as much to me as you do. Merry Christmas."

"She got a present," Zack pointed out. They were waiting in the crowded corridor outside the auditorium to congratulate Kim. "That means we could get one tonight. We could get her."

"Not if she goes home right after." Zack had already worked this out. He was waiting for his moment. When he saw her, he pounced. "Miss Davis! Over here, Miss Davis!"

Mac didn't move. Couldn't. Something had happened while he sat three rows back, watching her on the stage. Seeing her smile, seeing tears in her eyes. Just seeing her.

He was in love with her. It was nothing he'd ever experienced. Nothing he knew how to handle. Running seemed the smartest solution, but he didn't think he could move.

"Hi!" She crouched down for hugs, squeezing the boys tight, kissing each cheek. "Did you like the concert?"

"It was real good. Kim was the best."

Nell leaned close to Zeke's ear. "I think so, too, but it has to be a secret."

"We're good at keeping secrets." He smiled smugly at his brother. "We've had one for weeks and weeks."

"Can you come to our house now, Miss Davis?" Zack clung to her hand and put all his charm into his eyes. "Please? Come see our tree and the lights. We put lights everywhere so you can see them from all the way down on the road."

"I'd like that." Testing the water, she glanced up at Mac. "But your dad might be tired."

He wasn't tired, he was flattened. Her lashes were still damp, and the little pin the kids had given her glinted against her velvet jacket. "You're welcome to come out, if you don't mind the drive."

"I'd like it. I'm still wired up." She straightened, searching for some sign of welcome or rebuff in Mac's face. "If you're sure it isn't a bad time."

"No." His tongue was thick, he realized. As if he'd been drinking. "I want to talk to you."

"I'll head out as soon as I'm finished here, then." She winked at the boys and melted back into the crowd.

"She's done wonders with those kids." Mrs. Hollis nodded to Mac. "It'll be a shame to lose her."

"Lose her?" Mac glanced down at his boys, but they were already in a huddle, exchanging whispers. "What do you mean?"

"I heard from Mr. Perkins, who got it from Addie McVie at the high school office, that Nell Davis was offered her old position back at that New York school starting next fall. Nell and the principal had themselves a conference just this morning." Mrs. Hollis babbled on as Mac stared blankly over her head. "Hate to think about her leaving us. Made a difference with these kids." She spied one of her gossip buddies and elbowed her way through the crowd.

Chapter Nine

Control came easily to Mac—or at least it had for the past seven years. He used all the control at his disposal to keep his foul mood and bubbling temper from the boys.

They were so excited about her coming, he thought bitterly. Wanted to make certain all the lights were lit, the cookies were out, the decorative bell was hung on Zark's collar.

They were in love with her, too, he realized. And that made it a hell of a mess.

He should have known better. He *had* known better. Somehow he'd let it happen anyway. Let himself slip, let himself fall. And he'd dragged his kids along with him.

Well, he'd have to fix it, wouldn't he? Mac got himself a beer, tipped the bottle back. He was good at fixing things.

"Ladies like wine," Zack informed him. "Like Aunt Mira does."

He remembered Nell had sipped white wine at Mira's party. "I don't have any," he muttered.

Because his father looked unhappy, Zack hugged Mac's leg. "You can buy some before she comes over next time."

Reaching down, Mac cupped his son's upturned face. The

love was so strong, so vital, Mac could all but feel it grip him by the throat. "Always got an answer, don't you, pal?"

"You like her, don't you, Dad?"

"Yeah, she's nice."

"And she likes us, too, right?"

"Hey, who wouldn't like the Taylor guys?" He sat at the kitchen table, pulled Zack into his lap. He'd discovered when his sons were infants that there was nothing more magical than holding your own child. "Most of the time *I* even like you."

That made Zack giggle and cuddle closer. "She has to live all by herself, though." Zack began to play with the buttons of his father's shirt. A sure sign, Mac knew, that he was leading up to something.

"Lots of people live alone."

"We've got a big house, and two whole rooms nobody sleeps in except when Grandma and Pop come to visit."

His radar was humming. Mac tugged on his son's ear. "Zack, what are you getting at?"

"Nothing." Lip poked out, Zack toyed with another button. "I was just wondering what it would be like if she came and lived here." He peeked up under his lashes. "So she wouldn't be lonely."

"Nobody said she was lonely," Mac pointed out. "And I think you should—"

The doorbell rang, sending the dog into a fit of excited barking and jingling. Zeke flew into the kitchen, dancing from foot to foot. "She's here! She's here!"

"I got the picture." Mac ruffled Zack's hair, set him on his feet. "Well, let her in. It's cold out."

"I'll do it!"

"*I'll* do it!"

The twins had a fierce race through the house to the front door. They hit it together, fought over the knob, then all but dragged Nell over the threshold once they'd yanked the door open.

"You took so long," Zeke complained. "We've been waiting forever. I put on Christmas music. Hear? And we've got the tree lit and everything."

"So I see." It was a lovely room, one she tried not to resent having only now been invited into.

She knew Mac had built most of the house himself. He'd told her that much. He'd created an open, homey space, with lots of wood, a glass-fronted fireplace where stockings were already hung. The tree, a six-foot blue spruce, was wildly decorated and placed with pride in front of the wide front window.

"It's terrific." Letting the boys pull her along, Nell crossed over to give the tree a closer look. "Really wonderful. It makes the little one in my apartment look scrawny."

"You can share ours." Zack looked up at her, his heart in his eyes. "We can get you a stocking and everything, and have your name put on it."

"They do it at the mall," Zeke told her. "We'll get you a big one."

Now they were pulling at her heart, as well as her hands. Filled with the emotion of the moment, she crouched down to hug them to her. "You guys are the best." She laughed as Zark pushed in for attention. "You, too." Her arms full of kids and dog, she looked up to smile at Mac as he stepped in from the kitchen. "Hi. Sorry I took so long. Some of the kids hung around, wanting to go over every mistake and triumph of the concert."

She shouldn't look so right, so perfect, snuggling his boys under the tree. "I didn't hear any mistakes."

"They were there. But we'll work on them."

She scooted back, sitting on a hassock and taking both boys with her. As if, Mac thought, she meant to keep them.

"We don't have any wine," Zack informed her solemnly. "But we have milk and juice and sodas and beer. Lots of other things. Or…" He cast a crafty look in his father's direction. "Somebody could make hot cocoa."

"One of my specialties." Nell stood to shrug out of her coat. "Where's the kitchen?"

"I'll make it," Mac muttered.

"I'll help." Baffled by his sudden distance, she walked to him. "Or don't you like women in your kitchen?"

"We don't get many around here. You looked good up onstage."

"Thanks. It felt good being there."

He looked past her, into the wide, anticipation-filled eyes of his children. "Why don't you two go change into your pajamas? The cocoa'll be finished by the time you are."

"We'll be faster," Zeke vowed, and shot toward the stairs.

"Only if you throw your clothes on the floor. And don't." He turned back into the kitchen.

"Will they hang them up, or push them under the bed?" Nell asked.

"Zack'll hang them up and they'll fall on the floor. Zeke'll push them under the bed."

She laughed, watching him get out milk and cocoa. "I meant to tell you, a few days ago they came in with Kim to rehearsal. They'd switched sweaters—you know, the color code. I really impressed them when I knew who was who anyway."

He paused in the act of measuring cocoa into a pan. "How did you?"

"I guess I didn't think about it. They're each their own person. Facial expressions. You know how Zeke's eyes narrow and Zack looks under his lashes when they're pleased about something. Inflections in the voice." She opened a cupboard at random, looking for mugs. "Posture. There are all sorts of little clues if you pay attention and look closely enough. Ah, found them." Pleased with herself, she took out four mugs and set them on the counter. She tilted her head when she saw him studying her. Analytically, she thought. As if she were something to be measured and fit into place. "Is something wrong?"

"I wanted to talk to you." He busied himself with heating the cocoa.

"So you said." She found she needed to steady herself with a hand on the counter. "Mac, am I misreading something, or are you pulling back?"

"I don't know that I'd call it that."

Something was going to hurt. Nell braced for it. "What would you call it?" she said, as calmly as she could.

"I'm a little concerned about the boys. About the fallout when you move on. They're getting too involved." Why did that sound so stupid? he wondered. Why did he feel so stupid?

"*They* are?"

"I think we've been sending the wrong signals, and it would be best for them if we backed off." He concentrated on the cocoa as if it were a nuclear experiment. "We've gone out a few times, and we've…"

"Slept together," she finished, cool now. It was the last defense.

He looked around, sharply. But he could still hear the stomping of little feet in the room overhead. "Yeah. We've slept together, and it was great. The thing is, kids pick up on more things than most people think. And they get ideas. They get attached."

"And you don't want them to get attached to me." Yes, she realized. It was going to hurt. "You don't want to get attached."

"I just think it would be a mistake to take it any further."

"Clear enough. The No Trespassing signs are back up, and I'm out."

"It's not like that, Nell." He set the spoon down, took a step toward her. But there was a line he couldn't quite cross. A line he'd created himself. If he didn't make certain they both stayed on their own sides of it, the life he'd so carefully built could crumble. "I've got things under control here, and I need to keep them that way. I'm all they've got. They're all I've got. I can't mess that up."

"No explanations necessary." Her voice had thickened. In a moment, she knew, it would begin to shake. "You made it clear from the beginning. Crystal clear. Funny, the first time you invite me into your home, it's to toss me out."

"I'm not tossing you out, I'm trying to realign things."

"Oh, go to hell, and keep your realignments for your houses." She sprinted out of the kitchen.

"Nell, don't go like this." But by the time he reached the living room, she was grabbing her coat, and his boys were racing down the stairs.

"Where are you going, Miss Davis? You haven't—" Both boys stopped, shocked by the tears streaming down her face.

"I'm sorry." It was too late to hide them, so she kept heading for the door. "I have to do something. I'm sorry."

And she was gone, with Mac standing impotently in the living room and both boys staring at him. A dozen excuses spun around in his head. Even as he tried to grab one, Zack burst into tears.

"She went away. You made her cry, and she went away."

"I didn't mean to. She—" He moved to gather his sons up and was met with a solid wall of resistance.

"You ruined everything." A tear spilled out of Zeke's eyes, heated by temper. "We did everything we were supposed to, and you ruined it."

"She'll never come back." Zack sat on the bottom step and sobbed. "She'll never be the mom now."

"What?" At his wit's end, Mac dragged his hand through his hair. "What are you two talking about?"

"You ruined it," Zeke said again.

"Look, Miss Davis and I had a…disagreement. People have disagreements. It's not the end of the world." He wished it didn't feel like the end of his world.

"Santa sent her." Zack rubbed his eyes with his fists. "He sent her, just like we asked him. And now she's gone."

"What do you mean, Santa sent her?" Determined, Mac sat

on the steps. He pulled a reluctant Zack into his lap and tugged Zeke down to join them. "Miss Davis came from New York to teach music, not from the North Pole."

"We know that." Temper set aside, Zeke sought comfort, turning his face into his father's chest. "She came because we sent Santa a letter, months and months ago, so we'd be early and he'd have time."

"Have time for what?"

"To pick out the mom." On a shuddering sigh, Zack sniffed and looked up at his father. "We wanted someone nice, who smelled good and liked dogs and had yellow hair. And we asked, and she came. And you were supposed to marry her and make her the mom."

Mac let out a long breath and prayed for wisdom. "Why didn't you tell me you were thinking about having a mother?"

"Not *a* mom," Zeke told him. "*The* mom. Miss Davis is the mom, but she's gone now. We love her, and she won't like us anymore because you made her cry."

"Of course she'll still like you." She'd hate him, but she wouldn't take it out on the boys. "But you two are old enough to know you don't get moms from Santa."

"He sent her, just like we asked him. We didn't ask for anything else but the bikes." Zack burrowed into his lap. "We didn't ask for any toys or any games. Just the mom. Make her come back, Dad. Fix it. You always fix it."

"It doesn't work like that, pal. People aren't broken toys or old houses. Santa didn't send her, she moved here for a job."

"He did, too, send her." With surprising dignity, Zack pushed off his father's lap. "Maybe you don't want her, but we do."

His sons walked up the stairs, a united front that closed him out. Mac was left with emptiness in the pit of his stomach and the smell of burned cocoa.

Chapter Ten

She should get out of town for a few days, Nell thought. Go somewhere. Go anywhere. There was nothing more pathetic than sitting alone on Christmas Eve and watching other people bustle along the street outside your window.

She'd turned down every holiday party invitation, made excuses that sounded hollow even to her. She was brooding, she admitted, and it was entirely unlike her. But then again, she'd never had a broken heart to nurse before.

With Bob it had been wounded pride. And that had healed itself with embarrassing speed.

Now she was left with bleeding emotions at the time of year when love was most important.

She missed him. Oh, she hated to know that she missed him. That slow, hesitant smile, the quiet voice, the gentleness of him. In New York, at least, she could have lost herself in the crowds, in the rush. But here, everywhere she looked was another reminder.

Go somewhere, Nell. Just get in the car and drive.

She ached to see the children. Wondered if they'd taken their sleds out in the fresh snow that had fallen yesterday. Were they counting the hours until Christmas, plotting to stay awake until they heard reindeer on the roof?

She had presents for them, wrapped and under her tree. She'd send them via Kim or Mira, she thought, and was miserable all over again because she wouldn't see their faces as they tore off the wrappings.

They're not your children, she reminded herself. On that point Mac had always been clear. Sharing himself had been difficult enough. Sharing his children had stopped him dead.

She would go away, she decided, and forced herself to move. She would pack a bag, toss it in the car and drive until she felt like stopping. She'd take a couple of days. Hell, she'd take a week. She couldn't bear to stay here alone through the holidays.

For the next ten minutes, she tossed things into a suitcase without any plan or sense of order. Now that the decision was made, she only wanted to move quickly. She closed the lid on the suitcase, carried it into the living room and started for her coat.

The knock on her door had her clenching her teeth. If one more well-meaning neighbor stopped by to wish her Merry Christmas and invite her to dinner, she was going to scream.

She opened the door and felt the fresh wound stab through her. "Well, Macauley... Out wishing your tenants happy holidays?"

"Can I come in?"

"Why?"

"Nell." There was a wealth of patience in the word. "Please, let me come in."

"Fine, you own the place." She turned her back on him. "Sorry, I haven't any wassail, and I'm very low on good cheer."

"I need to talk to you." He'd been trying to find the right way and the right words for days.

"Really? Excuse me if I don't welcome it. The last time you needed to talk to me is still firmly etched in my mind."

"I didn't mean to make you cry."

"I cry easily. You should see me after a greeting-card commercial on TV." She couldn't keep up the snide comments, and she gave in, asking the question that was uppermost in her mind. "How are the kids?"

"Barely speaking to me." At her blank look, he gestured toward the couch. "Will you sit down? This is kind of a complicated story."

"I'll stand. I don't have a lot of time, actually. I was just leaving."

His gaze followed hers and landed on the suitcase. His mouth tightened. "Well, it didn't take long."

"What didn't?"

"I guess you took them up on that offer to teach back in New York."

"Word does travel. No, I didn't take them up. I like my job here, I like the people here, and I intend to stay. I'm just going on a holiday."

"You're going on a holiday at five o'clock on Christmas Eve?"

"I can come and go as I please. No, don't take off your coat," she snapped. Tears were threatening. "Just say your piece and get out. I still pay the rent here. On second thought, just leave now. Damn it, you're not going to make me cry again."

"The boys think Santa sent you."

"Excuse me?"

As the first tear spilled over, he moved to her, brushed it away with his thumb. "Don't cry, Nell. I hate knowing I made you cry."

"Don't touch me." She whirled away and fumbled a tissue out of the box.

He was discovering exactly how it felt to be sliced in two. "I'm sorry." Slowly he lowered his hand to his side. "I know how you must feel about me now."

"You don't know the half of it." She blew her nose, struggled for control. "What's this about the boys and Santa?"

"They wrote a letter back in the fall, not long before they met you. They decided they wanted a mom for Christmas. Not *a* mom," Mac explained as she turned back to stare at him. "*The* mom. They keep correcting me on that one. They had pretty specific ideas about what they wanted. She was supposed to have yellow hair and smile a lot, like kids and dogs and bake cookies. They wanted bikes, too, but that was sort of an after-thought. All they really wanted was the mom."

"Oh." She did sit now, lowering herself onto the arm of the sofa. "That explains a couple of things." Steadying herself, she looked back at him. "Put you in quite a spot, didn't it? I know you love them, Mac, but starting a relationship with me to try to please your children takes things beyond parental devotion."

"I didn't know. Damn it, do you think I'd play with their feelings, or yours, that way?"

"Not theirs," she said hollowly. "Certainly not theirs."

He remembered how delicate she had seemed when they made love. There was more fragility now. No roses in her cheeks, he saw with a pang of distress. No light in her eyes. "I know what it's like to be hurt, Nell. I never would have hurt you deliberately. They didn't tell me about the letter until the night… You weren't the only one I made cry that night. I tried to explain that Santa doesn't work that way, but they've got it fixed in their heads that he sent you."

"I'll talk to them if you want me to."

"I don't deserve—"

"Not for you," she said. "For them."

He nodded, accepting. "I wondered how it would make you feel to know they wished for you."

"Don't push me, Mac."

He couldn't help it, and he kept his eyes on hers as he moved closer. "They wished for you for me, too. That's why they didn't tell me. You were our Christmas present." He reached down, touched her hair. "How does that make you feel?"

"How do you think I feel?" She batted his hand away and rose to face the window. "It hurts. I fell in love with the three of you almost from the first glance, and it hurts. Go away, leave me alone."

Somehow a fist had crept into his chest and was squeezing at his heart. "I thought you'd go away. I thought you'd leave us alone. I wouldn't let myself believe you cared enough to stay."

"Then you were an idiot," she mumbled.

"I was clumsy." He watched the tiny lights on her tree shining in her hair and gave up any thought of saving himself. "All right, I was an idiot. The worst kind, because I kept hiding from what you might feel, from what I felt. I didn't fall in love with you right away. At least I didn't know it. Not until the night of the concert. I wanted to tell you. I didn't know how to tell you. Then I heard something about the New York offer and it was the perfect excuse to push you out. I thought I was protecting the kids from getting hurt." No, he wouldn't use them, he thought in disgust. Not even to get her back. "That was only part of it. I was protecting myself. I couldn't control the way I felt about you. It scared me."

"Now's no different from then, Mac."

"It could be different." He took a chance and laid his hands on her shoulders, turned her to face him. "It took my own sons to show me that sometimes you've just got to wish. Don't leave me, Nell. Don't leave us."

"I was never going anywhere."

"Forgive me." She started to turn her head away, but he cupped her cheek, held it gently. "Please. Maybe I can't fix this, but give me a chance to try. I need you in my life. We need you."

There was such patience in his voice, such quiet strength in the hand on her face. Even as she looked at him, her heart began to heal. "I love you. All of you. I can't help it."

Relief and gratitude flavored the kiss as he touched his lips to hers. "I love you. I don't want to help it." Drawing her close, he cradled her head on his shoulder. "It's just been the three of us for so long, I didn't know how to make room. I think I'm figuring it out." He eased her away again and reached into his coat pocket. "I bought you a present."

"Mac." Still staggered from the roller-coaster emotions, she rubbed her hands over her damp cheeks. "It isn't Christmas yet."

"Close enough. I think if you'd open it now, I'd stop having all this tightness in my chest."

"All right." She dashed another tear aside. "We'll consider it a peace offering, then. I may even decide to…" She trailed off when the box was open in her hand. A ring, the traditional single diamond crowning a gold band.

"Marry me, Nell," he said quietly. "Be the mom."

She raised dazzled eyes to his. "You move awfully quickly for someone who always seems to take his time."

"Christmas Eve." He watched her face as he took the ring out of the box. "It seemed like the night to push my luck."

"It was a good choice." Smiling, she held out her hand. "A very good choice." When the ring was on her finger, she lifted her hand to his cheek. "When?"

He should have known it would be simple. With her, it would always be simple. "New Year's Eve's only a week away. It would be a good start to a new year. A new life."

"Yes."

"Will you come home with me tonight? I left the kids at Mira's. We could pick them up, and you'd spend Christmas where you belong." Before she could answer, he smiled and kissed her hand. "You're already packed."

"So I am. It must be magic."

"I'm beginning to believe it." He framed her face with his

hands, lowered his mouth for a long, lingering kiss. "Maybe I didn't wish for you, but you're all I want for Christmas, Nell."

He rubbed his cheek over her hair, looked out at the colored lights gleaming on the houses below. "Did you hear something?" he murmured.

"Mmm..." She held him close, smiled. "Sleigh bells."

★ ★ ★ ★ ★

CAPTIVATED

To Marianne Willman, for the past, the present and the future

Prologue

She was born the night the Witch Tree fell. With the first breath she drew, she tasted the power—the richness of it, and the bitterness. Her birth was one more link in a chain that had spanned centuries, a chain that was often gilded with the sheen of folklore and legend. But when the chain was rubbed clean, it held fast, tempered by the strength of truth.

There were other worlds, other places, where those first cries of birth were celebrated. Far beyond the sweeping vistas of the Monterey coast, where the child's lusty cry echoed through the old stone house, the new life was celebrated. In the secret places where magic still thrived—deep in the green hills of Ireland, on the windswept moors of Cornwall, deep in the caves of Wales, along the rocky coast of Brittany—that sweet song of life was welcomed.

And the old tree, hunched and gnarled by its age and its marriage to the wind, was a quiet sacrifice.

With its death, and a mother's willing pain, a new witch was born.

Though the choice would be hers—a gift, after all, can be refused, treasured or ignored—it would remain as much a part of the child, and the woman she became, as the color of her eyes. For now she was only an infant, her sight still dim, her thoughts still half-formed, shaking angry fists in the air even as her father laughed and pressed his first kiss on her downy head.

Her mother wept when the babe drank from her breast. Wept in joy and in sorrow. She knew already that she would have only this one girl child to celebrate the love and union she and her husband shared.

She had looked, and she had seen.

As she rocked the nursing child and sang an old song, she understood that there would be lessons to be taught, mistakes to be made. And she understood that one day—not so long from now, in the vast scope of lifetimes—her child would also look for love.

She hoped that of all the gifts she would pass along, all the truths she would tell, the child would understand one, the vital one.

That the purest magic is in the heart.

Chapter One

There was a marker in the ground where the Witch Tree had stood. The people of Monterey and Carmel valued nature. Tourists often came to study the words on the marker, or simply to stand and look at the sculptured old trees, the rocky shoreline, the sunning harbor seals.

Locals who had seen the tree for themselves, who remembered the day it had fallen, often mentioned the fact that Morgana Donovan had been born that night.

Some said it was a sign, others shrugged and called it coincidence. Still more simply wondered. No one denied that it was excellent local color to have a self-proclaimed witch born hardly a stone's throw away from a tree with a reputation.

Nash Kirkland considered it an amusing fact and an interesting hook. He spent a great deal of his time studying the supernatural. Vampires and werewolves and things that went bump in the night were a hell of a way to make a living. And he wouldn't have had it any other way.

Not that he believed in goblins or ghoulies—or witches, if it came to that. Men didn't turn into bats or wolves at moonrise, the dead did not walk, and women didn't soar through the night on broomsticks. Except in the pages of a book, or in the flickering light and shadow of a movie screen.

There, he was pleased to say, anything was possible.

He was a sensible man who knew the value of illusions, and the importance of simple entertainment. He was also enough of a dreamer to conjure images out of the shades of folklore and superstition for the masses to enjoy.

He'd fascinated the horror-film buff for seven years, starting with his first—and surprisingly successful—screenplay, *Shape Shifter.*

The fact was, Nash loved seeing his imagination come to life on-screen. He wasn't above popping into the neighborhood movie theater and happily devouring popcorn while the audience caught their breath, stifled screams or covered their eyes.

He delighted in knowing that the people who plunked down the price of a ticket to see one of his movies were going to get their money's worth of chills.

He always researched carefully. While writing the gruesome and amusing *Midnight Blood,* he'd spent a week in Romania interviewing a man who swore he was a direct descendant of Vlad, the Impaler—Count Dracula. Unfortunately, the count's descendant hadn't grown fangs or turned into a bat, but he had proven to possess a wealth of vampire lore and legend.

It was such folktales that inspired Nash to spin a story—particularly when they were related by someone whose belief gave them punch.

And people considered him weird, he thought, grinning to himself as he passed the entrance to Seventeen Mile Drive. Nash knew he was an ordinary, grounded-to-earth type. At least by California standards. He just made his living from illusion, from playing on basic fears and superstitions—and the pleasure people took in being scared silly. He figured his value to society was his ability to take the monster out of the closet and flash it on the silver screen in Technicolor, usually adding a few dashes of unapologetic sex and sly humor.

Nash Kirkland could bring the bogeyman to life, turn the gentle Dr. Jekyll into the evil Mr. Hyde, or invoke the mummy's curse. All by putting words on paper. Maybe that was why he was a cynic. Oh, he enjoyed stories about the supernatural—but he, of all people, knew that was all they were. Stories. And he had a million of them.

He hoped Morgana Donovan, Monterey's favorite witch, would help him create the next one. For the past few weeks, between unpacking and taking pleasure in his new home, trying his skill at golf—and finally giving it up as a lost cause—and simply treasuring the view from his balcony, Nash had felt the urge to tell a tale of witchcraft. If there was such a thing as fate, he figured, it had done him a favor by plunking him down only a short, pleasant drive from an expert.

Whistling along with the car radio, he wondered what she'd be like. Turbaned or tasseled? Draped in black crepe? Or maybe she was some New Age fanatic who spoke only through Gargin, her channeler from Atlantis.

Either way, he wouldn't mind a bit. It was the loonies in the world that gave life its flavor.

He'd purposely avoided doing any extensive research on the witch. He wanted to form his own opinions and impressions, leaving his mind clear to start forming plot angles. All he knew was that she'd been born right here in Monterey, some twenty-eight years before, and she ran a successful shop that catered to people who were into crystals and herbs.

He had to give her two thumbs-up for staying in her hometown. After less than a month as a resident of Monterey, he wondered how he could ever have lived anywhere else. And God knew, he thought as his angular face creased in a grimace, he'd already lived just about everywhere.

Again, he had to thank his luck for making his scripts appealing to the masses. His imagination had made it possible for him to move away from the traffic and smog of L.A. to this priceless spot in northern California.

It was barely March, but he had the top down on his Jag, and the bright, brisk breeze whipped through his dark blond hair. There was the smell of water—it was never far away here—of grass, neatly clipped, of the flowers that thrived in the mild climate.

The sky was cloudless, a beautiful blue, his car was purring like a big, lean cat, he'd recently disentangled himself from a relationship that had been rushing downhill, and he was about to start a new project. As far as Nash was concerned, life was perfect.

He spotted the shop. As he'd been told, it stood neatly on the corner, flanked by a boutique and a restaurant. The businesses were obviously doing well, as he had to park more than a block away. He didn't mind the walk. His long, jeans-clad legs ate up the sidewalk. He passed a group of tourists who were arguing over where to have lunch, a pencil-slim woman in fuchsia silk leading two Afghan hounds, and a businessman who strolled along chatting on his cell phone.

Nash loved California.

He stopped outside the shop. The sign painted on the window simply read WICCA. He nodded, smiling to himself. He liked it. The Old English word for witch. It brought to mind images of bent old women, trundling through the villages to cast spells and remove warts.

Exterior scene, day, he thought. The sky is murky with clouds, the wind rushes and howls. In a small, run-down village with broken fences and shuttered windows, a wrinkled old woman hurries down a dirt road, a heavy covered basket in her arms. A huge black raven screams as it glides by. With a flutter of wings, it stops to perch on a rusted gatepost. Bird and woman stare at each other. From somewhere in the distance comes a long, desperate scream.

Nash lost the image when someone came out of the shop, turned and bumped into him.

"Sorry," came the muffled apology.

He simply nodded. Just as well, Nash thought. It wouldn't do to take the story too far until he'd talked to the expert. For now, what he wanted was to take a good look at her wares.

The window display was impressive, he noted, and showed a flair for the dramatic. Deep blue velvet was draped over stands of various heights and widths so that it resembled a wide river with dark waterfalls. Floating over it were clusters of crystals, sparkling like magic in the morning sun. Some were as clear as glass, while others were of almost heartbreaking hues. Rose and aqua, royal-purple, ink-black. They were shaped like wands or castles or small, surrealistic cities.

Lips pursed, he rocked back on his heels. He could see how they would appeal to people—the colors, the shapes, the sparkle. That anybody could actually believe a hunk of rock held any kind of power was one more reason to marvel at the human brain. Still, they were certainly pretty enough. Above the clusters, faceted drops hung from thin wires and tossed rainbows everywhere.

Maybe she kept the cauldrons in the back.

The idea made him chuckle to himself. Still, he took a last look at the display before pushing open the door. It was tempting to pick up a few pieces for himself. A paperweight, or a sun-catcher. He might just settle for that—if she wasn't selling any dragon's scales or wolf's teeth.

The shop was crowded with people. His own fault, Nash reminded himself, for dropping in on a Saturday. Still, it would give him time to poke around and see just how a witch ran a business in the twentieth century.

The displays inside were just as dramatic as those glistening in the window. Huge chunks of rock, some sliced open to reveal hundreds of crystal teeth. Dainty little bottles filled with colored liquid. Nash was slightly disappointed when he read one label and discovered that it was a rosemary bath balm, for relaxing the senses. He'd hoped for at least one love potion.

There were more herbs, packaged for potpourri, for tea and for culinary uses, as well as candles in soft colors and crystals in all shapes and sizes. Some interesting jewelry—again leaning heavily on crystals—was sparkling behind glass. Artwork, paintings, statues, sculpture, all so cleverly placed that the shop might more accurately have been termed a gallery.

Nash, always interested in the unusual, took a fancy to a pewter lamp fashioned in the shape of a winged dragon with glowing red eyes.

Then he spotted her. One look had him certain that this was the very image of the modern witch. The sulky-looking blonde was holding a discussion with two customers over a table of tumbling stones. She had a luscious little body poured into a sleek black jumpsuit. Glittery earrings hung to her shoulders, and rings adorned every finger. The fingers ended in long, lethal-looking red nails.

"Attractive, isn't he?"

"Hmm?" The smoke-edged voice had Nash turning away from the dragon. This time one look had him forgetting the stacked young witch in the corner. He found himself lost for several heartbeats in a pair of cobalt-blue eyes. "Excuse me?"

"The dragon." Smiling, she ran a hand over the pewter head. "I was just wondering if I should take him home with me." She smiled, and he saw that her lips were full and soft and unpainted. "Do you like dragons?"

"Crazy about them," he decided on the spot. "Do you shop in here often?"

"Yes." She lifted a hand to her hair. It was black as midnight and fell in careless waves to her waist. Nash made an effort and tried to put the pieces of her together. The ebony hair went with pale, creamy skin. The eyes were wide and heavily lashed, the nose was small and sharp. She was nearly as tall as he, and wand slender. The simple blue dress she wore showed taste and style, as well as subtle curves.

There was something, well, dazzling about her, he realized. Though he couldn't analyze what while he was so busy enjoying it.

As he watched, her lips curved again. There was something very aware as well as amused in the movement. "Have you been in Wicca before?"

"No. Great stuff."

"You're interested in crystals?"

"I could be." Idly he picked up a hunk of amethyst. "But I flunked my earth science course in high school."

"I don't think you'll be graded here." She nodded toward the stone he held. "If you want to get in touch with your inner self, you should hold it in your left hand."

"Oh, yeah?" To indulge her, he shifted it. He hated to tell her he didn't feel a thing—other than a shaft of pleasure at the way the dress skimmed around her knees. "If you're a regular here, maybe you could introduce me to the witch."

Brow lifted, she followed his look as he glanced at the blonde, who was finishing up her sale. "Do you need a witch?"

"I guess you could say that."

She turned those wonderful blue eyes on him again. "You don't look like the type who'd come looking for a love spell."

He grinned. "Thanks. I think. Actually, I'm doing some research. I write movies. I want to do a story on witchcraft in the nineties. You know...secret covens, sex and sacrifices."

"Ah." When she inclined her head, clear crystal drops swung at her ears. "Nubile women doing ring dances sky-clad. Naked," she explained. "Mixing potions by the dark of the moon to seduce their hapless victims into orgies of prurient delights."

"More or less." He leaned closer and discovered that she

smelled as cool and dark as a forest in moonlight. "Does this Morgana really believe she's a witch?"

"She knows what she is, Mr.—?"

"Kirkland. Nash Kirkland."

Her laugh was low and pleased. "Of course. I've enjoyed your work. I particularly liked *Midnight Blood*. You gave your vampire a great deal of wit and sensuality without trampling on tradition."

"There's more to being undead than graveyard dirt and coffins."

"I suppose. And there's more to being a witch than stirring a cauldron."

"Exactly. That's why I want to interview her. I figure she's got to be a pretty sharp lady to pull all this off."

"Pull off?" she repeated as she bent to pick up a huge white cat that had sauntered over to flow around her legs.

"The reputation," he explained. "I heard about her in L.A. People bring me weird stories."

"I'm sure they do." She stroked the cat's massive head. Now Nash had two pair of eyes trained on him. One pair of cobalt, and one of amber. "But you don't believe in the Craft, or the power."

"I believe I can make it into a hell of a good story." He smiled, putting considerable charm into it. "So, how about it? Put in a good word for me with the witch?"

She studied him. A cynic, she decided, and one entirely too sure of himself. Life, she thought, was obviously one big bed of roses for Nash Kirkland. Maybe it was time he felt a few thorns.

"I don't think that'll be necessary." She offered him a hand, long and slender and adorned with a single ring of hammered silver. He took it automatically, then hissed out a breath as a jolt of electricity zinged up to his shoulder. She just smiled. "I'm your witch," she said.

Static electricity, Nash told himself a moment later, after Morgana had turned away to answer a question from a customer about St. John's wort. She'd been holding that giant cat, rubbing the fur…. That was where the shock had come from.

But he flexed his fingers unconsciously.

Your witch, she'd said. He wasn't sure he liked her use of that particular pronoun. It made things a bit too uncomfortably intimate. Not that she wasn't a stunner. But the way she'd smiled at him when he jolted had been more than a little unnerving. It had also told him just why he'd found her dazzling.

Power. Oh, not *that* kind of power, Nash assured himself as he watched her handle a bundle of dried herbs. But the power some beautiful women seemed to be born with—innate sexuality and a terrifying self-confidence. He didn't like to think of himself as the kind of man who was intimidated by a woman's strength of will, yet there was no denying that the soft, yielding sort was easier to deal with.

In any case, his interest in her was professional. Not purely, he amended. A man would have to have been dead a decade to look at Morgana Donovan and keep his thoughts on a straight professional plane. But Nash figured he could keep his priorities in order.

Nash waited until she was finished with the customer, fixed a self-deprecating smile in place and approached the counter. "I wonder if you've got a handy spell for getting my foot out of my mouth."

"Oh, I think you can manage that on your own." Ordinarily she would have dismissed him, but there must be some reason she'd been drawn across the shop to him. Morgana didn't believe in accidents. Anyway, she decided, any man with such soft brown eyes couldn't be a complete jerk. "I'm afraid your timing's poor, Nash. We're very busy this morning."

"You close at six. How about if I come back then? I'll buy you a drink, dinner?"

Her impulse to refuse was automatic. She would have preferred to meditate on it or study her scrying ball. Before she could speak, the cat leapt onto the counter, clearing the four feet in that weightless soar felines accomplish so easily. Nash reached out absently to scratch the cat's head. Rather than walking off, insulted, or spitting bad-temperedly, as was her habit with strangers, the white cat arched sinuously under the stroking hand. Her amber eyes slitted and stared into Morgana's.

"You seem to have Luna's approval," Morgana muttered. "Six o'clock, then," she said as the cat began to purr lustily. "And I'll decide what to do about you."

"Fair enough." Nash gave Luna one last long stroke, then strolled out.

Frowning, Morgana leaned down until her eyes were level with the cat's. "You'd better know what you're about."

Luna merely shifted her not-inconsiderable weight and began to wash herself.

Morgana didn't have much time to think about Nash. Because she was a woman who was always at war with her impulsive nature, she would have preferred a quiet hour to mull over how best to deal with him. With her hands and mind busy with a flood of customers, Morgana reminded herself that she would have no trouble handling a cocksure storyteller with puppy-dog eyes.

"Wow." Mindy, the lavishly built blonde Nash had admired, plopped down on a stool behind the counter. "We haven't seen a crowd like that since before Christmas."

"I think we're going to have full Saturdays throughout the month."

Grinning, Mindy pulled a stick of gum out of the hip pocket of her snug jumpsuit. "Did you cast a money spell?"

Morgana arranged a glass castle to her liking before responding. "The stars are in an excellent position for business." She smiled. "Plus the fact that our new window display is fabulous. You can go on home, Mindy. I'll total out and lock up."

"I'll take you up on it." She slid sinuously off the stool to stretch, then lifted both darkened brows. "My, oh, my…look at this. Tall, tanned and tasty."

Morgana glanced over and spotted Nash through the front window. He'd had more luck with parking this time, and was unfolding himself from the front seat of his convertible.

"Down, girl." Chuckling, Morgana shook her head. "Men like that break hearts without spilling a drop of blood."

"That's okay. I haven't had my heart broken in days. Let's see…" She took a swift and deadly accurate survey. "Six foot, a hundred and sixty gorgeous pounds. The casual type—maybe just a tad intellectual. Likes the outdoors, but doesn't overdo it. Just a few scattered sun streaks through the hair, and a reasonable tan. Good facial bones—he'll hold up with age. Then there's that yummy mouth."

"Fortunately I know you, and understand you actually do think more of men than you do puppies in a pet-store window."

With a chuckle, Mindy fluffed her hair. "Oh, I think more of them, all right. A whole lot more." As the door opened, Mindy shifted position so that her body seemed about to burst out of the jumpsuit. "Hello, handsome. Want to buy a little magic?"

Always ready to accommodate a willing woman, Nash flashed her a grin. "What do you recommend?"

"Well…" The word came out in a long purr to rival one of Luna's.

"Mindy, Mr. Kirkland isn't a customer." Morgana's voice was mild and amused. There were few things more entertaining than Mindy's showmanship with an attractive man. "We have a meeting."

"Maybe next time," Nash told her.

"Maybe anytime." Mindy slithered around the counter, shot Nash one last devastating look, then wiggled out the door.

"I bet she boosts your sales," Nash commented.

"Along with the blood pressure of every male within range. How's yours?"

He grinned. "Got any oxygen?"

"Sorry. Fresh out." She gave his arm a friendly pat. "Why don't you have a seat? I have a few more things to— Damn."

"Excuse me?"

"Didn't get the Closed sign up quick enough," she muttered. Then she beamed a smile as the door opened. "Hello, Mrs. Littleton."

"Morgana." The word came out in a long, relieved sigh as a woman Nash judged to be somewhere between sixty and seventy streamed across the room.

The verb seemed apt, he thought. She was built like a cruise ship, sturdy of bow and stern, with colorful scarves wafting around her like flags. Her hair was a bright, improbable red that frizzed cheerfully around a moon-shaped face. Her eyes were heavily outlined in emerald, and her mouth was slicked with deep crimson. She threw out both hands—they were crowded with rings—and gripped Morgana's.

"I simply couldn't get here a moment sooner. As it was, I had to scold the young policeman who tried to give me a ticket. Imagine, a boy hardly old enough to shave, lecturing me on the law." She let out a huff of breath that smelled of peppermint. "Now then, I hope you have a few minutes for me."

"Of course." There was no help for it, Morgana thought. She was simply too fond of the batty old woman to make excuses.

"You're a dream. She's a dream, isn't she?" Mrs. Littleton demanded of Nash.

"You bet."

Mrs. Littleton beamed, turning toward him with a musical symphony of jaggling chains and bracelets. "Sagittarius, right?"

"Ah…" Nash heedlessly amended his birthday to suit her. "Right. Amazing."

She puffed out her ample bosom. "I do pride myself on being an excellent judge. I won't keep you but a moment from your date, dear."

"I don't have a date," Morgana told her. "What can I do for you?"

"Just the teensiest favor." Mrs. Littleton's eyes took on a gleam that had Morgana stifling a moan. "My grandniece. There's the matter of the prom, and this sweet boy in her geometry class."

This time she'd be firm, Morgana promised herself. Absolutely a rock. Taking Mrs. Littleton's arm, she edged her away from Nash. "I've explained to you that I don't work that way."

Mrs. Littleton fluttered her false eyelashes. "I know you *usually* don't. But this is such a worthy cause."

"They all are." Narrowing her eyes at Nash, who'd shifted closer, Morgana pulled Mrs. Littleton across the room. "I'm sure your niece is a wonderful girl, but arranging a prom date for her is frivolous—and such things have repercussions. No," she said when Mrs. Littleton began to protest. "If I did arrange it—changing something that shouldn't be changed—it could affect her life."

"It's only one night."

"Altering fate one night potentially alters it for centuries." Mrs. Littleton's downcast look had Morgana feeling like a miser refusing a starving man a crust of bread. "I know you only want her to have a special night, but I just can't play games with destiny."

"She's so shy, you see," Mrs. Littleton said with a sigh. Her ears were sharp enough to have heard the faint weakening in Morgana's resolve. "And she doesn't think she's the least bit pretty. But she is." Before Morgana could protest, she whipped out a snapshot. "See?"

She didn't want to see, Morgana thought. But she looked, and the pretty young teenager with the somber eyes did the rest. Morgana cursed inwardly. Dragon's teeth and hellfire. She was as soppy as a wet valentine when it came to puppy love.

"I won't guarantee—only suggest."

"That will be wonderful." Seizing the moment, Mrs. Littleton pulled out another picture, one she'd cut from the high school yearbook at the school library. "This is Matthew. A nice name, isn't it? Matthew Brody, and Jessie Littleton. She was named for me. You will start soon, won't you? The prom's the first weekend in May."

"If it's meant, it's meant," Morgana said, slipping the photos into her pocket.

"Blessed be." Beaming, Mrs. Littleton kissed Morgana's cheek. "I won't keep you any longer. I'll be back Monday to shop."

"Have a good weekend." Annoyed with herself, Morgana watched Mrs. Littleton depart.

"Wasn't she supposed to cross your palm with silver?" Nash asked.

Morgana tilted her head. The anger that had been directed solely at herself shot out of her eyes. "I don't profit from power."

He shrugged, then walked toward her. "I hate to point it out, but she twisted you around her finger."

A faint flush crept into her cheeks. If there was anything she hated more than being weak, it was being weak in public. "I'm aware of that."

Lifting a hand, he rubbed his thumb over her cheek to wipe away the faint smear of crimson Mrs. Littleton had left there. "I figured witches would be tough."

"I have a weak spot for the eccentric and the good-hearted. And you're not a Sagittarius."

He was sorry he had to remove his thumb from her cheek. Her skin was as cool and smooth as milk. "No? What, then?"

"Gemini."

His brow lifted, and he stuck his hand in his pocket. "Good guess."

His discomfort made her feel a little better. "I rarely guess. Since you were nice enough not to hurt her feelings, I won't take out my annoyance on you. Why don't you come in the back? I'll brew us some tea." She laughed when she saw his expression. "All right. I'll pour us some wine."

"Better."

He followed her through a door behind the counter into a room that served as storage, office and kitchenette. Though it was a small area, it didn't seem overly crowded. Shelves lined two walls and were stacked with boxes, uncrated stock and books. A curvy cherry desk held a brass lamp shaped like a mermaid, an efficient-looking two-line phone and a pile of paperwork held in place by a flat-bottomed glass that tossed out color and reflection.

Beyond that was a child-size refrigerator, a two-burner stove and a drop-leaf table with two chairs. In the single window, pots of herbs were crowded and thriving. He could smell...he wasn't sure what—sage, perhaps, and oregano, with a homey trace of lavender. Whatever it was, it was pleasant.

Morgana took two clear goblets from a shelf over the sink.

"Have a seat," she said. "I can't give you very much time, but you might as well be comfortable." She took a long, slim-necked bottle out of the refrigerator and poured a pale golden liquid into the goblets.

"No label?"

"It's my own recipe." With a smile, she sipped first. "Don't worry, there's not a single eye of newt in it."

He would have laughed, but the way she studied him over the rim of her glass was making him uneasy. Still, he hated to refuse a challenge. He took a sip. The wine was cool, faintly sweet, and smooth as silk. "Nice."

"Thank you." She took the chair beside him. "I haven't decided whether I'm going to help you or not. But I'm interested in your craft, particularly if you're going to incorporate mine into it."

"You like the movies," he said, figuring that gave him a head start. He hooked an arm around the back of the chair, scratching Luna absently with his foot as the cat wound around his legs.

"Among other things. I enjoy the variety of human imagination."

"Okay—"

"But," she went on, interrupting him, "I'm not sure I want my personal views going Hollywood."

"We can talk." He smiled again, and again she understood that he was a power to be reckoned with. As she considered that, Luna leapt onto the table. For the first time Nash noticed that the cat wore an etched round crystal around her neck. "Look, Morgana, I'm not trying to prove or disprove, I'm not trying to change the world. I just want to make a movie."

"Why horror and the occult?"

"Why?" He shrugged his shoulders. It always made him uncomfortable when people asked him to analyze. "I don't know. Maybe because when people go into a scary movie, they stop thinking about the lousy day they had at the office after the opening scream." His eyes lit with humor. "Or maybe because the first time I got past first base with a girl was when she wrapped herself all over me during a midnight showing of Carpenter's *Halloween*."

Morgana sipped and considered. Maybe, just maybe, there was a sensitive soul under that smug exterior. There certainly was talent, and there was undeniably charm. It bothered her that she felt…pushed somehow, pushed to agree.

Well, she'd damn well say no if she chose to, but she'd test the waters first.

"Why don't you tell me about your story?"

Nash saw the opening and pounced. "I haven't got one to speak of yet. That's where you come in. I like to have plenty of background. I can get a lot of information out of books." He spread his hands. "I already have some—my research tends to overlap and take me into all areas of the occult. What I want is the personal angle. You know, what made you get into witchcraft, do you attend ceremonies, what kind of trappings you prefer."

Morgana ran a fingertip thoughtfully around the rim of the goblet. "I'm afraid you're starting off with the wrong impression. You're making it sound as though I joined some sort of club."

"Coven, club.... A group with the same interests."

"I don't belong to a coven. I prefer working alone."

Interested, he leaned forward. "Why?"

"There are groups who are quite sincere, and those who are not. Still others dabble in things best left locked."

"Black magic."

"Whatever name you give it."

"And you're a white witch."

"You're fond of labels." With a restless move, she picked up her wine again. Unlike Nash, she didn't mind discussing the essence of her Craft—but once she agreed to, she expected to have her thoughts received respectfully. "We're all born with certain powers, Nash. Yours is to tell entertaining stories. And to attract women." Her lips curved as she sipped. "I'm sure you respect, and employ, your powers. I do exactly the same."

"What are yours?"

She took her time, setting her goblet down, lifting her eyes to his. The look she leveled at him made him feel like a fool for having asked. The power was there—the kind that could make a man crawl. His mouth went so dry that the wine he was drinking could have been sand.

"What would you like, a performance?" The faintest hint of impatience had seeped into her tone.

He managed to draw a breath and shake himself out of what he would almost have thought was a trance—if he believed in trances. "I'd love one." Maybe it was twitching the devil's tail, but he couldn't resist. The color that temper brought to her cheeks made her skin glow like a freshly picked peach. "What did you have in mind?"

She felt the quick, unwelcome tug of desire. It was distinctly annoying. "Lightning bolts from the fingertips? Should I whistle up the wind or draw down the moon?"

"Dealer's choice."

The nerve of the man, she thought as she rose, the power humming hot in her blood. It would serve him right if she—

"Morgana."

She whirled, anger sizzling. With an effort, she tossed her hair back and relaxed. "Ana."

Nash couldn't have said why he felt as though he'd just avoided a calamity of major proportions. But he knew that, for an instant, his whole being had been so wrapped up in Morgana that he wouldn't have felt an earthquake. She'd pulled him right in, and now he was left, a little dazed, a little dull-witted, staring at the slim blond woman in the doorway.

She was lovely, and, though a head shorter than Morgana, she exuded an odd kind of soothing strength. Her eyes were a soft, calm gray, and they were focused on Morgana. In her arms she carried a box that was overflowing with flowering herbs.

"You didn't have the sign up," Anastasia said, "so I came in the front."

"Let me take that." Messages passed between the two women. Nash didn't have to hear them to know it. "Ana, this is Nash Kirkland. Nash, my cousin, Anastasia."

"I'm sorry to interrupt." Her voice, low and warm, was as soothing as her eyes.

"You're not," Morgana said as Nash got to his feet. "Nash and I were just finished."

"Just beginning," he told her. "But we can pick it up later. Nice to meet you," he said to Anastasia. Then he smiled at Morgana and tucked her hair behind her ear. "Till next time."

"Nash." Morgana set the box down and took out a small pot of blooms. "A gift." She offered it, and her sweetest smile. "Sweet peas," she explained. "To symbolize departure."

He couldn't resist. Leaning over the box, he touched his lips to hers. "For the hell of it." He sauntered out.

In spite of herself, Morgana chuckled.

Anastasia settled into a chair with a contented sigh. "Want to tell me about it?"

"Nothing to tell. He's a charming annoyance. A writer with very typical views on witches."

"Oh. *That* Nash Kirkland." To please herself, Anastasia picked up Morgana's half-full goblet and sipped. "The one who wrote that gory movie you and Sebastian dragged me to."

"It was really quite intelligent and sly."

"Hmm." Anastasia drank again. "And gory. Then again, you've always enjoyed that kind of thing."

"Watching evil is an entertaining way to reaffirm good." She frowned. "Unfortunately, Nash Kirkland does very superior work."

"That may be. I'd rather watch the Marx Brothers." Automatically she walked over to check the herbs in Morgana's window. "I couldn't help but notice the tension. You looked as if you were about to turn him into a toad when I walked in."

The thought gave Morgana a moment of sterling pleasure. "I was tempted. Something about that smugness set me off."

"You're too easily set off. You did say you were going to work on control, didn't you, love?"

Scowling, Morgana snatched up Nash's glass. "He walked out of here on two legs, didn't he?" She sipped, and realized instantly it was a mistake. He'd left too much of himself in the wine.

A powerful man, she thought as she set the goblet down again. Despite the easy smile and the relaxed manner, a very powerful man.

She wished she'd thought to charm the flowers she'd given him, but she dismissed the idea immediately. Perhaps something was pushing them together, but she would deal with it. And she would deal with it, and with Nash Kirkland, without magic.

Chapter Two

Morgana enjoyed the peace of Sunday afternoons. It was her day to indulge herself—and from her first breath, Morgana had appreciated indulgences. Not that she avoided work. She had put a great deal of time and effort into seeing that her shop ran smoothly and turned a profit—without using her special skills to smooth her path. Still, she firmly believed that the proper reward for any effort was relaxation.

Unlike some business owners, Morgana didn't agonize over books and inventory and overhead. She simply did what she felt needed to be done, making sure she did it well. Then when she walked away from it—if only for an hour at a time—she forgot business completely.

It amazed Morgana that there were people who would spend a beautiful day inside, biting their nails over ledgers. She hired an accountant to do that.

She hadn't hired a housekeeper, but only because she didn't care for the idea of someone poking through her personal things. She, and only she, was their caretaker. Though her gardens were extensive—and she'd long ago accepted that she would never have the way with growing things that her cousin Anastasia had—she tended the blooms herself. She found the cycle—planting, watering, weeding, harvesting—rewarding.

She knelt now, in a strong stream of sunlight, at the extensive rockery where her herbs and spring bulbs thrived. There was the scent of rosemary, of hyacinth, the delicacy of jasmine, the richness of anise. Music drifted through the windows, the penny whistles and flutes of a traditional Irish folk tune, clashing cheerfully with the surge and thrust of water spewing up from the rocks a few hundred yards behind her.

It was one of those precious and perfect days, with the sky spread overhead like clear blue glass and the wind, light and playful, carrying the scents of water and wildflowers. From beyond the low wall and sheltering trees at the front of her property, she could hear the occasional swish of a car as tourists or natives took in the scenery.

Luna was sprawled nearby in a patch of sunlight, her eyes slitted, nearly closed, her tail switching occasionally as she watched birds. If Morgana weren't there, she might have tried for a snack—for all her bulk, she could move like lightning. But her mistress was very firm about such habits.

When the dog padded over to drop his head into Morgana's lap, Luna gave a mutter of disgust and went to sleep. Dogs had no pride.

Content, Morgana sat back on her heels, ruffling the dog's fur with one hand as she surveyed her rockery. Perhaps she would pluck a few sprigs—she was running low on angelica balm and hyssop powder. Tonight, she decided. If there was a moon. Such things were best done by moonlight.

For now, she would enjoy the sun, lifting her face to it, letting its warmth and life pour over her skin. She could never sit here without feeling the beauty of this spot, this place where she had been born. Though she had traveled to many other lands, seen many magic places, it was here she belonged.

For it was here, she had learned long ago, that she would

find love, share love, and bear her children. With a sigh, Morgana closed her eyes. Those days could wait, she mused. She was content with her life precisely as it was. When the time came for it to change, she intended to remain fully in charge.

When the dog sprang to his feet, a warning growl humming in his throat, Morgana didn't bother to look around. She'd known he'd come. She hadn't needed the crystal or the black mirror to tell her. Nor could she claim it was clairvoyance— that was more her cousin Sebastian's territory. She'd needed only to be a woman to know.

She sat, smiling, while the dog sent out a series of rapid, unfriendly barks. She would see just how Nash Kirkland handled the situation.

How was a man supposed to react when the woman he'd come to see was being guarded by a...he was sure it couldn't really be a wolf, but it sure as hell looked like one. He was doubly sure that if she gave the word the sleek silver beast would take one long leap and go for his throat.

Nash cleared that throat, then jolted when something brushed his leg. Glancing down, he noted that Luna, at least, had decided to be friendly. "Nice dog you got there," he said cautiously. "Nice, big dog."

Morgana deigned to glance over her shoulder. "Out for a Sunday drive?"

"More or less."

The dog had subsided into those low, dangerous growls again. Nash felt a bead of sweat slide down his back as the mass of muscle and teeth stalked toward him to sniff at his shoes. "I, ah..." Then the dog looked up, and Nash was struck by the gleam of deep blue eyes against that silver fur. "God, you're a beauty, aren't you?" He held out a hand, sincerely hoping the dog would let him keep it. It was sniffed thoroughly, then rewarded with a lick.

Lips pursed, Morgana studied them. Pan had never so much

as nipped anyone's ankle, but neither was he given to making friends so quickly. "You have a way with animals."

Nash was already crouched down to give the dog a brisk scratching. All throughout his childhood he'd yearned for a dog. It surprised him to realize that his boyhood desire had never quite faded. "They know I'm just a kid at heart. What breed is he?"

"Pan?" Her smile was slow and secret. "We'll just say he's a Donovan. What can I do for you, Nash?"

He looked over. She was in the sunlight, her hair bundled under a wide-brimmed straw hat. Her jeans were too tight, and her T-shirt was too baggy. Because she hadn't used gardening gloves, her hands were smeared with rich, dark earth. Her feet were bare. It hadn't occurred to him that bare feet could be sexy. Until now.

"Besides that," she said, with such an easy ripple of amusement in her voice that he had to grin.

"Sorry. My mind was wandering."

It didn't offend her to be found desirable. "Why don't you start with telling me how you found me?"

"Come on, honey, you know you've got a reputation." He rose to walk over and sit on the grass beside her. "I had dinner in the place beside your shop, struck up a conversation with my waitress."

"I'll bet you did."

He reached over to toy with the amulet she wore. An interesting piece, he thought, shaped like a half-moon and inscribed in—Greek? Arabic? He was no scholar. "Anyway, she was a fount of information. Fascinated and spooked. Do you affect a lot of people that way?"

"Legions." And she'd learned to enjoy it. "Did she tell you that I ride over the bay on my broomstick every full moon?"

"Close enough." He let the amulet drop. "It interests me how ordinarily intelligent people allow themselves to get caught up in the supernatural."

"Isn't that how you make your living?"

"Exactly. And, speaking of my living, I figure you and I started off wrong. How about a clean slate?"

It was hard to be annoyed with an attractive man on a beautiful day. "How about it?"

He thought it might be wise to take the conversation where he wanted by way of the back door. "You know a lot about flowers and stuff?"

"A few things." She shifted to finish planting a fresh pot of lemon balm.

"Maybe you can tell me what I've got in my yard, and what I should do about it?"

"Hire a gardening service," she said. Then she relented and smiled. "I suppose I might find time to take a look."

"I'd really appreciate it." He brushed at a smear of dirt on her chin. "You really could help me with the script, Morgana. It's no problem getting things out of books—anyone can do that. What I'm looking for is a different slant, something more personal. And I—"

"What is it?"

"You have stars in your eyes," he murmured. "Little gold stars...like sunlight on a midnight sea. But you can't have the sun at midnight."

"You can have anything if you know how to get it." Those fabulous eyes held his. He couldn't have looked away to save his soul. "Tell me what you want, Nash."

"To give people a couple of enjoyable hours. To know they'll forget problems, reality, everything, when they step into my world. A good story's like a door, and you can go through it whenever you need to. After you've read it or seen it or heard it, you can still go back through it. Once it's yours, it's always yours."

He broke off, startled and embarrassed. This kind of philosophizing didn't fit in with his carefree image. He'd had expert interviewers dig at him for hours without unearthing a statement as simple and genuine as that. And all she'd done was ask.

"And, of course, I want to make pots of money," he added, trying to grin. His head felt light, his skin too warm.

"I don't see that one desire has to be exclusive of the other. There have been storytellers in my family from the fairy days down to my mother. We understand the value of stories."

Perhaps that was why she hadn't dismissed him from the outset. She respected what he did. That, too, was in her blood.

"Consider this." She leaned forward, and he felt the punch of something in his gut, something that went beyond her beauty. "If I agree to help you, I refuse to let you fall back on the lowest common denominator. The old crone, cackling as she mixes henbane in the cauldron."

He smiled. "Convince me."

"Be careful what you dare, Nash," she murmured, rising. "Come inside. I'm thirsty."

Since he was no longer worried about being chewed up by her guard dog, who was now strolling contentedly beside them, Nash took time to admire her house. He already knew that many of the homes along the Monterey Peninsula were extraordinary and unique. He'd bought one himself. Morgana's had the added allure of age and grace.

It was three stories of stone, turreted and towered—to suit a witch, he supposed. But it was neither Gothic nor grim. Tall, graceful windows flashed in the sunlight, and climbing flowers crept up the walls to twine and tangle in lacy ironwork. Carved into the stone were winged fairies and mermaids, adding charm. Lovely robed figures served as rainspouts.

Interior scene, night, he mused. Inside the topmost tower of the old stone house by the sea, the beautiful young witch sits in a ring of candles. The room is shadowy, with the light fluttering over the faces of statues, the stems of silver goblets, a clear orb of crystal. She wears a sheer white robe open to the waist.

A heavy carved amulet hangs between the swell of her breasts. A deep hum seems to come from the stones themselves as she lifts two photographs high in the air.

The candles flicker. A wind rises within the closed room to lift her hair and ripple the robe. She chants. Ancient words, in a low, smoldering voice. She touches the photos to the candle flame.... No, scratch that. She...yeah, she sprinkles the photos with the glowing liquid from a cracked blue bowl. A hiss of steam. The humming takes on a slow, sinuous beat. Her body sways with it as she places the photos face-to-face, laying them on a silver tray. A secret smile crosses her face as the photos fuse together.

Fade out.

He liked it, though he figured she could add a bit more color to the casting of a love spell.

Content with his silence, Morgana took him around the side of the house, where the sound of water on rock rumbled and the cypress grove, trees bent and gnarled by time and wind, stood watch. They crossed a stone patio shaped like a pentagram, at whose top point stood a brass statue of a woman. Water gurgled in a tiny pool at her feet.

"Who's she?" Nash asked.

"She has many names." Moving to the statue, Morgana took up a small ladle, dipped it in the clear pool. She sipped, then poured the rest onto the ground for the goddess. Without a word, she crossed the patio again and entered a sunny, spotless kitchen. "Do you believe in a creator?"

The question surprised him. "Yeah, sure. I suppose." He shifted uncomfortably while she walked across a white tiled floor to the sink to rinse her hands. "This—your witchcraft—it's a religious thing?"

She smiled as she took out a pitcher of lemonade. "Life's a religious thing. But don't worry, Nash—I won't try to convert you." She filled two glasses with ice. "It shouldn't make you uncomfortable. Your stories are invariably about good and evil. People are always making choices, whether to be one or the other."

"What about you?"

She offered him his glass, then turned to walk through an archway and out of the kitchen. "You could say I'm always trying to check my less attractive impulses." She shot him a look. "It doesn't always work."

As she spoke, she led him down a wide hallway. The walls were decorated with faded tapestries depicting scenes from folklore and mythology, ornate sconces and etched plates of silver and copper.

She opted for what her grandmother had always called the drawing room. Its walls were painted a warm rose, and the tone was picked up in the pattern of the Bokhara rug tossed over the wide-planked chestnut floor. A lovely Adam mantel draped over the fireplace, which was stacked with wood ready to be put to flame should the night turn cool or should Morgana wish it.

But for now a light breeze played through the open windows, billowing the sheer curtains and bringing with it the scents of her gardens.

As in her shop, there were crystals and wands scattered around the room, along with a partial collection of her sculpture. Pewter wizards, bronze fairies, porcelain dragons.

"Great stuff." He ran his hand over the strings of a gold lap harp. The sound it made was soft and sweet. "Do you play?"

"When I'm in the mood." It amused her to watch him move around the room, toying with this, examining that. She appreciated honest curiosity. He picked up a scribed silver goblet and sniffed. "Smells like…"

"Hellfire?" she suggested. He set it down again, preferring a slender amethyst wand encrusted with stones and twined with silver threads. "Magic wand?"

"Naturally. Be careful what you wish for," she told him, taking it delicately from his hand.

He shrugged and turned away, missing the way the wand glowed before Morgana put it aside. "I've collected a lot of this kind of thing myself. You might like to see." He bent over a clear glass ball and saw his own reflection. "I picked up a shaman's mask at an auction last month, and a—what do you call it?—a scrying mirror. Looks like we have something in common."

"A taste in art." She sat on the arm of the couch.

"And literature." He was poking through a bookshelf. "Lovecraft, Bradbury. I've got this edition of *The Golden Dawn*. Stephen King, Hunter Brown, McCaffrey. Hey, is this—?" He pulled out the volume and opened it reverently. "It's a first edition of Bram Stoker's *Dracula*." He looked over at her. "Will you take my right arm for it?"

"I'll have to get back to you on that."

"I always hoped he'd have approved of *Midnight Blood*." As he slipped the book back into place, another caught his eyes. *"Four Golden Balls. The Faerie King."* He skimmed a finger over the slim volumes. *"Whistle Up the Wind*. You've got her entire collection." Envy stirred in his blood. "And in first editions."

"You read Bryna?"

"Are you kidding?" It was too much like meeting an old friend. He had to touch, to look, even to sniff. "I've read everything she's written a dozen times. Anyone who thinks they're just for kids is nuts. It's like poetry and magic and morality all rolled into one. And, of course, the illustrations are fabulous. I'd kill for a piece of the original artwork, but she just won't sell."

Interested, Morgana tilted her head. "Have you asked?"

"I've filtered some pitiful pleas through her agent. No dice. She lives in some castle in Ireland, and probably papers the walls with her sketches. I wish…" He turned at Morgana's quiet laugh.

"Actually, she keeps them in thick albums, waiting for the grandchildren she hopes for."

"Donovan." He tucked his thumbs in his pockets. "Bryna Donovan. That's your mother."

"Yes, and she'd be delighted to know you approve of her work." She lifted her glass. "From one storyteller to another. My parents lived in this house off and on for several years. Actually, she wrote her first published work upstairs while she was pregnant with me. She always says I insisted she write the story down."

"Does your mother believe you're a witch?"

"It would be better to ask her that yourself, if you get the opportunity."

"You're being evasive again." He walked over to sprawl comfortably on the couch beside her. It was impossible not to be comfortable with a woman who surrounded herself with things he himself loved. "Let's put it this way. Does your family have any problem with your interests?"

She appreciated the way he relaxed, legs stretched, body at ease, as if he'd been making himself at home on her couch for years. "My family has always understood the need to focus energies in an individual direction. Do your parents have a problem with your interests?"

"I never knew them. My parents."

"I'm sorry." The mocking light in her eyes turned instantly to sympathy. Her family had always been her center. She could hardly imagine living without them.

"It wasn't a big deal." But he rose again, uneasy with the way she'd laid a comforting hand on his shoulder. He'd come too far from the bad old days to want any sympathy. "I'm interested in your family's reactions. I mean, how would most parents feel, what would they do if they found their kid casting spells. Did you decide to start dabbling as a child?"

Sympathy vanished like a puff of smoke. "Dabbling?" she repeated, eyes slitted.

"I may want to have a prologue, you know, showing how the main character got involved."

He was paying less attention to her than to the room itself, the atmosphere. As he worked out his thoughts, he paced. Not nervously, not even restlessly, but in a way that made it obvious that he was taking stock of everything he could see.

"Maybe she gets pushed around by the kid next door and turns him into a frog," he continued, oblivious to the fact that Morgana's jaw had tensed. "Or she runs into some mysterious woman who passes on the power. I kind of like that." As he roamed, he played with ideas, slender threads that could be woven into whole cloth for a story. "I'm just not sure of the angle I want to use, so I figured we'd start by playing it straight. You tell me what started you off—books you read, whatever. Then I can twist it to work as fiction."

She was going to have to watch her temper, and watch it carefully. When she spoke, her voice was soft, and carried a ring that made him stop in the center of the rug. "I was born with elvish blood. I am a hereditary witch, and my heritage traces back to Finn of the Celts. My power is a gift passed on from generation to generation. When I find a man of strength, we'll make children between us, and they will carry it beyond me."

He nodded, impressed. "That's great." So she didn't want to play it straight, he thought. He'd humor her. The stuff about elvish blood had terrific possibilities. "So, when did you first realize you were a witch?"

The tone of his voice had her temper slipping a notch. The room shook as she fought it back. Nash snatched her off the couch so quickly that she didn't have time to protest. He'd pulled her toward the doorway when the shaking stopped.

"Just a tremor," he said, but he kept his arms around her. "I was in San Francisco during the last big one." Because he felt like an idiot, he gave her a lopsided grin. "I haven't been able to be casual about a shake since."

So, he thought it was an earth tremor. Just as well, Morgana decided. There was absolutely no reason for her to lose her temper, or to expect him to accept her for what she was. In any case, it was sweet, the way he'd jumped to protect her.

"You could move to the Midwest."

"Tornados." Since he was here, and so was she, he saw no reason to resist running his hands up her back. He enjoyed the way she leaned into the stroke, like a cat.

Morgana tilted her head back. Staying angry seemed a waste of time when her heart gave such an eager leap. It was perhaps unwise of them to test each other this way. But wisdom was often bland. "The East Coast," she said, letting her own hands skim up his chest.

"Blizzards." He nudged her closer, wondering for just an instant why she seemed to meld with him so perfectly, body to body.

"The South." She twined her arms around his neck, watching him steadily through a fringe of dark lashes.

"Hurricanes." He tipped the hat off her head so that her hair tumbled down to fill his hands like warm silk. "Disasters are everywhere," he murmured. "Might as well stay put and deal with the one that's yours."

"You won't deal with me, Nash." She brushed her lips teasingly over his. "But you're welcome to try."

He took her mouth confidently. He didn't consider women a disaster.

Perhaps he should have.

It was more turbulent than any earthquake, more devastating than any storm. He didn't feel the ground tremble or hear the wind roar, but he knew the moment her lips parted beneath his that he was being pulled in by some irresistible force that man had yet to put a name to.

She was molded against him, soft and warm as melted wax. If he'd believed in such things, he might have said her body had been fashioned for just this purpose—to mate perfectly with his. His hands streaked under her loose shirt to race over the smooth skin of her back, to press her even closer, to make sure she was real and not some daydream, some fantasy.

He could taste the reality, but even that had some kind of dreamy midnight flavor. Her mouth yielded silkily under his, even as her arms locked like velvet cords around his neck.

A sound floated on the air, something she murmured, something he couldn't understand. Yet he thought he sensed surprise in the whisper, and perhaps a little fear, before it ended with a sigh.

She was a woman who enjoyed the tastes and textures of a man. She had never been taught to be ashamed of taking pleasure, with the right man, at the right time. She hadn't ever learned to fear her own sexuality, but to celebrate it, cherish it, and respect it.

And yet now, for the first time, she felt the sly quickening of fear with a man.

The simplicity of a kiss filled a basic need. But there was nothing simple in this. How could it be simple, when excitement and unease were dancing together along her skin?

She wanted to believe that the power came from her, was in her. She was responsible for this whirlwind of sensation that surrounded them. Conjuring was often as quick as a wish, as strong as the will.

But the fear was there, and she knew it came from the knowledge that this was something beyond her reach, out of her control, past her reckoning. She knew that spells could be cast on the strong, as well as the weak. To break a charm took care. And action.

She slid out of his arms, moving slowly, deliberately. Not for an instant would she let him see that he had had power over her. She closed a hand over her amulet and felt steadier.

Nash felt like the last survivor of a train wreck. He jammed his hands in his pockets to keep himself from grabbing her again. He didn't mind playing with fire—he just liked to be sure he was the one holding the match. He knew damn well who'd been in charge of that little experiment, and it wasn't Nash Kirkland.

"You play around with hypnosis?" he asked her.

She was fine, Morgana told herself. She was just fine. But she sat on the couch again. It took an effort, but she managed a smile that was sultry around the edges. "Did I mesmerize you, Nash?"

Flustered, he paced to the window and back. "I just want to be sure when I kiss you that it's my idea."

Her head came up. The pride that swam in her blood was something else that was ageless. "You can have all the ideas you like. I don't have to resort to magic to make a man want me." She lifted a finger to touch the heat he'd left on her lips. "And if I decided to have you, you'd be more than willing." Under her finger, her lips curved. "Then you'd be grateful."

He didn't doubt it, and that scraped at his pride. "If I said something like that to you, you'd claim I was sexist and ego-centric."

Lazily she picked up her glass. "The truth has nothing to do with sex or ego." The white cat jumped soundlessly on the back of the couch. Without taking her eyes off Nash, Morgana lifted a hand and stroked Luna's head. "If you're unwilling to take the risk, we can break off our...creative partnership."

"You think I'm afraid of you?" The absurdity of it put him in a slightly better mood. "Babe, I stopped letting my glands do the thinking a long time ago."

"I'm relieved to hear it. I'd hate to think of you as some cal-culating woman's love slave."

"The point is," he said between his teeth, "if we're going to work this out, we'd better have some rules."

He had to be out of his mind, Nash decided. Five minutes

ago he had had a gorgeous, sexy, incredibly delicious woman in his arms, and now he was trying to think up ways to keep her from seducing him.

"No." Lips pursed, Morgana considered. "I'm not very good with rules. You'll just have to take your chances. But I'll make a deal with you. I won't lure you into any compromising situations if you'll stop taking smug little potshots at witchcraft." She combed her hair back with her fingers. "It irritates me. And I sometimes do things I regret when I'm irritated."

"I have to ask questions."

"Then learn to accept the answers." Calm but determined, she rose. "I don't lie—or at least I rarely do. I'm not sure why I've decided to share my business with you. Perhaps because there's something appealing about you, and certainly because I have a great deal of respect for a teller of tales. You have a strong aura—and a questing, if cynical, brain—along with a great deal of talent. And perhaps because those closest to me have approved of you."

"Such as?"

"Anastasia—and Luna and Pan. They're all excellent judges of character."

So he'd passed muster with a cousin, a cat and a dog. "Is Anastasia also a witch?"

Her eyes remained steady. "We'll discuss me, and the Craft in general. Ana's business is her own."

"All right. When do we start?"

They already had, she thought, and nearly sighed. "I don't work on Sundays. You can come by tomorrow night, at nine."

"Not midnight? Sorry," he said quickly. "Force of habit. I'd like to use a tape recorder, if that's all right."

"Of course."

"Should I bring anything else?"

"Tongue of bat and some wolfbane." She smiled. "Sorry. Force of habit."

He laughed and kissed her chastely on the cheek. "I like your style, Morgana."

"We'll see."

She waited until sundown, then dressed in a thin white robe. Forewarned was always best, she'd told herself when she'd finally broken down and slipped into the room at the top of the tower. She didn't like to admit that Nash was important enough to worry about, but since she was worrying, she might as well see.

She cast the protective circle, lit the candles. Drawing in the scent of sandalwood and herbs, she knelt in the center and lifted her arms.

"Fire, water, earth and wind, not to break and not to mend. Only now to let me see. As I will, so mote it be."

The power slid inside her like breath, clean and cool. She lifted the sphere of clear crystal, cupping it in both hands so that the light from the candles flickered over it.

Smoke. Light. Shadow.

The globe swam with them, and then, as if a wind had blown, cleared to a pure, dazzling white.

Within she saw the cypress grove, the ancient and mystical trees filtering moonlight onto the forest floor. She could smell the wind, could hear it, and the call of the sea some said was the goddess singing.

Candlelight. In the room. Inside the globe.

Herself. In the room. Inside the globe.

She wore the white ceremonial robe belted with a rope of crystals. Her hair was unbound, her feet were bare. The fire had been lit by her hand, by her will, and it burned as cool as the moonlight. It was a night for celebration.

An owl hooted. She turned, saw its white wings flash and cut the dark like knives, she watched it glide off into the shadows. Then she saw him.

He stepped away from the trunk of a cypress, into the clearing. His eyes were full of her.

Desire. Demand. Destiny.

Trapped in the sphere, Morgana held out her arms, and took Nash into her embrace.

The walls of the tower room echoed with one brief curse. Betrayed—by herself—Morgana threw up a hand. The candles winked out. She stayed where she was, sulking in the dark.

She cursed herself, thinking she'd have been better off not knowing.

A few miles away, Nash woke from a catnap he'd taken in front of a blaring television. Groggy, he rubbed his hands over his face and struggled to sit up.

Hell of a dream, he thought as he worked out the kinks in his neck. Vivid enough to make him ache in several sensitive areas. And it was his own fault, he decided on a yawn as he reached absently for the bowl of popcorn he'd burned.

He hadn't made enough of an effort to get Morgana out of his mind. So if he was going to end up fantasizing about watching her do some kind of witch dance in the woods, about peeling her out of white silk and making love with her on the soft ground in the moonlight, he had no one to blame but himself.

He gave a quick shudder and groped for his lukewarm beer. It was the damnedest thing, he mused. He could have sworn he smelled candles burning.

Chapter Three

Morgana was already annoyed when she turned into her driveway Monday evening. An expected shipment had been delayed in Chicago, and she'd spent the last hour on the phone trying to track it down. She was tempted to deal with the matter her own way—nothing irked her more than ineptitude—but she was fully aware that such impulses often caused complications.

As it was, she'd lost valuable time, and it was nearly dusk before she parked her car. She'd hoped for a quiet walk among the trees to clear her mind—and, yes, damn it, to settle her nerves before she dealt with Nash. But that wasn't to be.

She sat for a moment, scowling at the gleaming black-and-chrome motorcycle in front of her car.

Sebastian. Perfect. Just what she *didn't* need.

Luna slid out of the car ahead of her to pad up the drive and rub herself against the Harley's back wheel.

"You would," Morgana said in disgust as she slammed the door. "As long as it's a man."

Luna muttered something that sounded uncomplimentary and stalked on ahead. Pan greeted them both at the front door with his wise eyes and his loving tongue. While Luna moved on, ignoring him, Morgana took a moment to stroke his fur before tossing her purse aside. She could hear the soft strains of Beethoven drifting from her stereo.

She found Sebastian exactly where she'd expected. He was sprawled on her couch, booted feet comfortably crossed on her coffee table, his eyes half-closed and a glass of wine in his hand. His smile might have devastated an ordinary woman, with the way it shifted the planes and angles of his dusky face, curved those sculptured, sensuous lips, deepened the color of the heavy-lidded eyes that were as sharp as Luna's.

Lazily he lifted a long, lean-fingered hand in an ancient sign of greeting. "Morgana, my own true love."

He'd always been too handsome for his own good, she thought, even as a boy. "Make yourself at home, Cousin."

"Thank you, darling." He raised his glass to her. "The wine's excellent. Yours or Ana's?"

"Mine."

"My compliments." He rose, graceful as a dancer. It always irritated her that she had to tilt her head to keep her eyes level with his. At six-three, he had five full inches on her. "Here you go." He passed her the glass. "You look like you could use it."

"I've had an annoying day."

He grinned. "I know."

She would have sipped, but her teeth had clenched. "You know I hate it when you poke into my mind."

"I didn't have to." In a gesture of truce, he spread his hands. A ring with a square amethyst and intricately twisted gold winked on his little finger. "You were sending out signals. You know how loud you get when you're annoyed."

"Then I must be screaming now."

Since she wasn't drinking the wine, he took it back. "Darling, I haven't seen you since Candlemas." His eyes were laughing at her. "Haven't you missed me?"

The hell of it was, she had. No matter how often Sebastian

teased her—and he'd been doing it since she was in the cradle—she enjoyed him. But that wasn't any reason to be too friendly too soon.

"I've been busy."

"So I hear." He chucked her under the chin because he knew it annoyed her. "Tell me about Nash Kirkland."

Fury snapped into her eyes. "Damn you, Sebastian, you keep your psychic fingers out of my brain."

"I didn't peek." He made a good show of looking offended. "I'm a seer, an artist, not a voyeur. Ana told me."

"Oh." She pouted a moment. "Sorry." She knew that, at least since he'd gained some maturity and control, Sebastian rarely invaded anyone's private thoughts. Unless he considered it necessary. "Well, there's nothing to tell. He's a writer."

"I know that. Haven't I enjoyed his movies? What's his business with you?"

"Research. He wants a witch tale."

"T-a-l-e, as in story, I hope."

She fought back a chuckle. "Don't be crude, Sebastian."

"Just looking out for my baby cousin."

"Well, don't." She tugged, hard, on a lock of his hair that lay over his collar. "I can look after myself. And he's going to be here in a couple of hours, so—"

"Good. That'll give you time to feed me." He swung a friendly arm over her shoulders. He'd decided she'd have to blast him out of the house to make him leave before meeting the writer. "I talked to my parents over the weekend."

"By phone?"

His eyes widened in shock. When he spoke, the faint wisps of Ireland that occasionally surfaced in his voice enlivened his tone. "Really, Morgana, you know how much they charge you for overseas calls? They positively soak you."

Laughing, she slipped an arm around his waist. "All right, I'll give you some dinner and you can catch me up."

She could never stay annoyed with him. After all, he was family. When one was different, family was sometimes all that could be relied on. They ate in the kitchen while he told her of the latest exploits of her parents, her aunts and uncles. By the end of an hour, she was completely relaxed again.

"It's been years since I've seen Ireland by moonlight," Morgana murmured.

"Take a trip. You know they'd all love to see you."

"Maybe I will, for the summer solstice."

"We could all go. You, Anastasia and me."

"Maybe." Sighing, she pushed her plate aside. "The problem is, summer's my busiest time."

"You're the one who tied yourself up with free enterprise." There was the better part of a pork chop on her plate. Sebastian stabbed it and ate it himself.

"I like it, really. Meeting people. Even though some of them are weird."

He topped off their wineglasses. "Such as?"

She smiled and leaned forward on her elbows. "There was this little pest. He came around day after day for weeks. He claimed that he recognized me from another incarnation."

"A pathetic line."

"Yes. Fortunately, he was wrong—I'd never met him before, in any life. One night a couple of weeks ago, when I was closing up, he burst in and made a very strong, sloppy pass."

"Hmm." Sebastian finished off the last bite of pork. He was well aware that his cousin could take care of herself. That didn't stop him from being annoyed that some pseudo–New Ager had put the moves on her. "What'd you do?"

"Punched him in the stomach." She lifted her shoulders as Sebastian laughed.

"Style, Morgana. You have such style. You didn't turn him into a bullfrog?"

All dignity, she straightened. "You know I don't work that way."

"What about Jimmy Pakipsky?"

"That was different—I was only thirteen." She couldn't fight back the grin. "Besides, I turned him right back to a nasty little boy again."

"Only because Ana pleaded his case." Sebastian gestured with his fork. "And you left the warts on."

"It was the least I could do." She reached out to grab his hand. "Damn it, Sebastian, I have missed you."

His fingers curled tight around hers. "And I've missed you. And Anastasia."

She felt something—their bond was too old and too deep for her to miss it. "What is it, love?"

"Nothing we can change." He kissed her fingers lightly, then let them go. He hadn't intended to think about it, or to let his guard down enough to have his cousin tune in. "Got anything with whipped cream around here?"

But she shook her head. She had picked up grief. Though he was skilled enough to block it from her now, she refused to let it pass. "The case you were working on—the little boy who'd been kidnapped."

The pain was sudden and sharp. He forced it away again. "They didn't get to him in time. The San Francisco police did everything they could, but the kidnappers had panicked. He was only eight years old."

"I'm sorry." There was a wave of sorrow. His, and her own. She rose to go over and curl into his lap. "Oh, Sebastian, I'm so sorry."

"You can't let it get to you." Seeking comfort, he rubbed his cheek against her hair. He could feel the sharper edges of his regret dulling because she shared it with him. "It'll eat you up if you do, but, damn it, I got so close to that kid. When something like this happens, you wonder why, why you've been given this gift if you can't make a difference."

"You have made a difference." She cupped his face in her hands. Her eyes were wet, and strong. "I can't count the times you've made a difference. It wasn't meant to be this time."

"It hurts."

"I know." Gently she stroked his hair. "I'm glad you came to me."

He hugged her tight, then drew her back. "Look, I came here to mooch a meal and have a few laughs, not to dump. I'm sorry."

"Don't be an ass."

Her voice was so brusque that he had to chuckle. "All right. If you want to make me feel better, how about that whipped cream?"

She gave him a smacking kiss between the eyes. "How about a hot fudge sundae?"

"My hero."

She rose and, knowing Sebastian's appetites, got out an enormous bowl. She also knew she would help him more by saying nothing else about the case. He would struggle past it and go on. Because there was no other way. Flicking her mind toward the living room, she switched channels on the stereo, moving from classical to rock.

"Better," Sebastian said, and propped his feet on an empty chair. "So, are you going to tell me why you're helping this Kirkland with research?"

"It interests me." She heated a jar of fudge sauce in the conventional way. She used the microwave.

"Do you mean he interests you?"

"Somewhat." She scooped out a small mountain of French vanilla. "Of course, he doesn't believe in anything supernatural, he just exploits it for movies. I don't have a problem with that, really." Thoughtful, she licked ice cream from her thumb. "With the movies, I mean. They're very entertaining. His attitude, now... Well, I might have to adjust it before we're through."

"Dangerous ground, Cousin."

"Hell, Sebastian, life's dangerous ground." She poured a river of sauce over the mountain of ice cream. "We might as well have some fun with it." To prove her point, she covered the entire confectionary landscape with heaping clouds of whipped cream. With a flourish, she set the bowl in front of Sebastian.

"No nuts?"

She slapped a spoon into his hand. "I don't like nuts, and you're sharing." After sitting again, she dug deep into the sundae. "You'd probably like him," she said with her mouth full. "Nash. He has that relaxed sort of arrogance men think is so manly." Which, of course, it was, she thought resentfully. "And, obviously, he has a very fluid imagination. He's good with animals—Pan and Luna reacted very favorably. He's a big fan of Mother's, has a nice sense of humor, a good brain. And he drives a very sexy car."

"Sounds like you're smitten."

If she hadn't just swallowed, she would have choked. "Don't be insulting. Just because I find him interesting and attractive doesn't mean I'm—as you so pitifully put it—smitten."

She was sulking, Sebastian noted, pleased. It was always a good sign. The closer Morgana got to anger, the easier it was to slide information out of her. "So, have you looked?"

"Of course I looked," she shot back. "Merely as a precaution."

"You looked because you were nervous."

"Nervous? Don't be ridiculous." But she began to drum her fingers on the table. "He's just a man."

"And you, despite your gifts, are a woman. Shall I tell you what happens when men and women get together?"

She curled her fingers into fists to keep from doing something drastic. "I know the facts of life, thank you. If I do take him as a lover, it's my business. And perhaps my pleasure."

Happy that she'd lost interest in the ice cream, Sebastian nodded as he ate. "Trouble is, there's always a risk of falling in love with a lover. Tread carefully, Morgana."

"There's a difference between love and lust," she replied primly. From his spot under the table, Pan lifted his head and gave a soft woof.

"Speaking of which…"

Eyes full of warning, Morgana rose. "Behave yourself, Sebastian. I mean it."

"Don't worry about me. Go answer the door." The bell rang a heartbeat later. Chuckling to himself, Sebastian watched her stalk off.

Damn it, Morgana thought when she'd opened the front door. He looked so cute. His hair was tumbled by the wind. He carried a battered knapsack over one shoulder and had a hole in the knee of his jeans.

"Hi. I guess I'm a little early."

"It's all right. Come in and sit down. I just have a little… mess to clear up in the kitchen."

"What a way to speak about your cousin." Sebastian strolled down the hall, carrying the bowl of rapidly depleting ice cream. "Hello." He gave Nash a friendly nod. "You must be Kirkland."

Morgana narrowed her eyes but spoke pleasantly enough. "Nash, my cousin Sebastian. He was just leaving."

"Oh, I can stay for a minute. I've enjoyed your work."

"Thank you. Don't I know you?" His gaze changed from mild to shrewd as he studied Sebastian. "The psychic, right?"

Sebastian's lips quirked. "Guilty."

"I've followed some of your cases. Even some hard-boiled cops give you the credit for the arrest of the Yuppie Killer up in Seattle. Maybe you could—"

"Sebastian hates to talk shop," Morgana told him. There were dire threats in her eyes when she turned them on her cousin. "Don't you?"

"Actually—"

"I'm so glad you could stop by, darling." A quick jolt of power passed as she snatched the bowl out of his hands. "Don't be a stranger."

He gave in, thinking it was still early enough to stop by Anastasia's and discuss Morgana's current situation in depth. "Take care, love." He gave her a kiss, lingering over it until he felt Nash's thoughts darken. "Blessed be."

"Blessed be," Morgana returned automatically, and all but shoved him out the door. "Now, if you'll just give me a minute, we can get started." She tossed her hair back, pleased when she heard him gun the engine of his motorcycle. "Would you like some tea?"

His brows were knitted, and his hands in his pockets. "I'd rather have coffee." He trailed after her as she walked toward the kitchen. "What kind of a cousin is he?"

"Sebastian? Often an annoying one."

"No, I mean…" In the kitchen he frowned at the remnants of their cozy dinner for two. "Is he a first cousin, or one of the three-times-removed sort?"

She set an old-fashioned iron kettle on the stove to heat, then started to load a very modern dishwasher. "Our fathers are brothers." Catching Nash's look of relief nearly had her chuckling. "In this life," she couldn't help but add.

"In this… Oh, sure." He set his knapsack aside. "So you're into reincarnation."

"Into it?" Morgana repeated. "Well, that's apt enough. In any case, my father, Sebastian's and Ana's were born in Ireland. They're triplets."

"No kidding?" He leaned a hip on the table as she opened a small tin. "That's almost as good as being the seventh son of a seventh son."

With a shake of her head, she measured out herbs for tea.

"Such things aren't always necessary. They married three sisters," she went on. "Triplets also."

Nash rubbed Pan's head when the dog leaned against his leg. "That's great."

"An unusual arrangement, some might say, but they recognized each other, and their destiny." She glanced back with a smile before she set a small pot of tea aside to steep. "They were fated to have only one child apiece—a disappointment to them in some ways. Between the six of them, they had a great deal of love, and would have showered it over quantities of children. But it wasn't meant."

She added a pot of coffee to a silver tray where she'd arranged delicate china cups along with a creamer and sugar bowl, both in the shape of grinning skulls.

"I'll carry it in," Nash told her. As he hefted the tray, he glanced down. "Heirlooms?"

"Novelty shop. I thought they'd amuse you."

She led the way into the drawing room, where Luna was curled in the center of the sofa. Morgana chose the cushion beside her and gestured for Nash to set the tray on the table.

"Cream and sugar?" she asked.

"Both, thanks." Watching her use the grim containers, he was amused. "I bet you're a stitch around Halloween."

She offered him a cup. "Children come for miles to be treated by the witch, or try to trick her." And her fondness for children had her postponing her own All Hallows' Eve celebration every year until the last goody bag had been filled. "I think some of them are disappointed that I don't wear a pointed hat and ride out on my broomstick." The silver band on her finger winked in the lamplight as she poured a delicate amber tea brewed from jasmine flowers.

"Most people have one of two views on witches. It's either the hooked-nosed crone passing out poisoned apples, or the glittering spirit with a star-shaped wand telling you there's no place like home."

"I'm afraid I don't fit either category."

"Exactly why you're what I need." After setting his cup aside, he dug in his knapsack. "Okay?" he asked, setting his tape recorder on the table.

"Sure."

He punched the record button, then dug again. "I spent the day slogging through books—the library, bookstores." He offered her a slim soft-cover volume. "What do you think about this?"

One brow arched, Morgana studied the title. *"Fame, Fortune and Romance: Candle Rituals for Every Need."* She dropped the book into his lap smartly enough to make him wince. "I hope you didn't pay much for it."

"Six-ninety-five, and it comes off my taxes. You don't go in for this sort of thing, then?"

Patience, she told herself, slipping off her shoes and curling up her legs. The little red skirt she wore slid up to midthigh. "Lighting candles and reciting clever little chants. Do you really believe that any layman can perform magic by reading a book?"

"You gotta learn somewhere."

Snarling, she snatched it up again, flipped it open. "To arouse jealousy," she read, disgusted. "To win the love of a woman. To obtain money." She slapped it down again. "Think about this, Nash, and be grateful it doesn't work for everyone. You're a little strapped for cash, bills are piling up. You'd really like to have that new car, but the credit's exhausted. So, light a few candles, make a wish—maybe dance naked for effect. Abracadabra." She spread her hands. "You find yourself getting a check for ten thousand. Only problem is, your beloved grandmother had to die to leave it to you."

"Okay, so you've got to be careful how you phrase your charm."

"Follow me here," she said with a toss of her head. "Actions have consequences. You wish your husband were more romantic. Shazam, he's suddenly a regular Don Juan—with every woman in town. But you'll be noble, and cast a charm to stop a war. It works just fine, but as a result dozens of others spring up." She let out a huff of breath. "Magic is not for the unprepared or the irresponsible. And it certainly can't be learned out of some silly book."

"Okay." Impressed by her reasoning, he held up both hands. "I'm convinced. My point was that I could buy this in a bookstore for seven bucks. People are interested."

"People have always been interested." When she shifted, her hair slid down over her shoulder. "There have been times when their interest caused them to be hanged, burned or drowned." She sipped her tea. "We're a bit more civilized today."

"That's the thing," he agreed. "That's why I want to write the story about now. Now, when we've got cell phones and microwave ovens, fax machines and voice mail. And people are still fascinated with magic. I can go a couple of ways. Use lunatics who sacrifice goats—"

"Not with my help."

"Okay, I figured that. Anyway, that's too easy…too, ah, ordinary. I've been thinking about leaning more toward the comic angle I used in *Rest In Peace,* maybe adding some romance. Not just sex." Luna had crawled into his lap, and he was stroking her, running long fingers down her spine. "The idea is to focus on a woman, this gorgeous woman who happens to have a little extra. How does she deal with men, with a job, with… I don't know, grocery shopping? She has to know other witches. What do they talk about? What do they do for laughs? When did you decide you were a witch?"

"Probably when I levitated out of my crib," Morgana said mildly, and watched laughter form in his eyes.

"That's just the kind of thing I want." He settled back, and

Luna draped herself over his legs like a lap rug. "Must've sent your mother into shock."

"She was prepared for it." When she shifted, her knees brushed his thigh. He didn't figure there was anything magical about the quick flare of heat he felt. It was straight chemistry. "I told you I was a hereditary witch."

"Right." His tone had her taking a deep breath. "So, did it ever bother you? Thinking you were different?"

"*Knowing* I was different," she corrected. "Of course. As a child, it was more difficult to control power. One often loses control through emotion—in the same way a woman might lose control of the intellect with certain men."

He wanted to reach out and touch her hair, but he thought better of it. "Does it happen often? Losing control?"

She remembered the way it had felt the day before, with his mouth on hers. "Not as often as it did before I matured. I have a problem with temper, and I sometimes do things I regret, but there is something no responsible witch forgets. 'An it harm none,'" she quoted. "Power must never be used to hurt."

"So you're a serious and responsible witch. And you cast love spells for your customers."

Her chin shot out. "Certainly not."

"You took those pictures—that woman's niece, and the geometry heartthrob."

He didn't miss a trick, Morgana thought in disgust. "She didn't give me much choice." Because she was embarrassed, she set down her cup with a snap. "And just because I took the pictures doesn't mean I'm about to sprinkle them both with moondust."

"Is that how it works?"

"Yes, but—" She bit her tongue. "You're making fun of me. Why do you ask questions when you're not going to believe the answers?"

"I don't have to believe them to be interested." And he

was—very. He found himself sliding a few inches closer. "So you didn't do anything about the prom?"

"I didn't say that." She sulked a little while he gave in and toyed with her hair. "I simply removed a small barrier. Anything else would have been interference."

"What barrier?" He didn't have a clue as to what moondust might smell like, but he thought it would carry the same perfume as her hair.

"The girl's desperately shy. I only gave her confidence a tiny boost. The rest is up to her."

She had a beautiful neck, slim and graceful. He imagined what it would be like to nibble on it. For an hour or two. Business, he reminded himself. Stick to business.

"Is that how you work? Giving boosts?"

She turned her head and looked directly into his eyes. "It depends on the situation."

"I've been reading a lot. Witches used to be considered the wise women of the villages. Making potions, charming, foretelling events, healing the sick."

"My speciality isn't healing, or seeing."

"What is your speciality?"

"Magic." Whether it was a matter of pride or annoyance, she wasn't sure, but she sent thunder walking across the sky.

Nash glanced toward the window. "Sounds like a storm coming."

"Could be. Why don't I answer some of your questions, so you can beat it home?"

Damn it, she wanted him gone. She knew what she'd seen in the scrying ball, and that with care, with skill, such things could sometimes be changed. But whatever was to be, she didn't want things moving so fast.

And the way he was touching her, just those long fingertips to her hair, had little flicks of fear lighting in her gut.

That made her angry.

"No hurry," he said easily, wondering whether, if he took a chance and kissed her again, he'd experience that same other-worldly sensation. "I don't mind a little rain."

"It's going to pour," she muttered to herself. She'd damn well see to it. "Some of your books might be helpful," she began. "Giving you history and recorded facts, a general outline of ritu-als." She poked a finger at the first one he'd given her. "Not this one. There are certain...trappings that are used in the Craft."

"Graveyard dirt?"

She rolled her eyes. "Oh, please."

"Come on, Morgana, it's a great visual." He shifted, slipping a hand over hers, wanting her to see as he saw. "Exterior scene, night. Our beautiful heroine wading through the fog, crossing over the shadows of headstones. An owl screams. In the dis-tance echoes the long, ululant howl of a dog. Close-up of that pale, perfect face, framed by a dark hood. She stops by a fresh grave and, chanting, sifts a handful of newly turned earth into her magic pouch. Thunder claps. Fade out."

She tried, really tried, not to be offended. Imagine anyone thinking she skulked around graveyards. "Nash, I'm trying to remember that what you do is entertainment, and you're cer-tainly entitled to a great deal of artistic license."

He had to kiss her fingers. Really had to. "So you don't spend much time in cemeteries."

She snagged her temper, and a bolt of desire. "I'll accept the fact that you don't believe what I am. But I will not, I abso-lutely will not, tolerate being laughed at."

"Don't be so intense." He brushed the hair off her shoulder and gave the back of her neck a quick massage. "I admit, I usu-ally do a better job at this. Hell, I did twelve hours of interviews with this whacked-out Romanian who swore he was a vampire. Didn't have a mirror in the house. He made me wear a cross the whole time. Not to mention the garlic," Nash remembered with a grimace. "Anyway, I didn't have a problem humoring him, and he was a treasure chest of information. But you…"

"But me," she prompted, doing her best to ignore the fact that he was trailing a finger up her arm with the same skill and sensuousness he had used to stroke Luna.

"I just can't buy it, Morgana. You're a strong, intelligent woman. You've got style, taste—not to mention the fact that you smell terrific. I just can't pretend to believe that you believe all this."

Her blood was starting to boil. She would not, simply could not, tolerate the fact that he could infuriate her and seduce her at the same time. "Is that what you do to get what you want? Pretend?"

"When some ninety-year-old woman tells me her lover was shot as a werewolf in 1922, I'm not going to call her a liar. I figure either she's a hell of a storyteller or she believes it. Either way it's fine with me."

"As long as you get the angle for your movie."

"That's my living. Illusion. And it doesn't hurt anyone."

"Oh, I'm sure it doesn't, not when you walk away, then have a few drinks with the boys and laugh about the lunatic you interviewed." Her eyes were flaming. "Try it with me, Nash, and you'll get warts on your tongue."

Because he could see that she was really angry, he swallowed his grin. "All I'm saying is, I know you've got a lot of data, a lot of facts and fantasy, which is exactly what I'm looking for. I figure building a reputation as a witch probably adds fifty percent to your sales annually. It's a great hook. You just don't have to play the game with me."

"You think I pretend to be a witch to increase sales." She was getting slowly to her feet, afraid that if she stayed too close she might do him bodily harm.

"I don't— Hey!" He jumped when Luna dug her claws into his thighs.

Morgana and her cat exchanged looks of approval. "You sit in my home and call me a charlatan, a liar and a thief."

"No." He unhooked himself from the cat and stood. "That's not what I meant at all. I just meant that you can be straight with me."

"Straight with you." She began to pace the room, trying and failing to regain control. On one hand he was seducing her without her willing it, and on the other he was sneering at her. He thought she was a fraud. Why, the insolent jackass was lucky she didn't have him braying and twitching twelve-inch ears. Smiling wickedly, she turned. "You want me to be straight with you?"

The smile relieved him, a little. He'd been afraid she'd start throwing things. "I just want you to know you can relax. You give me the facts, and I'll take care of the fiction."

"Relax," she said with a nod. "That's a good idea. We should both relax." Her eyes glowed as she stepped toward him. "Why don't we have a fire? Nothing like a cozy fire to help you relax."

"Good idea." And definitely a sexy one. "I'll light it."

"Oh, no." She laid a hand on his arm. "Allow me."

She whirled away, flung out both arms toward the hearth. She felt the cool, clear knowledge whip through her blood. It was an ancient skill, one of the first mastered, one of the last to be lost with age. Her eyes, then her mind, focused on the dry wood. In the next moment, flames erupted with a roar, logs snapped, smoke billowed.

Pleased, she banked it so that the hearth glowed with the cheerful blaze.

Lowering her arms, she turned back. It delighted her to see not only that Nash was white as a sheet, but also that his mouth had yet to close.

"Better?" she asked sweetly.

He sat on the cat. Luna howled her disapproval and stalked off, despite his muttered apology. "I think—"

"You look like you could use a drink." On a roll now, Morgana held out a hand. A decanter hopped off a table five feet away and landed on her palm. "Brandy?"

"No." He let out a deep breath. "Thanks."

"I believe I will." She snapped her fingers. A snifter drifted over and hung suspended in midair while she poured. It was showing off, she knew, but it was immensely satisfying. "Sure you don't want some?"

"Yeah."

With a shrug, she sent the decanter back. Glass clinked lightly against wood as it landed. "Now," she said, curling on the couch beside him. "Where were we?"

Hallucination, he thought. Hypnosis. He opened his mouth, but all he could manage was a stutter. Morgana was still smiling that sleek cat smile at him. Special effects. It was suddenly so clear, he laughed at his own stupidity.

"Gotta be a wire," he said, and rose to look for himself. "Hell of a trick, babe. Absolutely first-rate. You had me for a minute."

"Did I really?" she murmured.

"I hired some of the F/X guys to help me with this party last year. You should have seen some of the stuff we pulled off."

He picked up the decanter, looking for trips and levers. All he found was old Irish crystal and smooth wood. With a shrug, he walked over to crouch in front of the fire. He suspected she'd had a small charge set under the wood, something she could set off with a small device in the palm of her hand. Inspired, he sprang up.

"How about this? We bring this guy into town. He's a scientist, and he falls for her, then drives himself crazy trying to explain everything she does. Make it logical." His mind was leaping ahead. "Maybe he sneaks into one of her ceremonies. You ever been to one?"

She'd exorcised the temper, and she found only humor in its place. "Naturally."

"Great. You can give me inside stuff. We could have him see her do something off-the-wall. Levitate. Or this fire bit was good. We could have this bonfire, and she lights it without a match. But he doesn't know for sure if it's a trick or real. Neither does the audience."

She let the brandy slide warm into her system. Temper tantrums were so exhausting. "What's the point of the story?"

"Besides some chills and thrills, I think it's a matter of, can this guy, this regular guy, deal with the fact that he's in love with a witch."

Suddenly sad, she stared into her glass. "You might ask yourself if a witch could deal with the fact that she's in love with an ordinary man."

"That's just what I need you for." He sauntered over to drop down beside her. "Not only the witch's angle, but the woman's, too." Comfortable again, he patted her knee. "Now, let's talk about casting spells."

With a shake of her head, she set the drink aside and laughed. "All right, Nash. Let's talk magic."

Chapter Four

He hadn't been lonely. How could he have been, when he'd spent hours that day poring over books, enlivening his mind and his world with facts and fantasies? Since childhood, Nash had been content with his own company. What had once been a necessity to survive had become a way of life.

The time he'd spent with his grandmother or his aunt, or his sporadic stays in foster homes, had taught him that he was much better off devising his own entertainment than looking to the adults in his life to devise some for him. More often than not, that entertainment had equaled chores, a lecture, solitary confinement or—in his grandmother's case—a swift backhand.

Since he'd never been permitted an abundance of playthings or playmates, he'd turned his mind into a particularly fine toy.

He'd often thought it had given him an advantage over better-endowed children. After all, the imagination was portable, unbreakable and amazingly malleable. It couldn't be taken away from you by an irritated adult when you had committed some infraction. It didn't have to be left behind when you were packed off to some other place.

Now that he could afford to buy himself whatever he liked—and Nash would have been among the first to admit that adult toys were a terrific source of entertainment—he was still content with the fluidity of imagination.

He could happily close himself off from the real world and real people for hours at a stretch. It didn't mean he was alone, not with all the characters and events racing around in his head. His imagination had always been company enough. If he occasionally indulged in binges of parties and people, it was as much to gather grist for the mill as it was to balance out those solitary times.

But lonely? No, that was absurd.

He had friends now, he had control over his own destiny. It was his choice, his alone, whether to stay or to go. It delighted him that he had his big house to himself. He could eat when he was hungry, sleep when he was tired, and toss his clothes wherever it suited him. Most of his friends and associates were unhappily married or bitterly divorced and wasted a great deal of time and effort complaining about their partners.

Not Nash Kirkland.

He was a single man. A carefree bachelor. A lone wolf who was happy as a clam.

And what, he wondered, made a clam so damn happy, anyway?

Nash knew what made him happy. Being able to set his laptop out on the patio table and work in the sunlight and fresh air, with the drumming of water in the background. Being able to toy with the treatment for a new screenplay without sweating about time clocks or office politics or a woman who was waiting for him to snap back and pay attention to her.

Did that sound like the lament of a lonely man?

Nash knew he'd never been meant for a conventional job, or a conventional relationship. God knows his grandmother had told him often enough he'd never amount to anything remotely respectable. And she'd mentioned, more than once, that no decent woman with a grain of sense would have him.

Nash didn't figure that that stiff-necked woman would have considered penning occult tales remotely respectable. If she were still alive, she'd sniff and nod her head smugly at the fact that he'd reached the age of thirty-three without taking a wife.

Still, he'd tried the other way. His brief and terrible stint as a desk jockey with an insurance company in Kansas City had proven that he would never be a nine-to-fiver. Certainly his last attempt at a serious relationship had proven that he wasn't suited to the demands of permanence with a woman.

As that former lover, DeeDee Driscol, had sniped during their final battle, he was... How had she put it again? "You're nothing but a selfish little boy, emotionally arrested. You think since you're good in bed you can behave irresponsibly out of it. You'd rather play with your monsters than have a serious adult relationship with a woman."

She'd said a lot more, Nash remembered, but that had been the gist of it. He couldn't really blame her for throwing his irresponsibility at him. Or the marble ashtray, if it came to that. He'd let her down. He wasn't, as she'd hoped, husband material. And, no matter how much she'd altered and stitched during their six-month run, he just hadn't measured up.

So DeeDee was marrying her oral surgeon. Nash didn't think it was overly snide to chuckle at the idea that an impacted wisdom tooth had led to orange blossoms.

Better you than me, he told the nameless dentist. DeeDee was a bright, friendly woman with a cuddly body and a great smile. And she had the arm of a major-league outfielder when you ticked her off.

It certainly didn't make him lonely to think of DeeDee taking that long, slippery walk down the matrimonial aisle.

He was a free agent, a man-about-town, unattached, unencumbered, and pleased as punch. Whatever the hell that meant.

So why was he rattling around this big house like the last living cell in a dying body?

And, much more important, why had he started to pick up the phone a dozen times to call Morgana?

It wasn't their night to work. She'd been very firm about giving him only two evenings a week. And he had to admit, once they'd gotten past those initial rough spots, they'd cruised along together smoothly enough. As long as he watched the sarcasm.

She had a nice sense of humor, and a nice sense of drama— which was great, since he wanted both for the story. It wasn't exactly a sacrifice to spend a few hours a week in her company. True, she was adamant about insisting she was a witch, but that only made the whole business more interesting. He was almost disappointed that she hadn't set up any more special effects.

He'd exercised admirable control in keeping his hands off her. Mostly. Nash didn't figure touching her fingers or playing with her hair really counted. Not when he'd resisted that soft, sulky mouth, that long white throat, those high, lovely breasts....

Nash cut himself off, wishing he had something more satisfying to kick than the side of the sofa.

It was perfectly normal to want a woman. Hell, it was even enjoyable to imagine what it would be like to tangle up the sheets with her. But the way his mind kept veering toward Morgana at all hours of the day and night, making his work suffer in the process, was close to becoming an obsession.

It was time to get it under control.

Not that he'd lost control, he reminded himself. He'd been a saint. Even when she'd answered the door wearing those faded, raggedy cutoffs—a personal weakness of his—he'd slapped back his baser instincts. It was a bit lowering to admit that his reasoning had had less to do with altruism than with self-preservation. A personal entanglement with her would mess up the professional one. In any case, a woman who could knock him sideways with a single kiss was best treated with caution.

He had a feeling that that kind of punch would be a lot more lethal than DeeDee's deadly aim.

But he wanted to call her, to hear her voice, to ask if he could see her for just an hour or two.

Damn it, he was *not* lonely. Or at least he hadn't been until he'd shut off his machine and his tired brain to go for a walk on the beach. All those people he'd seen—the families, the couples, those tight little groups of belonging. And he'd been alone, watching the sun slide down into the water, longing for something he was sure he didn't really want. Something he certainly wouldn't know what to do with if he had it.

Some people weren't made to have families. That much Nash knew from firsthand experience. He'd decided long ago to avoid the mistake, and save some nameless, faceless child from being saddled with a lousy father.

But standing alone and watching those families had made him restless, had made the house he'd come home to seem too big and much too empty. It made him wish he'd had Morgana with him, so that they could have strolled along, hand in hand, by the water. Or sat on an old, bleached log, his arm tucked around her shoulders, as they watched the first stars come out.

On an oath, he yanked up the phone and punched out her number. His lips curved when he heard her voice, but the smile faded the moment he realized it was a recording, informing him that she was unavailable.

He thought about leaving a message, but hung up instead. What was he supposed to say? he asked himself. I just wanted to talk to you. I need to see you. I can't get you out of my mind.

Shaking his head, he paced the room again. Grim, beautiful masks from Oceania stared down at him from their place on the wall. In low cases, keen-edged knives with ornate handles glinted in the lamplight. To relieve some tension, Nash scooped up a voodoo doll and jammed a pin through its heart.

"See how you like it, bub."

He tossed it aside, jammed his hands in his pockets and decided it was time to get out of the house. What the hell, he'd go to the movies.

"It's your turn to buy the tickets," Morgana told Sebastian patiently. "Mine to spring for popcorn, and Ana's to choose the movie."

Sebastian scowled as they walked down Cannery Row. "I bought the tickets last time."

"No. You didn't."

Anastasia smiled when Sebastian appealed to her, but shook her head. "I bought them last time," she confirmed. "You're just trying to weasel out again."

"Weasel?" Insulted, he stopped in the middle of the sidewalk. "What a disgusting word. And I distinctly remember—"

"What you want to remember," Anastasia finished for him, tucking her arm through his. "Give it up, Cousin. I'm not passing on my turn."

He muttered something but started walking again, Morgana on one arm, Anastasia on the other. He really wanted to catch the new Schwarzenegger flick, and he was very much afraid that Ana was going to opt for the fluffy romantic comedy in theater two. Not that he minded romance, but he'd heard that Arnold had outdone himself this time, saving the entire planet from a group of evil, shape-shifting extraterrestrials.

"Don't sulk," Morgana said lightly. "You get to pick next time."

She liked the arrangement very much. Whenever the mood or their schedules allowed, the three cousins would take in a movie. Years of bickering, seething tempers and ruined evenings had resulted in the current system. It wasn't without its flaws, but it usually prevented a heated argument at the ticket booth.

"And no fair trying to influence," Anastasia added when she felt Sebastian pushing at her mind. "I've already decided."

"Just trying to keep you from wasting my money." Resigned, Sebastian glanced down at the smattering of people forming in line. His spirits lifted when he spotted the man who was strolling up from the opposite direction. "Well, well," he said. "Isn't this cozy?"

Morgana had already seen Nash, and wasn't sure whether she was annoyed or pleased. She'd managed to keep everything on an even keel during their meetings. No mean trick, she decided, considering the sexual sparks that crackled through the air whenever they got within two feet of each other.

She could handle it, she reminded herself, and offered Nash a smile. "Busman's holiday?"

His gloomy mood vanished. She looked like a dark angel, her hair flowing around her shoulders, the short red dress clinging to each curve. "More or less. I always like falling into someone else's movie when I'm struggling with one of my own." Though it took an effort to tear his eyes from Morgana's, he glanced at Sebastian and Anastasia. "Hi."

"It's nice to see you again." Anastasia stepped into line. "It's funny, the last time the three of us hit the movies, we saw your *Play Dead*."

"Oh, yeah?"

"It was very good."

"She'd know," Sebastian put in. "Ana watched the last thirty minutes with her eyes closed."

"The highest of compliments." Nash shuffled his way down the line with them. "So, what're you going to see?"

Anastasia shot Sebastian a look as he pulled out his wallet. "The Schwarzenegger movie."

"Really?" Nash hadn't a clue why Sebastian was chuckling, but he smiled at Morgana. "Me, too."

Nash figured his luck was in when he settled down in the theater beside Morgana. It hardly mattered that he'd already seen the movie at its Hollywood premiere. He'd probably have ended up choosing it anyway. It was a hell of a show, as he recalled. Fast paced, with plenty of humor to leaven the violence, along with a nicely twisted coil of suspense. And there was a particular scene that had had the celebrity audience on the edge of their seats. If his luck held, Morgana would be cuddled up against him by the second reel.

As the lights dimmed, Morgana turned her head and smiled at him. Nash felt several of his brain cells melt and wished they still ran double features.

In the normal scheme of things, Nash took the long step out of reality the moment a movie caught his imagination. There was nothing he liked better than diving into the action. It rarely mattered whether it was his first shot at a film or he was visiting an old friend for the twentieth time—he was always at home in a movie. But tonight he kept losing track of the adventure on the screen.

He was much too aware of the woman beside him to click off reality.

Theaters had their own smell. The oily, not unpleasant aroma of what the concessions jokingly called butter over the warm fragrance of popcorn, the sweet tang of candies, the syrupy scent of spilled soft drinks. However appealing it was—and it had always been appealing to Nash—he couldn't get beyond the dreamy sexuality of Morgana's perfume.

The theater was cool, almost chilly. It had never made sense to him that the air-conditioning was so often turned toward frigid in a place where people would be sitting still for two hours. But the scent of Morgana's skin was hot, arousingly hot, as if she were sitting in a strong beam of sunlight.

She didn't gasp or jolt or huddle against him, no matter how much mayhem the invaders or the hero wrought. Instead, she kept her gaze fixed intently on the screen, nibbling occasionally from a dwindling container of popcorn.

At one point she did hiss a breath through her teeth and grip the armrest between them. Gallantly Nash covered her hand with his. She didn't look toward him, but she did turn her hand, palm up, and link her fingers with his.

She couldn't help it, Morgana thought. She wasn't made of stone. What she was was a flesh-and-blood woman who found the man beside her outrageously attractive. And sweet, damn it. There was something undeniably sweet about sitting in a darkened theater holding hands.

And what could it hurt?

She was being careful when they were alone, making sure things didn't move too quickly or in a direction not of her choosing. Not that she'd had to fight him off, Morgana reminded herself with a touch of resentment. He'd made no attempt to hold her, or kiss her again, or to seduce her in any way.

Unless she counted the fact that he always seemed to be touching her in that careless and friendly manner. The manner that had her tossing restlessly in bed for several hours after he'd left her last.

Her problem, she reminded herself, and tried to ignore the long, slow tug inside as Nash ran his thumb lazily up and down the side of her hand.

The upside was, she enjoyed working with him, helping him with his research. Not only because he was an amusing companion with a mind and talent she respected, but also because it was giving her the opportunity to explain what she was in her own way.

Of course, he didn't believe a word of it.

Not that it mattered, Morgana told herself, and lost track of the film as Nash's forearm rubbed warmly over hers. He didn't have to believe to incorporate her knowledge and write a good story. Yet it disappointed her, on some deep level. Having him believe, and accept, would have been so soothing.

When the world was saved and the lights came up, she slipped her hand from Nash's. Not that it hadn't felt nice keeping it there, but Morgana wasn't in the mood to risk any of Sebastian's teasing comments.

"Excellent choice, Ana," Sebastian told her.

"Say that again when my heart rate's normal."

Her cousin slipped an arm over her shoulders as they shuffled up the aisle. "Scare you?"

"Of course not." She refused to admit it this time. "Seeing that incredible body stripped to the waist for the best part of two hours is enough to give any woman a rush."

They moved into the brightly lit, noisy lobby. "Pizza," Sebastian decided. He glanced back at Nash. "You up for food?"

"I'm always up for food."

"Great." Sebastian pushed open the door and led them into the night. "You're buying."

They were quite a trio, Nash decided as the four of them devoured slices of pizza dripping with cheese. They argued about everything, from what kind of pizza to buy to which alien demise had been the most effective in the movie they'd just seen. He decided that Morgana and Sebastian enjoyed sniping at each other as much as they enjoyed the meal, with Anastasia slipping in and out of the role of referee.

It was obvious that the bond ran deep, for under the bickering and complaining was an inescapable stream of affection.

When Morgana said to Sebastian, "Don't be such a jerk, love," Nash sensed that she meant "jerk" and "love" in equal measure. Listening to it, Nash fought back the same little stab of envy he'd felt on the beach at sunset.

They were each only children, as he was. Yet they were not, as he was, alone.

Anastasia turned to him. Something flickered in her eyes for a moment that was so much like sympathy that he felt a wave of embarrassment. Then it was gone, and she was only a lovely woman with an easy smile.

"They don't mean to be rude," she said lightly. "They can't help themselves."

"Rude?" With her hair tucked around to spill over one shoulder, Morgana swirled her glass of heavy red wine. "It isn't rude to point out Sebastian's flaws. Not when they're so obvious." She slapped his hand away from the slice of pizza on her plate. "See that?" she asked Nash. "He's always been greedy."

"Generous to a fault," Sebastian said.

"Conceited," she said, grinning at her cousin while she took a healthy bite of pizza. "Bad-tempered."

"Lies." Contenting himself with his wine, Sebastian leaned back in his chair. "I'm enviably even-tempered. It's you who have always had the tantrums. Right, Ana?"

"Well, actually, you both—"

"She never grew out of it," Sebastian interjected. "As a child, when she didn't get her way, she'd wail like a banshee, or sulk in corners. Control was never her strong point."

"I hate to point this out," Anastasia told him, "but at least half the time Morgana was driven to wails it was because you'd provoked her."

"Naturally." Unrepentant, Sebastian shrugged. "It was so easy." He winked at Morgana. "Still is."

"I should never have let you down from the ceiling all those years ago."

Nash paused over his drink. "Excuse me?"

"A particularly nasty little prank," Sebastian explained. It still annoyed him that his cousin had gotten the better of him.

"Which you richly deserved." Morgana was pouting over her wine. "I'm not sure I've forgiven you yet."

Anastasia was forced to agree. "It was lousy of you, Sebastian."

Outnumbered, Sebastian relented. He could even, with an effort, dredge up some humor along with the memory. "I was only eleven years old. Little boys are entitled to be lousy. Anyway, it wasn't a real snake."

Morgana sniffed. "It looked real."

Chuckling, Sebastian leaned forward to tell Nash the tale. "We were all over at Aunt Bryna's and Uncle Matthew's for May Day. Admittedly, I was always looking for a way to get a rise out of the brat here, and I knew she was terrified of snakes."

"And it's just like you to exploit one small phobia," Morgana muttered.

"The thing was, the kid was fearless—except for this one thing." Sebastian's eyes, tawny as a cat's, glowed with humor. "So, seeing as boys will be boys, I plopped a rubber snake right in the center of her bed—while she was in it, of course."

Nash couldn't suppress the grin, but he did manage to turn the laugh into a cough when he saw Morgana's arch look. "It doesn't seem so terrible."

"He made it hiss and wriggle," Ana put in, biting down on her lip to keep it from curving.

Sebastian sighed nostalgically. "I'd worked on that charm for weeks. Magic's never been my strong point, so it was a pretty weak attempt, all in all. Still—" he leered at Morgana "—it worked."

Nash discovered he had absolutely no comment to make. It appeared he wasn't sitting at a table with three sensible people after all.

"So, after I got finished screaming, and saw through what was really a very pitiful spell, I sent Sebastian to the ceiling, let him hang there, upside down." Her tone was smug and satisfied. "How long was it, darling?"

"Two hideous hours."

She smiled. "You'd still be there if my mother hadn't found you and made me bring you down."

"And for the rest of the summer," Anastasia put in, "the two of you tried to outdo each other, and you both stayed in trouble."

Sebastian and Morgana grinned at each other. Then Morgana tilted her head and sent Nash a sidelong glance. She could all but hear the wheels turning. "Sure you won't have a glass of wine?"

"No, thanks, I'm driving." They were putting him on, he realized. He flicked a smile at Morgana. Why should he mind? It made him part of the little group, and it gave him new angles for the story. "So, you, ah...played a lot of tricks on each other as kids?"

"It's difficult, when one has certain talents, to be content with ordinary games."

"Whatever we played," Sebastian said to Morgana, "you cheated."

"Of course I did." Unoffended, she passed him the rest of her pizza. "I like to win. It's getting late." She rose to kiss each of her cousins on the cheek. "Why don't you give me a ride home, Nash?"

"Sure." It was exactly what he'd had in mind.

"Be careful, Kirkland," Sebastian said lazily. "She likes to play with fire."

"So I've noticed." He took Morgana's hand and led her away.

Anastasia gave a little sigh and propped her chin on her hand. "With all the sparks popping back and forth between the two of them, I'm surprised we didn't have a blaze right here at the table."

"There'll be flames soon enough." Sebastian's eyes darkened, going fixed and nearly opaque. "Whether she likes it or not."

Instantly concerned, Ana put a hand on his. "She'll be all right?"

He wasn't seeing as clearly as he would have liked. It was always more difficult with family, and particularly with Morgana. "She'll have a few bumps and bruises." And he was sorry for it. Then his eyes cleared and the easy smile was back in place. "She'll get through it, Ana. As she said, Morgana likes to win."

* * *

Morgana wasn't thinking of battles or victories, but of how cool and silky the air felt blowing against her cheeks. With her head back, she stared up at a black sky haunted by a half-moon and dazzled by stars.

It was easy to enjoy. The fast, open car on the curving road, the shadowy moonlight and the sea-flavored air. And it was easy to enjoy him, this man who drove with a natural, confident flair, who played the radio too loud, who smelled of the night and all its secrets.

Turning her head, she studied his profile. Oh, she would have enjoyed running her fingers over that angular face, testing the shape of the bones, brushing a touch over that clever mouth, perhaps feeling the slight roughness of his chin. She would have enjoyed it very much.

So why did she hesitate? Though she'd never been promiscuous or seen every attractive man as a potential lover, she recognized the deeper desire to be his. And she had seen that it was to happen before much longer in any case.

That was her answer, Morgana realized. She would always rebel against being destiny's puppet.

But surely if she chose him for herself, if she kept the power in her own hands, it was not the same as being led by fate. She was, after all, her own mistress.

"Why did you go into town tonight?" she asked him.

"I was restless. Tired of myself."

She understood the feeling. It didn't spring up in her often, but when it did it was unbearable. "The script is going well?"

"Pretty well. I should have a treatment to send to my agent in a few days." He glanced toward her, then immediately wished he hadn't. She looked so beautiful, so alluring, with the wind in her hair and the moonlight sprinkling over her skin, that he didn't want to look away again. It wasn't a wise way to operate a moving vehicle. "You've been a lot of help."

"Does that mean you're through with me?"

"No. Morgana, I—" He stopped and swore, catching himself a moment after he passed her driveway. He backed up and turned in, but left the motor running. For a moment he sat brooding in silence, looking at the house, where only a single window glowed gold and the rest were black as pitch.

If she asked him in, he would go with her, would have to go. Something was happening tonight. Something had been happening since the moment he'd turned and looked into her eyes. It gave him the unsettling feeling that he was walking through someone else's script and the ending had yet to be written.

"You are restless," she murmured. "Out of character for you." On impulse, she reached over and switched off the ignition. The absence of the engine's purr had the silence roaring in his head. Their bodies brushed, and the promise of more sizzled hot in his gut. "Do you know what I like to do when I'm restless?"

Her voice had lowered, and it seemed liquid enough now to slide over his skin like mulled wine. He turned to see those vivid blue eyes glowing with moonlight. And his hands were already reaching for her.

"What?"

She eased away, slipping from his hands like a ghost. After opening her door, she walked slowly around to his side, leaned down until their lips nearly touched. "I take a walk." With her eyes still on his, she straightened and offered a hand. "Come with me. I'll show you a magic place."

He could have refused. But he knew if there was a man who wouldn't have stepped from the car and taken that offered hand, he had yet to be born.

They crossed the lawn, walking away from the house where the single light glowed, and entered the mystic shadows and whispering silence of the cyprus grove. Moonlight flickered down, casting eerie silhouettes of the twisted branches on the soft forest floor. The faintest of breezes hummed through the leaves and made him think of the harp she kept in her drawing room.

Her hand was warm and firm in his as she moved forward, not with hurry, but with purpose.

"I like the night." She took a deep breath of it. "The scent and the flavor of night. Sometimes I'll wake in the dark, and come to walk here."

He could hear water on rock, a steady heartbeat of sound. For reasons he couldn't fathom, his own heart was thudding relentlessly in his chest.

Something was happening.

"The trees." The sound of his own voice seemed odd and secretive in the shadowy grove. "I fell in love with them."

She stopped walking to eye him curiously. "Did you?"

"I was up here on vacation last year. Wanted to get out of the heat. I couldn't get enough of the trees." He laid a hand on one, feeling the rough bark of a trunk that bent dramatically away. "I'd never been much of the nature type. I'd always lived in cities, or just outside them. But I knew I had to live somewhere where I could look out of my window and see these trees."

"Sometimes we come back where we belong." She began to walk again, her footsteps silent on the soft earth. "Some ancient cults worshiped trees like these." She smiled. "I think it's enough to love them, appreciate them for their age, their beauty, their tenacity. Here." She stopped again and turned to him. "This is the center, the heart. The purest magic is always in the heart."

He couldn't have said why he understood, or why he believed. Perhaps it was the moon, or the moment. He knew only that he felt a stirring along the skin, a fluttering in his mind. And, from somewhere deep in memory, he knew he'd been here before. With her.

Lifting a hand, he touched her face, letting his fingertips trace from cheek to jaw. She didn't move, not forward or away. She only continued to watch him. And wait.

"I don't know if I like what's happening to me," he said quietly.

"What is happening to you?"

"You are." Unable to resist, he lifted his other hand so that her face was framed, a captive of his tensed fingers. "I dream about you. Even in the middle of the day I dream about you. I can't turn it off, or switch the scene around as I'd like. It just happens."

She lifted a hand to his wrist, wanting to feel the good, strong beat of his pulse. "Is that so bad?"

"I don't know. I'm real good at avoiding complications, Morgana. I don't want that to change."

"Then we'll keep it simple."

He wasn't certain if she had moved, or if he had, but somehow she was in his arms, and his mouth was drinking from hers. No dream had ever been so stirring.

Her tongue toyed with his, tempting him to plunge deeper. She welcomed him with a moan that sizzled in his blood. At last he pleasured himself by tasting the long line of her throat, sliding his tongue over the pulse that hammered there, nibbling the sensitive flesh under her jaw, until he felt the first quick, helpless shudder pass through her. And then he was diving, more deeply, more desperately, when his mouth again met hers.

How could she have thought she had any choice, any control? What they were bringing to each other here was as old as time, as fresh as spring.

If only it could be pleasure, nothing more, she thought weakly as sensations battered against her will. But even as her body throbbed with that pleasure, she knew it was much, much more.

Not once in her years as a woman had she given her heart. It had not been jealously guarded, because it had always been safe. But now, with the moon overhead, with the silent old trees as witnesses, she gave it to him.

Her arms tightened at the swift, silvery ache. His name tumbled from her lips. In that moment, she knew why she had needed to bring him there, to her most private place. Where could it be more fitting for her to lose her heart than here?

For another moment, she held him close, letting her body absorb what he could give her, wishing she could have honored her word and kept it simple.

But it was not to be simple now. Not for either of them. All she could do was take the time that was still left and prepare them both.

When she would have drawn back, he pulled her in, taking her mouth again and again while images and sounds and needs whirled in his brain.

"Nash." She turned her head to rub her cheek soothingly against his. "It can't be now."

Her quiet voice slipped through the roaring in his brain. A wave of violence stunned him. Appalled, he loosened his grip, realizing his fingers were digging into her flesh.

"I'm sorry." He dropped his hands to his sides. "Did I hurt you?"

"No." Touched, she brought his hand to her lips. "Of course not. Don't worry."

He damn well would worry. He'd never, never been anything but gentle with a woman. There were some who might say he could be careless with feelings, and if it was true he was sorry for it. But no one would ever have accused him of being careless physically.

Yet he had nearly pulled her to the ground and taken what he so desperately needed, without a thought to her acceptance or agreement.

Shaken, he jammed his hands into his pockets. "I was right, I don't like what's happening here. That's the second time I've kissed you, and the second time I've felt like I had to. The same way I have to breathe or eat or sleep."

She would have to tread carefully here. "Affection is just as necessary for survival."

He doubted it, since he'd done without it for most of his life. Studying her, he shook his head. "You know, babe, if I believed you were really a witch, I'd say I was spellbound."

It surprised her that it hurt. Oh, not his words so much as the distance it put between them. Try as she might, she couldn't remember ever having been hurt by a man before. Perhaps that was what it meant to be in love. She hadn't guarded her heart before, but she could protect it now.

"Then it's fortunate you don't believe. It was just a kiss, Nash." She smiled, hoping the shadows would mask the sadness in her eyes. "There's nothing to fear in a kiss."

"I want you." His voice had roughened, and his hands were fisted in his pockets. There was a helplessness tangled with this need. Perhaps that was what had nearly touched off violence. "That might be dangerous."

She didn't doubt it. "When the time comes, we'll find out. Now I'm tired. I'm going in."

This time, when she walked through the grove, she didn't offer her hand.

Chapter Five

Morgana had opened the doors of Wicca for the first time five years and some months before Nash had walked through them looking for a witch. The success of the shop was due to Morgana's insistence on intriguing stock, her willingness to put in long hours, and her frank enjoyment of the game of buying and selling.

Since her family, for longer than anyone could clearly remember, had been financially successful, she could have spent her time in any number of idle pursuits while drawing from a number of trust funds. Her decision to become a businesswoman had been a simple one. She was ambitious enough, and more than proud enough, to want to earn her own living.

The choice of opening a shop had appealed to Morgana because it allowed her to surround herself with things she liked and enjoyed. She had also, from the first sale, found pleasure in passing those things along to others who would also enjoy them.

There were definite advantages to owning your own business. A sense of accomplishment, the basic pride of ownership, the constant variety of people who walked in and out of your life. But whenever there was an upside, there was also a down. If you were blessed with a sense of responsibility, it wasn't possible to simply shut the doors and pull down the shades when you were in the mood to be alone.

Among Morgana's many gifts was an undeniable sense of responsibility.

At the moment, she wished her parents had allowed her to become a flighty, self-absorbed, feckless woman. If they hadn't done such a good job raising her, she might have bolted the door, jumped in her car and driven away until this miserable mood passed.

She wasn't used to feeling unsettled. She certainly didn't like the idea that this uncomfortable mood had been brought on by a man. As long as she could remember, Morgana had been able to handle all members of the male species. It was— she smiled a little at the thought—a gift. Even as a child she'd been able to dance her way around her father and her uncles, getting her own way with a combination of charm, guilt and obstinacy. Sebastian had been tougher to manage, but she felt she'd at least broken even there.

Once she'd reached adolescence, she'd learned quickly how to deal with boys. What moves to make if she was interested, what moves to make if she was not. As the years had passed, it had been a simple matter of applying the same rules, with subtle variations, to men.

Her sexuality was a source of joy to her. And she was well aware that it equaled another kind of power. She would never abuse power. Her dealings with men, whether they led to friendship or to romance, had always been successful.

Until now. Until Nash.

When had she begun to slip? Morgana wondered as she wrapped and bagged a long, slim bottle of ginseng bath balm for a customer. When she'd followed that little tug on her sixth sense and crossed this very room to speak to him for the first time? When she'd bowed to that spark of curiosity and attraction and kissed him?

Perhaps she had made her first serious misstep only last night, by allowing herself to be led by pure emotion. Taking him into the grove, to that spot where the air hummed and the moon spilled.

She had taken no other man there before. She would take no other man there again.

At least, dreaming back, she could almost make herself believe it was the place and the night that had caused her to believe she had fallen in love.

She didn't want to accept that such a thing could happen to her so quickly, or leave her such little choice.

So she would refuse to accept and put an end to it.

Morgana could almost hear the spirits laughing. Ignoring the sensation, she walked around the counter to help a customer.

Throughout the morning, business was slow but steady. Morgana wasn't sure whether she preferred it when browsers drifted in or when she and Luna had the shop to themselves.

"I think I should blame you for the whole thing." Morgana braced her elbows on the table and leaned down until she was eye to eye with the cat. "If you hadn't been so friendly, I wouldn't have assumed he was harmless."

Luna merely switched her tail and looked wise.

"He's not the least bit harmless," Morgana continued. "Now it's too late to back out. Oh, sure," she said when Luna blinked, "I could tell him the deal's off. I could make up excuses why I couldn't meet with him anymore. If I wanted to admit I was a coward." She drew in a deep breath and rested her brow on the cat's. "I am not a coward." Luna gave Morgana's cheek a playful pat. "Don't try to make up. If this business gets any further out of hand, it's on your head."

Morgana glanced up when the shop door opened. Her lips curved in relief when she spotted Mindy. "Hi. Is it two already?"

"Just about." Mindy tucked her purse behind the counter,

then gave Luna a quick scratch between the ears. "So how's it going?"

"Well enough."

"I see you sold the big rose quartz cluster."

"About an hour ago. It's going to a good home, a young couple from Boston. I've got it in the back ready to pack for shipping."

"Want me to take care of it now?"

"No, actually, I could use a little break from retail. I'll do it while you mind the shop."

"Sure. You look a little down, Morgana."

She arched a brow. "Do I?"

"Yep. Let Madame Mindy see." Taking Morgana's hand, she peered, steely eyed, at the palm. "Aha. No doubt about it. Man trouble."

Despite the accuracy, the very annoying accuracy, of the statement, Morgana's lips twitched. "I hate to doubt your expertise in palmistry, Madame Mindy, but you always say it's man trouble."

"I play the odds," Mindy pointed out. "You'd be surprised how many people stick their hands in my face just because I work for a witch."

Intrigued, Morgana tilted her head. "I suppose I would."

"Well, lots of them are nervous about approaching you, and I'm safe. I guess they figure some of it might rub off, but not enough to worry about. Sort of like catching a touch of the flu or something, I guess."

For the first time in hours, a laugh bubbled up in Morgana's throat. "I see. I suppose it would disappoint them to learn I don't read palms."

"They won't hear it from me." Mindy lifted a jade-and-silver hand mirror to check her face. "But I'll tell you, honey, I don't need to be a fortune-teller to see a tall blond man with great buns and eyes to die for." She tugged a corkscrew curl toward the middle of her forehead before glancing at Morgana. "He giving you a rough time?"

"No. Nothing I can't handle."

"They're easy to handle." After setting the mirror aside, Mindy unwrapped a fresh stick of gum. "Until they matter." Then she flashed Morgana a smile. "Just say the word and I'll run interference for you."

Amused, Morgana patted Mindy's cheek. "Thanks, but I'll make this play on my own."

Her mood brighter, Morgana stepped into the back room. What was she worried about anyway? She *could* handle it. Would handle it. After all, she didn't know Nash well enough for him to matter.

He had plenty to keep him busy, Nash told himself. Plenty. He was sprawled on the sofa—six feet of faded, sagging cushions he'd bought at a garage sale because it was so obviously fashioned for afternoon naps. Books were spread over his lap and jumbled on the floor. Across the room, the agonies and pathos of an afternoon soap flickered on the television screen. A soft-drink bottle stood on the cluttered coffee table, should he want to quench his thirst.

In the next room, his computer sat sulking at the lack of attention. Nash thought he could almost hear it whine.

It wasn't like he wasn't working. Idly Nash ripped off a sheet of notepaper and began folding it. He might have been lying on the sofa, he might have spent a great deal of his morning staring into space. But he was thinking. Maybe he'd hit a bit of a snag in the treatment, but it wasn't like he was blocked or anything. He just needed to let it cook a while.

Giving the paper a last crease, he narrowed his eyes, then sent the miniature bomber soaring. To please himself, he added sound effects as the paper airplane glided off, crash-landing on the floor in a heap of other models.

"Sabotage," he said grimly. "Must be a spy on the assembly

line." Shifting for comfort, he began to build another plane while his mind drifted.

Interior scene, day. The big, echoing hangar is deserted. Murky light spills through the front opening and slants over the silver hull of a fighter jet. Slow footsteps approach. As they near, there is something familiar about them, something feminine. Stiletto heels on concrete. She slips in the entrance, from light into shadow. The glare and the tipped-down brim of a slouchy hat obscure her face, but not the body poured into a short red leather dress. Long, shapely legs cross the hangar floor. In one delicate hand, she holds a black leather case.

After one slow glance around, she goes to the plane. Her skirt hikes high on smooth white thighs as she climbs into the cockpit. There is purpose, efficiency, in her movements. The way she slips into the pilot's seat, spins the locks on the leather case.

Inside the case is a small, deadly bomb, which she secretes under the console. She laughs. The sound is sultry, seductive. The camera moves in on her face.

Morgana's face.

Swearing, Nash tossed the plane in the air. It did an immediate nosedive. What was he doing? he asked himself. Making up stories about her. Indulging in bad symbolism. So, sure, she'd climbed into his cockpit and set off an explosion. That was no reason to daydream about her.

He had work to do, didn't he?

Determined to do it, Nash shifted, sending books sliding to the floor. Using the remote, he switched off the television, then took up what was left of his notebook. He punched the play button on his recorder. It took less than five seconds for him to realize his mistake and turn it off again. He wasn't in any frame of mind to listen to Morgana's voice.

He rose, scattering books, then stepping over them. He was thinking, all right. He was thinking he had to get the hell out of the house. And he knew exactly where he wanted to go.

It was his choice, he assured himself as he snagged his keys. He was making a conscious decision. When a man had an itch, he was a lot better off scratching it.

Her mood had improved enough that Morgana could hum along with the radio she'd turned on low. This was just what she'd needed, she thought. A cup of soothing chamomile, an hour of solitude, and some pleasant and constructive work. After packing up the crystal cluster and labeling it for shipping, she pulled out her inventory ledger. She could have spent a happy afternoon sipping the soothing tea, listening to music and looking over her stock. Morgana was certain she would have done exactly that if she hadn't been interrupted.

Perhaps if she'd been tuned in, she would have been prepared to see Nash stride through the door. But it really didn't matter what she might have planned, as he stalked over to the desk, hauled her to her feet and planted a long, hard kiss on her surprised mouth.

"That," he said when he took a moment to breathe, "was my idea."

Nerve ends sizzling, Morgana managed a nod. "I see."

He let his hands slide down to her hips to hold her still. "I liked it."

"Good for you." She glanced over her shoulder and noted that Mindy was standing in the open doorway, smirking. "I can handle this, Mindy."

"Oh, I'm sure you can." With a quick wink, she shut the door.

"Well, now." Searching for composure, Morgana put her hands on his chest to ease him away. She preferred that he not detect the fact that her heart was pounding and her bones were doing a fast melt. That was no way to keep the upper hand. "Was there something else?"

"I think there's a whole lot else." His eyes on hers, he backed her up against the desk. "When do you want to get started?"

She had to smile. "I guess we could call this being direct and to the point."

"We'll call it whatever you like. I figure it this way." Because she was wearing heels and they were eye to eye, Nash had only to ease forward to nibble on her full lower lip. "I want you, and I don't see how I'm going to start thinking straight again until I spend a few nights making love with you. All kinds of love with you."

The stirring started deep and spread. She had to curl her fingers over the edge of the desk to keep her balance. But when she spoke her voice was low and confident. "I could say that once we did make love you'd never think straight again."

He cupped her face with one hand and brushed his lips over hers. "I'll take my chances."

"Maybe." Her breath hitched twice before she controlled it. "I have to decide whether I want to take mine."

His lips curved over hers. He'd felt her quick tremor of reaction. "Live dangerously."

"I am." She gave herself a moment to enjoy what he brought to her. "What would you say if I told you it wasn't the right time yet? And that we'd both know when it was the right time."

His hands slid up so that his thumbs teased the curves of her breasts. "I'd say you're avoiding the issue."

"You'd be wrong." Enchanted—his touch was incredibly gentle—she pressed her cheek to his. "Believe me, you'd be wrong."

"The hell with timing. Come home with me, Morgana."

She gave a little sigh as she drew away. "I will." She shook her head when his eyes darkened. "To help you, to work with you. Not to sleep with you. Not today."

Grinning, he leaned closer to give her earlobe a playful nip. "That gives me plenty of room to change your mind."

Her eyes were very calm, almost sad, when she stepped back.

"You may change yours before it's done. Let me ask Mindy to take over for the rest of the day."

She insisted on driving herself, following behind him with Luna curled in her passenger seat. She would give him two hours, she promised herself, and two hours only. Before she left him, she would do her best to clear his mind so that he could work.

She liked his house, the overgrown yard that shouted for a gardener, the sprawling stucco building with arching windows and red tile for the roof. It was closer to the sea than hers, so the music of the water was at full pitch. In the side yard were a pair of cypresses bent close together, like lovers reaching for one another.

It suited him, she thought as she stepped out of her car, off the drive and into the grass that rose above her ankles. "How long have you lived here?" she asked Nash.

"Couple months." He glanced around the yard. "I need to buy a lawn mower."

He'd need a bush hog before much longer. "Yes, you do."

"But I kind of like the natural look."

"You're lazy." She felt some sympathy for the daffodils that were struggling to get their heads above the weeds. She walked to the front entrance with Luna streaming regally behind her.

"I have to get motivated," he told her as he pushed open the front door. "I've mostly lived in apartments and condos. This is the first regular house I've had to myself."

She looked around at the high, cool walls of the foyer, the rich, dark wood of the curving banister that trailed upstairs and along an open balcony. "At least you chose well. Where are you working?"

"Here and there."

"Hmm." She strolled down the hallway and peeked in the first archway. It was a large, jumbled living area with wide, uncurtained windows and a bare hardwood floor. Signs, Morgana thought, of a man who had yet to decide if he was going to settle in.

The furniture was mismatched and heaped with books, papers, clothes and dishes—possibly long forgotten. More books were shoved helter-skelter into built-in cases along one wall. And toys, she noted. She often thought of her own clutter as toys. Little things that gave her pleasure, soothed her moods, passed the time.

She noted the gorgeous, grim-faced masks that hung on the wall, an exquisite print of nymphs by Maxfield Parrish, a movie prop—one of the wolves' claws from *Shape Shifter,* she imagined. He was using it as a paperweight. A silver box in the shape of a coffin sat next to the Oscar he'd won. Both could have used a proper dusting. Lips pursed, she picked up the voodoo doll, the pin still sticking lethally out of its heart.

"Anyone I know?"

He grinned, pleased to have her there, and too used to his own disorder to be embarrassed by it. "Whatever works. Usually it's a producer, sometimes a politician. Once it was this bean-counting IRS agent. I've been meaning to tell you," he added as his gaze skimmed over her slim, short dress of purple silk, "you have great taste in clothes."

"Glad you approve." Amused, she set the unfortunate doll down, patted the mangled head, then picked up a tattered deck of tarot cards. "Do you read them?"

"No. Somebody gave them to me. They're supposed to have belonged to Houdini or someone."

"Hmm." She fanned them, felt the faint trickle of old power on her fingertips. "If you're curious where they came from, ask Sebastian sometime. He could tell. Come here." She held out the deck to him. "Shuffle and cut."

Willing to oblige, he did what she asked. "Are we going to play?"

She only smiled and took the cards back. "Since the seats

are occupied, let's use the floor." She knelt, gesturing for him to join her. After tossing her hair behind her back, she dealt out a Celtic Cross. "You're preoccupied," she said. "But your creative juices aren't dried up or blocked. There are changes coming." Her eyes lifted to his. They were that dazzling Irish blue that tempted even a sane man to believe anything. "Perhaps the biggest of your life, and they won't be easy to accept."

It was no longer the cards she read, but rather the pale light of the seer, which burned so much more brightly in Sebastian.

"You need to remember that some things are passed through the blood, and some are washed out. We aren't always the total of the people who made us." Her eyes changed, softened, as she laid a hand on his. "And you're not as alone as you think you are. You never have been."

He couldn't joke away what hit too close to home. Instead, he avoided the issue entirely by bringing her hand to his lips. "I didn't bring you here to tell my fortune."

"I know why you asked me here, and it isn't going to happen. Yet." With more than a little regret, she drew her hand free. "And it isn't really your fortune I'm telling, it's your present." Quietly she gathered up the cards again. "I'll help you, if I can, with what I can. Tell me about the problem in your story."

"Other than the fact that I keep thinking of you when I'm supposed to be thinking of it?"

"Yes." She curled up her legs. "Other than that."

"I guess it's a matter of motivation. Cassandra's. That's what I decided to call her. Is she a witch because she wanted power, because she wanted to change things? Was she looking for revenge, or love, or the easy way out?"

"Why would it be any of those things? Why wouldn't it be a matter of accepting the gifts she was given?"

"It's too easy."

Morgana shook her head. "No, it's not. It's easier, so much easier, to be like everyone else. Once, when I was a little girl, some of the mothers refused to let their children play with me. I was a bad influence. Odd. Different. It hurt, not being a part of the whole."

Understanding, he nodded. "I was always the new kid. Hardly in one place long enough to be accepted. Somebody always wants to give the new kid a bloody nose. Don't ask me why. Moving around, you end up being awkward, falling behind in school, wishing you'd just get old enough to get the hell out." Annoyed with himself, he stopped. "Anyway, about Cassandra—"

"How did you cope?" She had had Anastasia, Sebastian, her family, and a keen sense of belonging.

With a restless movement of his shoulders, he reached out to touch her amulet. "You run away a lot. And, since that just gets your butt kicked nine times out of ten, you learn to run away safe. In books, in movies, or just inside your own head. As soon as I was old enough, I got a job working the concession stand at a theater. That way, I'd get paid for watching movies." As troubled memories left his eyes, his face cleared. "I love the flicks. I just plain love them."

She smiled. "So now you get paid for writing them."

"A perfect way to feed the habit. If I can ever get this one whipped into shape." In one smooth movement, he took a handful of her hair and wrapped it around his wrist. "What I need is inspiration," he murmured, tugging her forward for a kiss.

"What you need," she told him, "is concentration."

"I'm concentrating." He nibbled and tugged at her lips. "Believe me, I'm concentrating. You don't want to be responsible for hampering creative genius, do you?"

"Indeed not." It was time, she decided, for him to understand exactly what he was getting into. And perhaps it would also help him open his mind to his story. "Inspiration," she said, and slid her hands around his neck. "Coming up."

And so were they. As she met his lips with hers, she brought them six inches off the floor. He was too busy enjoying the taste to notice. Sliding over him, Morgana forgot herself long enough to lose herself in the heat. When she broke the kiss, they were floating halfway to the ceiling.

"I think we'd better stop."

He nuzzled her neck. "Why?"

She glanced down deliberately. "I didn't think to ask if you were afraid of heights."

Morgana wished she could have captured the look on his face when he followed her gaze—the wide-eyed, slack-jawed comedy of it. The string of oaths was a different matter. As they ran their course, she took them gently down again.

His knees buckled before he got them under control. White-faced, he gripped her shoulders. The muscles in his stomach were twanging like plucked strings. "How the hell did you do that?"

"A child's trick. A certain kind of child." She was sympathetic enough to stroke his cheek. "Remember the boy who cried wolf, Nash? One day the wolf was real. Well, you've been playing with—let's say the paranormal—for years. This time you've got yourself a real witch."

Very slowly, very sure, he shook his head from side to side. But the fingers on her shoulders trembled lightly. "That's bull."

She indulged in a windy sigh. "All right. Let me think. Something simple but elegant." She closed her eyes, lifted her hands.

For a moment she was simply a woman, a beautiful woman standing in the center of a disordered room with her arms lifted gracefully, her palms gently cupped. Then she changed. God, he could see her change. The beauty deepened. A trick of the light, he told himself. The way she was smiling, with those full, unpainted lips curved, her lashes shadowing her cheeks, her hair tumbling wildly to her waist.

But her hair was moving, fluttering gently at first as though teased by a playful breeze. Then it was flying, around her face, back from her face, in one long gorgeous stream. He had an impossible image of a stunning wooden maiden carved on the bow of an ancient ship.

But there was no wind to blow. Yet he felt it. It chilled along his skin, whisked along his cheeks. He could hear it whistle as it streaked into the room. When he swallowed, he heard a click in his throat, as well.

She stood straight and still. A faint gold light shivered around her as she began to chant. As the sun poured through the high windows, soft flakes of snow began to fall. From Nash's ceiling. They swirled around his head, danced over his skin as he gaped, frozen in shock.

"Cut it out," he ordered in a ragged voice before he sank to a chair.

Morgana let her arms drop, opened her eyes. The miniature blizzard stopped as if it had never been. The wind silenced and died. As she'd expected, Nash was staring at her as if she'd grown three heads.

"That might have been a bit overdone," she allowed.

"I— You—" He fought to gain control over his tongue. "What the hell did you do?"

"A very basic call to the elements." He wasn't as pale as he had been, she decided, but his eyes still looked too big for the rest of his face. "I didn't mean to frighten you."

"You're not frightening me. Baffling, yes," he admitted. He shook himself like a wet dog and ordered his brain to engage. If he had seen what he had seen, there was a reason. There was no way she could have gotten inside his house to set up the trick.

But there had to be.

He pushed out of the chair and began to search through the room. Maybe his movements were a bit jerky. Maybe his joints felt as though they'd rusted over. But he was moving. "Okay, babe, how'd you pull it off? It's great, and I'm up for a joke as much as the next guy, but I like to know the trick."

"Nash." Her voice was quiet, and utterly compelling. "Stop. Look at me."

He turned, and he looked, and he knew. Though it wasn't possible, wasn't reasonable, he knew. He let out a long, careful breath. "My God, it's true. Isn't it?"

"Yes. Do you want to sit down?"

"No." But he sat on the coffee table. "Everything you've been telling me. You weren't making any of it up."

"No, I wasn't making any of it up. I was born a witch, like my mother, my father, like my mother's mother, and hers, and back for generations." She smiled gently. "I don't ride on a broomstick—except perhaps as a joke. Or cast spells on young princesses or pass out poisoned apples."

It wasn't possible, really. Was it? "Do something else."

A flicker of impatience crossed her face. "Nor am I a trained seal."

"Do something else," he insisted, and cast his mind for options. "Can you disappear, or—"

"Oh, really, Nash."

He was up again. "Look, give me a break. I'm trying to help you out here. Maybe you could—" A book flew off the shelf and bopped him smartly in the head. Wincing, he rubbed the spot. "Okay, okay. Never mind."

"This isn't a sideshow," she said primly. "I only demonstrated so obviously in the first place because you're so thickheaded. You refused to believe, and since we seem to be developing some sort of relationship, I prefer that you do." She smoothed out the skirt of her dress. "And now that you do, we can take some time to think it all through before we move on."

"Move on," he repeated. "Maybe the next step is to talk about this."

"Not now." He'd already retreated a step, she thought, and he didn't even know it.

"Damn it, Morgana, you can't drop all this on me, then calmly walk out. Good God, you're a witch."

"Yes." She flicked back her hair. "I believe we've established that."

His mind began to spin again. Reality had taken a long, slow curve. "I have a million questions."

She picked up her bag. "You've already asked me several of those million. Play back your tapes. All of the answers I gave you were true ones."

"I don't want to listen to tapes, I want to talk to you."

"For now, it's what I want that matters." She opened her bag and took out a small, wand-shaped emerald on a silver chain. She should have known there was a reason she'd felt compelled to put it there that morning. "Here." Moving forward, she slipped the chain over his head.

"Thanks, but I'm not much on jewelry."

"Think of it as a charm, then." She kissed both of his cheeks.

Warily he eyed it. "What kind of a charm?"

"It's for clearing the mind, promoting creativity and— See the small purple stone above the emerald?"

"Yeah."

"Amethyst." Her lips curved as they brushed his. "For protection against witchcraft." With the cat already at her heels, Morgana moved to the archway. "Go sleep for an hour, Nash. Your brain is tired. When you wake, you'll work. And when the time is right, you'll find me." She slipped out the door.

Frowning, Nash tilted the slender green stone up to examine it. Clear thinking. Okay, he could use some of that. At the moment, his thoughts were as clear as smoke.

He ran a thumb over the companion stone of amethyst. Protection against witchcraft. He glanced up, through the window, to see Morgana drive away.

He was pretty sure he could use that, as well.

Chapter Six

What he needed to do was think, not sleep. Though he wondered that any man could think after what had happened in the last fifteen minutes. Why, any of the parapsychologists he'd interviewed over the years would have been wild to have a taste of what Morgana had given him.

But wasn't the first rational step to attempt to disprove what he had seen?

He wandered back into the living room to squint at the ceiling for a while. He couldn't deny what he had seen, what he had felt. But perhaps, with time, he could come up with some logical alternatives.

Taking the first step, he assumed his favorite thinking position. He lay down on the sofa. Hypnotism. He didn't care to think that he could be put in a trance or caused to hallucinate, but it was a possibility. An easier one to believe now that he was alone again.

If he didn't believe that, or some other logical explanation, he would have to accept that Morgana was exactly what she had said she was all along.

A hereditary witch, possessing elvish blood.

Nash toed off his shoes and tried to think. His mind was full

of her—the way she looked, the way she tasted, the dark, un-
canny light that had been in her eyes before she'd closed them
and lifted her arms to the ceiling.

The same light, he recalled now, that had come into her eyes
when she'd done the trick with the brandy decanter.

Trick, he reminded himself as his heart gave a single unpleasant thud. It was wiser to assume they were tricks and try to
logic out how she had produced them. Just how did a woman
lift a hundred-and-sixty-five-pound man six feet off the floor?

Telekinesis? Nash had always thought there were real possibilities there. After his preliminary work on his script *The Dark
Gift,* he'd come to believe there were certain people who were
able to use their minds, or their emotions, to move objects. A
more logical explanation than the existence of poltergeists, to
Nash's way of thinking. And scientists had done exhaustive
studies of pictures flying across the room, books leaping off
shelves, and so forth. Young girls were often thought to possess this particular talent. Girls became women. Morgana was
definitely a woman.

Nash figured a research scientist would need a lot more
than his word that Morgana had lifted him, and herself, off the
ground. Still, maybe he could...

He stopped, realizing he was thinking, reacting, the same
way the fictional Jonathan McGillis thought and reacted in his
story. Was that what Morgana wanted? he wondered.

Listen to the tapes, she'd told him. All right, then, that was
what he'd do. Shifting, he punched buttons on his recorder
until he'd reversed the tape inside and pushed play.

Morgana's smoky voice flowed from the tiny machine.

"It's not necessary to belong to a coven to be a witch, any
more than it's necessary to belong to a men's club to be a man.
Some find joining a group rewarding, comforting. Others simply enjoy the social aspects." There was a slight pause, then a
rustling of silks as she shifted. "Are you a joiner, Nash?"

"Nope. Groups usually have rules somebody else made up. And they like to assign chores."

Her light laugh drifted into the room. "And there are those of us who prefer our own company, and our own way. The history of covens, however, is ancient. My great-great-grandmother was high priestess of her coven in Ireland, and her daughter after her. A sabbat cup, a keppen rod and a few other ceremonial items were passed down to me. You might have noticed the ritual dish on the wall in the hallway. It dates back to before the burning time."

"Burning time?"

"The active persecution of witches. It began in the fourteenth century and continued for the next three hundred years. History shows that mankind usually feels the need to persecute someone. I suppose it was our turn."

She continued to speak, he to question, but Nash was having a hard time listening to words. Her voice itself was so alluring. It was a voice meant for moonlight, for secrets, for hot midnight promises. If he closed his eyes, he could almost believe she was there with him, curled up on the couch beside him, those long, luscious legs tangled with his, her breath warm on his cheek.

He drifted off to sleep with a smile on his face.

When he awakened, nearly two hours had passed. Heavy-eyed and groggy, he scrubbed his hands over his face, then swore at the crick in his neck. He blinked at his watch as he pushed himself to a half sitting, half slouching position.

It shouldn't be a surprise he'd slept so heavily, he thought. He'd been burning energy on nothing but catnaps for the last few days. Automatically he reached out for the liter bottle and gulped down warm soda.

Maybe it had all been a dream. Nash sat back, surprised at how quickly those afternoon-nap fuzzies lifted from his brain. It could have all been a dream. Except... He fingered the stones resting against his chest. She'd left those behind, as well as a faint, lingering scent that was exclusively hers.

All right, then, he decided. He was going to stop backtracking and doubting his own sanity. She had done what she had done. He had seen what he had seen.

It wasn't so complicated, really, Nash thought. More a matter of adjusting your thinking and accepting something new. At one time people had believed that space travel was the stuff of fantasy. On the other hand, a few centuries back, witchcraft had been accepted without question.

Maybe reality had a lot to do with what century you happened to live in. It was a possibility that started his brain ticking.

He took another swallow, grimacing as he capped the bottle again. He wasn't just thirsty, he realized. He was hungry. Famished.

And more, much more important than his stomach was his mind. The entire story seemed to roll out inside it, reel by reel. He could see it, really see it clearly, for the first time. With the quick thrum of excitement that always came when a story unfolded for him, he sprang up and headed for the kitchen.

He was going to fix himself one monster sandwich, brew the strongest pot of coffee on the planet, and then get to work.

Morgana sat on Anastasia's sunny terrace, envying and admiring her cousin's lush gardens and drinking an excellent glass of iced julep tea. From this spot on Pescadaro Point, she could look out over the rich blue water of Carmel Bay and watch the boats bob and glide in the light spring breeze.

Here she was tucked away from the tourist track, seemingly a world away from the bustle of Cannery Row, the crowds and scents of Fisherman's Wharf. Sheltered on the terrace by trees and flowers, she couldn't hear the rumble of a single car. Only birds, bees, water and wind.

She understood why Anastasia lived here. There was the serenity, and the seclusion, her younger cousin craved. Oh, there was drama in the meeting of land and sea, the twisted trees, the high call of the gulls. But there was also peace within the tumbling walls that surrounded the estate. Silent and steady ivy climbed the house. Splashy flowers and sweet-smelling herbs crowded the beds Ana tended so gently.

Morgana never failed to feel at ease here, and she was unfailingly drawn here whenever her heart was troubled. The spot, she thought, not for the first time, was so much like Anastasia. Lovely, welcoming, without guile.

"Fresh from the oven," Ana announced as she carried a tray through the open French doors.

"Oh, God, Ana—fudge cookies. My favorite."

With a chuckle, Anastasia set the tray on the glass table. "I had an urge to bake some this morning. Now I know why."

More than willing, Morgana took the first bite. Her eyes drifted closed as the smooth chocolate melted on her tongue. "Bless you."

"So." Ana took her seat so that she could look out over the gardens and grass to the bay. "I was surprised to see you out here in the middle of the day."

"I'm indulging in a long lunch break." She took another bite of cookie. "Mindy's got everything under control."

"Do you?"

"Don't I always?"

Ana laid a hand over Morgana's. Before Morgana could attempt to close them off, Ana felt the little wisps of sadness. "I can't help feeling how unsettled you are. We're too close."

"Of course you can't. Just as I couldn't help coming out here today, even though I knew I was bringing you problems."

"I'd like to help."

"Well, you're the herbalist," Morgana said lightly. "How about some essence of *Helleborus Niger?*"

Ana smiled. *Helleborus,* more commonly called Christmas

rose, was reputed to have the power to cure madness. "Fearing for your sanity, love?"

"At least." With a shrug, she chose another cookie. "Or I could take the easy way out and mix up a blend of rose and angelica, a touch of ginseng, sprinkled liberally with moondust."

"A love potion?" Ana sampled a cookie herself. "For anyone I know?"

"Nash, of course."

"Of course. Things aren't going well?"

A faint line appeared between Morgana's brows. "I don't know how things are going. I do know I wish I wasn't so bloody conscientious. It's really a very basic procedure to bind a man."

"But not very satisfying."

"No," Morgana admitted, "I can't imagine it would be. So I'm stuck with the ordinary way." As she sipped the reviving tea, she watched the snowy sails billowing from the boats on the bay. She'd always considered herself that free, she realized. Just that free. Now, though she had done no binding, she, herself, was bound.

"To tell the truth, Ana, I've never given much thought to what it would be like to have a man fall in love with me. Really in love. The trouble is, this time my heart's too involved for comfort."

And there was little comfort she could offer, Anastasia thought, for this type of ailment. "Have you told him?"

Surprised by the quick aching in her heart, Morgana closed her eyes. "I can't tell him what I'm not entirely sure of myself. So I wait. Moonglow to dawn's light," she chanted. "Night to day, and day to night. Until his heart is twined with mine, no rest or peace can I find." She opened her eyes and managed a smile. "That always seemed overly dramatic before."

"Finding love's like finding air. We can't survive without it."

"But what's enough?" This was the question that had troubled her most in the days since she had left Nash. "How do we know what's enough?"

"When we're happy, I'd think."

Morgana thought the answer was probably true—but was it attainable? "Do you think we're spoiled, Ana?"

"Spoiled? In what way?"

"In our…our expectations, I suppose." Her hand fluttered up in a helpless gesture. "Our parents, mine, yours, Sebastian's. There's always been so much love there, support, understanding, respect. The fun of being in love, and the generosity. It's not that way for everyone."

"I don't think that knowing love can run deep and true, that it can last, means being spoiled."

"But wouldn't it be enough to settle for the temporary? For affection and passion?" She frowned, watching a bee court a stalk of columbine. "I think it might be."

"For some. You'd have to be sure it would be enough for you."

Morgana rose with a grumble of annoyance. "It's so exasperating. I hate not being in charge."

A smile tugged at Anastasia's mouth as she joined her cousin. "I'm sure you do, darling. As long as I can remember, you've pushed things along your own way, just by force of personality."

Morgana slanted her a look. "I suppose you mean I was a bully."

"Not at all. Sebastian was a bully." Ana tucked her tongue in her cheek. "We'll just say you were—are—strong-willed."

Far from mollified, Morgana bent to sniff at a heavy-headed peony. "I suppose I could take that as a compliment. But being strong-willed isn't helping at the moment." She moved along the narrow stone path that wound through tumbling blooms and tangled vines. "I haven't seen him in more than a week, Ana. Lord," she said. "That makes me sound like some whiny, weak-kneed wimp."

Ana had to laugh even as she gave Morgana a quick squeeze. "No, it doesn't. It sounds as though you're an impatient woman."

"Well, I am impatient," she admitted. "Though I was prepared to avoid him if necessary, it hasn't been necessary." She shot Ana a rueful look. "A little sting to the pride."

"Have you called him?"

"No." Morgana's lips formed into a pout. "At first I didn't because I thought it was best to give us both some time. Then…" She'd always been able to laugh at herself, and she did so now. "Well, then I didn't because I was so damn mad he hadn't tried to beat down my door. He has called me a few times, at the shop or at home. He fires off a couple of questions on the Craft, mutters and grumbles while I answer. Grunts, then hangs up." She jammed fisted hands in her skirt pockets. "I can almost hear the tiny little wheels in his tiny little brain turning."

"So he's working. I'd imagine a writer could become pretty self-absorbed during a story."

"Ana," Morgana said patiently, "try to keep with the program. You're supposed to feel sorry for me, not make excuses for him."

Ana dutifully smothered a grin. "I don't know what came over me."

"Your mushy heart, as usual." Morgana kissed her cheek. "But I forgive you."

As they walked on, a bright yellow butterfly flitted overhead. Absently Ana lifted a hand, and the swallowtail danced shyly into her palm. She stopped to stroke the fragile wings. "Why don't you tell me what you intend to do about this self-absorbed writer who makes you so damn mad?"

With a shrug, Morgana brushed a finger over a trail of wisteria. "I've been thinking about going to Ireland for a few weeks."

Ana released the butterfly with her best wishes, then turned to her cousin. "I'd wish you a good trip, but I'd also have to remind you that running away only postpones. It doesn't solve."

"Which is why I haven't packed." Morgana sighed. "Ana, before I left him, he believed I am what I am. I wanted to give him time to come to terms with it."

That was the crux of it, Ana thought. She slipped a comforting hand around Morgana's waist. "It may take him more than a few days," she said carefully. "He may not be able to come to terms with it at all."

"I know." She gazed out over the water to the horizon. One never knew exactly what lay beyond the horizon. "Ana, we'll be lovers before morning. This I know. What I don't know is if this one night will make me happy or miserable."

Nash was ecstatic. As far as he could remember, he'd never had a story flow out of his mind with the speed and clarity of this one. The treatment, which he'd finished in one dazzling all-nighter, was already on his agent's desk. With his track record, Nash wasn't worried about a sale—which, in a gleeful phone call, his agent had told him was imminent. The fact was, for the first time, Nash wasn't even thinking about the sale, the production, the ultimate filming.

He was too absorbed in the story.

He wrote at all hours. Bounding awake at 3:00 a.m. to attack the keyboard, slurping coffee in the middle of the afternoon with the story still humming like a hive of bees in his head. He ate whatever came to hand, slept when his eyes refused to stay open, and lived within the tilted reality of his own imagination.

If he dreamed, it was in surreal snatches, with erotic images of himself and Morgana sliding through the fictional world he was driven to create.

He would wake wanting her, at times almost unbearably. Then he would find himself compelled to complete the task that had brought them together in the first place.

Sometimes, just before he fell into an exhausted sleep, he thought he could hear her voice.

It's not yet time.

But he sensed the time was coming.

When the phone rang, he ignored it, then rarely bothered to return any of the calls on his machine. If he felt the need for air, he took his laptop out to the patio. If he could have figured out a way, he'd have dragged it into the shower with him.

In the end, he snatched the hard copy from his printer as each page slid out. A few adjustments here, he thought, scrawling notes in the margins. A little fine-tuning there, and he'd have it. But as he read, he knew. He *knew* he'd never done better work.

Nor had he ever finished a project so quickly. From the time he'd sat down and begun the screenplay, only ten days had passed. Perhaps he'd slept only thirty or forty hours total in those ten days, but he didn't feel tired.

He felt elated.

After gathering the papers up, he searched for an envelope. Books, notes, dishes, all scattered as he dug through them.

He only had one thought now, and that was to take it to Morgana. One way or the other, she had inspired him to write it, and she would be the first person to read it.

He found a tattered manila envelope covered with notations and doodles. After dumping the papers inside, he headed out of his office. It was fortunate that he caught sight of himself in the mirror in the foyer.

His hair was standing on end, and he had the beginnings of a fairly decent beard. Which, as he rubbed a curious hand over his chin, made him wonder if he should give growing a real one a shot. All that might not have been too bad, but he was standing in the foyer, gripping a manila envelope—and wearing nothing but the silver neck chain Morgana had given him and a pair of red jockey shorts.

All in all, it would probably be best if he took the time to clean up and dress.

Thirty minutes later he rushed back downstairs, more conservatively attired in jeans and a navy sweatshirt with only one small hole under the left armpit. He had to admit, the sight of his bedroom, the bathroom and the rest of the house had come as quite a shock, even to him. It looked as though a particularly ragged army had billeted there for a few weeks.

He'd been lucky to find any clothes at all that weren't dirty or crumpled or hadn't been kicked under the bed. There certainly hadn't been a clean towel, so he'd had to make do with a trio of washcloths. Still, he'd located his razor, his comb and a matching pair of shoes, so it hadn't been all that bad.

It took him another frustrating fifteen minutes to unearth his keys. God alone knew why they were on the second shelf of the refrigerator beside a moldy peach, but there they were. He also noted that that very sad peach and an empty quart container of milk were all that was left after he took the keys.

There would be time to deal with that later.

Gripping the script, he headed out the door.

It wasn't until the engine sprang to life and the dash lit that Nash noticed it was nearly midnight. He hesitated, considered calling her first or just putting off the visit until morning.

The hell with it, he decided, and shot out of the drive. He wanted her now.

Only a few miles away, Morgana was closing the door behind her. She stepped out into the silvery light of the full moon. As she walked away from the house, the ceremonial robe drifted around her body, cinched at the waist with a belt of crystals. In her arms she carried a simple basket that contained everything she would need to observe the spring equinox.

It was a night of joy, of celebration, of thanksgiving for the renewal spring brought to the earth. But her eyes were troubled. In this night, where light and dark were balanced, her life would change.

She knew, though she had not looked again. There was no need to look, when her heart had already told her.

It was difficult to admit that she had nearly stayed inside. A challenge to fate, she supposed. But that would have been the coward's way. She would go on with the rite, as she and others like her had gone on for aeons.

He would come when he was to come. And she would accept it.

Twisted shadows stretched over the lawn as she moved toward the grove. There was the smell of spring in the night air. The nocturnal bloomers, the drift of the sea, the fragrance of earth she had turned herself for planting.

She heard the call of an owl, low and lonely. But she didn't look for the white wings. Not yet.

There were other sounds, the gentle breath of the wind easing through the trees, stroking leaves, caressing branches. And the murmur of music that only certain ears could hear. The song of the faeries, a song that was older than man.

She was not alone here, in the shadowy grove with the drift of stars swimming overhead. She had never been alone here.

As she approached the place of magic, her mood shifted, and the clouds drifted from her eyes. Setting the basket down, she took a moment for herself. Standing still, eyes closed, hands cupped loosely at her sides, she drew in the flavor and beauty of the night.

She could see, even with her eyes closed, the white moon sailing through the black sea of the sky. She could see the generous light it spilled onto the trees, and through them to her. And the power that bloomed inside her was as cool, as pure, as lovely, as the moonlight.

Serenely she opened the basket. From it she took a white cloth, edged in silver, that had been in her family for generations. Some said it had been a gift to Merlin from the young king he had loved. Once it was spread on the soft ground, she knelt.

A small round of cake, a clear flask containing wine, candles, the witch's knife with its scribed handle, the ceremonial dish and cup, a small halo woven from gardenia blossoms. Other blooms…larkspur, columbine, sprigs of rosemary and thyme. These she scattered, along with rose petals, over the cloth.

This done, she rose to cast the circle. She felt the power drumming in her fingertips, warmer now, more urgent. When the circle was complete, she set candles, pure as ice, along its edge. Fourteen in all, to symbolize the days between the moon's waxing and its waning. Slowly she walked beside them, holding out her hand.

One by one, the candles flickered to flame, then glowed steadily. Morgana stood in the center of the ring of light. She unhooked the belt of crystals. It slid onto the cloth like a rope of fire. She slipped her arms from the thin robe. It drifted to her feet like melting snow.

Candlelight gleamed gold on her skin as she began the ancient dance.

At five to midnight, Nash pulled up in Morgana's driveway. He swore, noting that not a single light glowed in a single window.

He'd have to wake her up, he thought philosophically. How much sleep did a witch need, anyway? He grinned to himself. He'd have to ask her.

Still, she was a woman. Women had a tendency to get ticked off if you dropped by in the middle of the night and got them out of bed. It might help to have something to pave the way.

Inspired, he tucked the envelope under his arm and began to raid her flower bed. He doubted she'd notice that he'd stolen a few blooms. After all, it seemed she had hundreds. Awash in the scent of them, he got carried away, gathering an overflowing armful of tulips and sweet peas, narcissi and wallflowers.

Pleased with himself, he adjusted the load and strolled to

her front door. Pan barked twice before Nash could knock. But no light flicked on at the dog's greeting, or at the pounding Nash set up.

He glanced back to the driveway to assure himself her car was there and then pounded again. Probably sleeps like a stone, he thought, and felt the first pricklings of annoyance. There was something working in him, some urgency. He had to see her, and it had to be tonight.

Refusing to be put off, he laid the script on the stoop and tried the knob. Pan barked again, but to Nash the dog sounded more amused than aroused. Finding the door locked, Nash started around the side. He was damn well getting in, and getting to her, before the night was done.

A sudden rush of immediacy quickened his step, but somewhere between the front of the house and the side terrace he found himself looking toward the grove.

It was there he needed to go. Had to go. Though his brain told him it was utterly foolish to go traipsing into the woods at night, he followed his heart.

Perhaps it was the shadows, or the sighing of the wind, that had him moving so quietly. He felt somehow it would be blasphemous to make unnecessary noise. There was a quality in the air here tonight, and it was almost unbearably lovely.

Yet, with every step he took, the blood seemed to pound faster in his head.

Then he saw, in the distance, a ghostly shimmer of white. He started to call out, but a rustle of movement had him glancing up. There, on a twisted cypress branch, stood a huge white owl. As Nash watched, the bird glided soundlessly from its perch and flew toward the heart of the grove.

His pulse was drumming in his ears, and his heart was rapping hard against his ribs. He knew that, even if he turned and walked away, he would be drawn again to that same center.

So he moved forward.

She was there, kneeling on a white cloth. Moonlight poured over her like silver wine. Again he started to call her name, but the sight of her forming a circle of candles, jewels at her waist, flowers in her hair, struck him mute.

Trapped in the shadows, he stood as she made the small golden fires spark atop the snowy candles. As she disrobed to stand gloriously naked in the center of flames. As she moved into a dance so graceful it stopped his breath.

Moonlight slithered over her skin, tipped her breasts, caressed her thighs. Her hair rained, an ebony waterfall, down her back as she lifted her face to the stars.

And he remembered his dream, remembered it so vividly that the fantasy and the reality merged into one potent image, with Morgana dancing at its center. The scent of flowers grew so strong that he was nearly dizzy with it. For an instant, his vision dimmed. He shook his head to clear it and struggled to focus.

The image had changed. She was kneeling again, sipping from a silver cup while the flames from the candles rose impossibly high, surrounding her like golden bars. Through them he could see the shimmer of her skin, the glint of silver between her breasts, at her wrists. He could hear her voice, softly chanting, then rising so that it seemed to be joined by thousands of others.

For a moment, the grove was filled with a soft, ethereal glow. Different from light, different from shadow, it pulsed and shivered, glinting like the edge of a silver sword in the sun. He could feel the warmth of it bathing his face.

Then the candle flames ebbed once again to small points, and the sound of chanting echoed away into silence.

She was rising. She slipped the white robe on, belted it.

The owl, the great white bird he had forgotten in his fascination with the woman, called twice before gliding like a cloud through the night.

She turned, her breath rising high in her throat. He stepped from the shadows, his heart hammering in his breast.

For a moment she hesitated. A warning whispered to her. Tonight would bring her pleasure. More than she had known. And its price would be pain. More than she would wish.

Then she smiled and stepped from the circle.

Chapter Seven

Thousands of thoughts avalanched into his brain. Thousands of feelings flooded into his heart. As she moved toward him, her robe flowing around her like moondust, all those thoughts, all those feelings, shivered down to one. Down to her.

He wanted to speak, to tell her something, anything, that would explain how he felt at that moment. But his heart stuttered in his throat, making words impossible. He knew this was more than the simple desire of a man for a woman, yet whatever was spiraling through him was so far out of his experience that he was sure he could never describe it, never explain it.

He knew only that in this place of magic, at this moment of enchantment, there was only one woman. Some quiet, patient voice was whispering inside his heart that there had always been only one woman and he had been waiting all his life for her.

Morgana stopped, only an arm span away. Soft, silent shadows waltzed between them. She had only to step into that lazy dance to be in his arms. He would not turn from her. And she was afraid she had gone beyond the point where it was possible for her to turn from him.

Her eyes remained on his, though the little fingers of nerves pinched her skin. He looked stunned, she realized, and she could hardly blame him. If he was feeling even a fraction of the needs and fears that were skidding through her, he had every right to be.

It would not be easy for them, she knew. After tonight, the bond would be sealed. Whatever decisions were made in the tomorrows, by both of them, that bond would not be broken.

She reached out to trail a hand over the flowers he still cradled in his arms. She wondered if he knew, by the blossoms he had chosen, that he was offering her love, passion, fidelity and hope.

"Blooms picked in moonlight carry the charms and secrets of the night."

He'd forgotten about them. Like a man waking from a dream, he glanced down. "I stole them from your garden."

Her lips curved beautifully. He wouldn't know the language of the flowers, she thought. Yet his hand had been guided. "That doesn't make their scent less sweet, or the gift less thoughtful." Lifting her hand from them, she touched his cheek. "You knew where to find me."

"I... Yes." He couldn't deny the urge that had brought him into the grove. "I did."

"Why did you come?"

"I wanted to..." He remembered his frantic rush to leave the house, his impatience to see her. But, no, it was more basic than that. And infinitely more simple. "I needed you."

For the first time, her gaze wavered. She could feel the need radiating from him like heat, to warm her and to tempt her. It could, if she did nothing to stop it, bind her to him so firmly that no charm, no spell, would ever free her.

Her power was not absolute. Her own wishes were not always granted. To take him tonight would be to risk everything, including her power to stand alone.

Until tonight, freedom had always been her most prized possession. Lifting her gaze to his again, she cast that possession away.

"What I give you tonight, I give with a free heart. What I take from you, I take without regrets." Her eyes glittered with visions he couldn't see. "Remember that. Come with me." She took his hand and drew him into the circle of light.

The moment he stepped through the flames, he felt the change. The air was purer here, its scent more vivid, as if they had climbed to the top of some high, untraveled cliff. Even the stars seemed closer, and he could see the trails of moonlight, silver-edged white streaks through the sheltering trees.

But she was the same, her hand firm in his.

"What is this place?" Instinctively he lowered his voice to a whisper, not in fear, but in reverence. It seemed to drift off, twining with the harp song that filled the air.

"It needs no name." She drew her hand from his. "There are many forms of magic," she said, and unfastened her belt of crystals. "We'll make our own here." She smiled again. "An it harm none."

Slowly she placed the crystal rope on the edge of the cloth, then turned to face him. With the moonlight silvering her eyes, she opened her arms.

She took him in, and the lips she offered were warm and soft. He could taste the lingering sweetness of the wine she had drunk, as well as her own richer, more potent flavor. He wondered that any man could survive without that heady, drugging taste. That any man would choose to. His head spun with it as she urged him to drink deeper.

On a moan that seemed to spring from his soul, he dragged her closer, crushing the flowers between them so that the night air swelled with their scent. His mouth branded hers before moving frantically over her face.

Behind her closed lids she could see the dance of candlelight, could see the single shadow her body and Nash's made sway. She could hear the deep, pure resonance of the breeze singing through the leaves, the night music that was its own kind of magic. And she heard the whisper of her name as it breathed through the lips that once again searched for hers.

But it was what she felt that was so much more real. This deep well of emotion that filled for him as it had never filled for anyone. As she gave him her heart for a second time, that well brimmed, then overflowed in a quiet, steady stream.

For a moment, she was afraid she might drown in it, and that fear brought on racking shudders. Murmuring to her, Nash drew her closer. Whether it was in need or comfort, Morgana didn't know, but she settled again. And accepted.

The captivator became the captivated.

He was struggling against some clawing beast prowling in his gut, demanding that he take her quickly, feed himself. He had never, never experienced such a violent surge of hunger for anything, or anyone, as he did for Morgana in that glowing circle of light.

He fisted his hands in her hair to keep them from tearing the robe from her. Some flicker shadowed by instinct told him she would accept the speed, respond to this gnawing appetite. But it wasn't the way. Not here. Not now.

Pressing his face to the curve of her neck, he held her close and fought it back.

Understanding didn't make her heartbeat less erratic. His desire to take warred with his desire to give, and both were ripe with power. His choice would make a difference. And, though she couldn't see, she knew that the texture of their loving tonight would matter to both of them in all the years to come.

"Nash, I—"

He shook his head, then leaned back and framed her face in his hands. They weren't steady. Nor was his breathing. His eyes were dark, intense. She wondered that they couldn't see into her and study her heart.

"You scare the hell out of me," he managed. "I scare the hell out of me. It's different now, Morgana. Do you understand?"

"Yes. It matters."

"It matters." He let out a long, unsteady breath. "I'm afraid I'll hurt you."

You will hurt me. The certainty of it shivered through her. The pain would come, no matter what defenses she used. But not tonight. "You won't." She kissed him gently.

No, he thought as his cheek rubbed against hers. He wouldn't. He couldn't. Though desire continued to beat in his blood, its tempo had slowed. His hands were steady again as he slipped the robe from her shoulders, followed it down her arms until they were both free of it.

The pleasure of looking at her was like a velvet fist pressed against his heart. He had seen her body before, when he had watched her dance naked in the circle. But that had been like a dream, as if she were some beautiful phantom just out of his reach.

Now she was only a woman, and his hand would not pass through if he tried to touch.

Her face first. He glided his fingertips over her cheeks, her lips, her jaw, and down the slender column of her throat. And she was real. Hadn't he felt her warm breath against his skin? Wasn't he now feeling the hammerbeat of her pulse when his fingers lingered?

Witch or mortal, she was his, to cherish, to enjoy, to pleasure. It was meant to be here, surrounded by the old, silent trees, by shadowed light. By magic.

Her eyes changed, as a woman's would when her system was crowded with desire and anticipation. He watched them as he trailed those curious fingers over the slope of her shoulders, down her arms and back again. Her breath began to shiver through her parted lips.

Just as lightly, just as slowly, his touch skimmed down to her breasts. Now her breath caught on a moan, and she swayed, but he made no move to possess her. Only skimming patiently over those soft slopes, brushing his thumbs over nipples that hardened and ached in response.

She couldn't move. If the hounds of hell had burst out of the trees, jaws snapping, she would have stood just as she was, body throbbing, eyes fixed helplessly on his. Did he know? Could he know what a spell he had cast over her with this exquisite tenderness?

There was nothing else for her but him. She could see only his face, feel only his hands. With each unsteady breath she took, she was filled with him.

He followed the line of her body, down her rib cage, detouring around to her back, where her hair drifted over his hands and her spine trembled under them. He wondered why he had thought it necessary to speak, when he could tell her so much more with a touch.

Her body was a banquet of slender curves, smooth skin, subtle muscles. But he no longer felt the urge to ravish. How much better it was, this time, to sample, to savor, to seduce. How much more power did a man need than to feel a woman's skin singing under his hands?

He skimmed over her hips, let his fingers glide over those long, lovely thighs, changing the angle on the return journey so that he absorbed all the little bolts of pleasure at finding her already hot and damp for him.

When her knees buckled, he gathered her close, lowering her to the cloth so that he could begin the same glorious journey with his lips.

Steeped in sensation, she tugged his shirt away so that she could feel the wonder of his flesh sliding over hers. His muscles were taut, showing her that the gentleness he gave her took more strength than wild passion would have. She murmured something, and he brought his mouth back to hers so that she could slide the jeans over his hips, cast them away and make him as vulnerable as she.

Sweet, mindless pleasure. Long, lingering delights. The moon showered its fragile light as they offered each other the most precious of gifts. The scattered flowers they lay upon sent up exotic perfumes to mix with the scent of the night. Though the breeze rustled the leaves, the encircling flames ran straight and true.

Even when passion gripped them, sending them rolling over crushed blooms and rumpled silk, there was no rush. Somewhere in the shadows, the owl called again, and the ring of flames shot up like lances. Closing them in, closing all else out.

Her body was shuddering, but there were no longer any nerves or fears. Her arms encircled him as he slipped inside her.

With his blood roaring in his head, he watched her eyes flutter open, saw those gold stars shining against the deep blue as magnificently as those overhead shone in the sky. He lowered his mouth to hers as they moved together in a dance older and more powerful than any other.

She felt the beauty of it, the magic that was more potent than anything she could conjure. He filled her utterly. Even when the ache drove them both, the tenderness remained. Two glistening tears slipped from her eyes as she arched for him, letting her body fly with that final staggering release. She heard him call out her name, like a prayer, as he poured himself into her.

When he buried his face in her hair, shuddering, she saw the flash of a shooting star, streaking like a flame through the velvet sky.

Time passed. Minutes, hours, it didn't concern him. All he knew was that she was as soft as a wish beneath him, her body relaxed but still curled into his. Nash thought it would be delightful for them to stay just like this until sunrise.

Then he thought, more practically, that he would probably end up smothering her.

When he started to shift, Morgana clamped herself around him like a vise. "Uh-uh," she said sleepily.

Since she insisted, he thought he might as well nibble on her neck. "I may be on the thin side, but I'd guess I have you by a good sixty pounds. Besides, I want to look at you."

He levered himself onto his elbows and pleased himself.

Her hair was spread out like tangled black silk on the white cloth. There were flowers caught in it, making him think of gypsies and faeries. And witches.

He let out a long, labored breath. "What happens when a mortal makes love to a witch?"

She had to smile, and did so slowly, sinuously. "Did you happen to notice the gargoyles on the tower of the house?" Nash's mouth opened, then closed again. Morgana let out a long, rich laugh as her fingers danced down his spine. "I love it when you're gullible."

He was feeling entirely too good to be annoyed. Instead, he played with her hair. "It seemed like a reasonable question. I mean, you are... I know you are. But it's still tough to swallow. Even after what I saw tonight." His eyes came back to hers. "I watched you."

She traced his lips with a fingertip. "I know."

"I've never seen anything more beautiful. You, the light. The music." His brows came together. "There was music."

"For those who know how to hear it. For those who are meant to hear it."

It wasn't so hard to accept, after everything else. "What are you doing here? It looked like some kind of ceremony."

"Tonight's the spring equinox. A magic night. What happened here, with us, was magic, too."

Because he couldn't resist, he kissed her shoulder. "It sounds like a tired line, but it's never been like this for me before. With anyone."

"No." She smiled again. "Not with anyone." Her pulse leapt as she felt him harden inside her. "Again," she murmured when his lips lowered to hers.

★ ★ ★

The night moved toward morning before they dressed. As Nash pulled on his sweatshirt, he watched Morgana gathering up the crushed and broken flowers.

"I guess we did them in. I'll have to steal you some more."

Smiling, she cradled them in her arms. "These will do nicely," she said. Nash's eyes widened when he saw that the flowers she held were now as full and fresh as when he had first picked them.

He passed a hand through his hair. "I don't think I'm going to get used to that anytime soon."

She merely placed them in his hands. "Hold them for me. I have to remove the circle." She gestured, and the candle flames died. As she took them from the ground, she chanted quietly.

"The circle cast in the moon's light is lifted now by my right. The work is done, with harm to none. With love and thanks I set thee free. As I will, so mote it be."

She set the last candle in the basket, then lifted the cloth. When it was folded, she put it away.

"That's, ah...all there is to it?"

She picked up the basket and turned to him. "Things are usually more simple than we believe." Morgana offered a hand, pleased when he curled his fingers around hers. "And, in the spirit of that simplicity, will you share my bed for what's left of the night?"

He brought their joined hands to his lips and gave her a simple answer. "Yes."

She couldn't get enough of him, Nash thought dreamily. During the night, they had turned to each other again and again. Drifting off to sleep, drifting into love while the moonlight faded. And now, when the sun was a pale red glow behind his closed lids, she was nuzzling his ear.

He smiled, murmuring to her as he let himself float toward

wakefulness. Her head was a warm, welcome weight on his chest. The way she was tickling and teasing his ear told him she would not object to some lazy morning loving. More than willing to oblige her, he lifted a hand to stroke her hair. His hand stopped in midair.

How could her head be on his chest *and* her mouth be at his ear? Anatomically speaking, it just didn't figure. But then again, he'd seen her do several things that didn't figure in terms of the simple laws of the real world. But this was *too* weird. Even half-awake, his lively imagination bounced.

Would he open his eyes to look and see something so fantastic, so out of his realm, that it would send him screaming out into the night?

Day, he reminded himself. It was day. But that was hardly the point.

Cautiously he let his hand lower until it touched her hair. Soft, thick, but... God, the shape of her head was wrong. She'd changed. She'd...she'd shifted into... When her head moved under his hand, Nash let out a muffled cry and, with his heart skating into his throat, opened his eyes.

The cat lay on his chest, staring at him with unblinking—and somehow smug—amber eyes. Nash jolted when something cold slid over his cheek. He found that Pan was standing with his forelegs on the bed, his big silver head tilted curiously to one side. Before Nash could speak, the dog licked him again.

"Oh, boy." While Nash waited for his mind to clear and his pulse to settle, Luna stood, stretched, then padded up his chest to peer into his face. Her muttered purr seemed distinctly like a chuckle. "Okay, sure, you got me." He reached out with each hand to rub a furry head.

Pan took that for a welcome and leapt onto the bed. He landed—light-footed, fortunately—on Nash's most vulnerable area. With a strangled *oof,* Nash sat bolt upright, dislodging the cat and making her rap up against Pan.

Things looked dicey for a moment, with the animals glaring and growling at each other. But Nash was too concerned with getting his wind back to worry about the prospect of fur flying.

"Ah, playing with the animals?"

Sucking in air, Nash looked up to see Morgana standing in the doorway. The moment she was spotted, Luna flicked her tail in Pan's face, strolled over to a pillow, circled, sat and began to wash her hindquarters. Tail thumping, Pan plopped down. Nash figured he had about seventy pounds of muscle pinning his legs to the mattress.

"My pets seem very fond of you."

"Yeah. We're one happy family."

With a steaming mug in one hand, she crossed to the bed. She was already dressed, in a little red number with beads and embroidery on the wide shoulders, and tiny snaps running down the front until they ran out at the hem, which stopped several inches above her very sexy knees.

Nash wondered if he should undo the snaps one at a time, or in one quick yank. Then he caught a scent that was nearly as exotic and every bit as seductive as her perfume.

"Is that coffee?"

Morgana sat on the edge of the bed and sniffed the contents of the cup. "Yes, I believe it is."

Grinning, he reached out to toy with the end of the hair she'd woven into an intricate braid. "That was awfully sweet of you."

Her eyes mirrored surprise. "What was? Oh, you think I brought this in for you." Watching him, she tapped a fingertip against the mug. "That I brewed a pot of coffee, poured a cup and decided to serve it to you, in bed, because you're so damn cute."

Properly chastened, he sent one last, longing look at the mug. "Well, I—"

"In this case," she said, interrupting him, "you happen to be exactly right."

He took the cup she offered, watching her over the rim as he drank. He wasn't a coffee snob—couldn't afford to be, with the mud he usually made for himself—but he was sure this was the best cup to be found west of the Mississippi. "Thanks. Morgana…" He reached up to set one of the complex arrangements of beads and stones at her ears jangling. "Just how damn cute am I?"

She laughed, pushing the mug aside so that she could kiss him. "You'll do, Nash." More than do, she thought as she kissed him again. With that tousled, sun-streaked hair tumbled around a sleepy face, that surprisingly well-muscled chest tempting her above the tangle of sheets, and that very warm, very skilled mouth rubbing against hers, he did magnificently.

She pulled back, not without regret. "I have to go to work."

"Today?" Lazily he cupped his hand around the back of her neck to urge her closer. "Don't you know it's a national holiday?"

"Today?"

"Sure." She smelled like night, he thought. Like flowers that bloom only in starlight. "It's National Love-In Day. A tribute to the sixties. You're supposed to celebrate it by—"

"I get the picture. And that's very inventive," she said, closing her teeth over his bottom lip. "But I have a shop to run."

"That's very unpatriotic of you, Morgana. I'm shocked."

"Drink your coffee." She stood to keep from letting him change her mind. "There's food in the kitchen if you feel like breakfast."

"You could have gotten me up." He snagged her hand before she could retreat.

"I thought you could use the sleep, and I didn't want to give you any more time to distract me."

His eyes slanted up to hers as he nibbled on her knuckles. "I'd like to spend several hours distracting you."

Her knees went weak. "I'll give you a chance later."

"We could have dinner."

"We could." Her blood was beginning to hum, but she couldn't make herself pull her hand free.

"Why don't I pick something up, bring it by?"

"Why don't you?"

He opened her hand to press a kiss on the palm. "Seven-thirty?"

"Fine. You'll let Pan out, won't you?"

"Sure." His teeth grazed her wrist and sent her pulse soaring. "Morgana, one more thing."

Her body yearned toward his. "Nash, I really can't—"

"Don't worry." But he could see that she was worried, and it delighted him. "I'm not going to muss you up. It's going to be too much fun thinking about doing just that for the next few hours. I left something for you on the front stoop last night. I was hoping you'd find time to read it."

"Your script? You've finished?"

"All but some fine-tuning, I think. I'd like your opinion."

"Then I'll try to have one." She leaned over to kiss him again. "Bye."

"See you tonight." He settled back with the cooling coffee, then swore.

Morgana turned at the doorway. "What?"

"My car's parked behind yours. Let me get some pants on."

She laughed. "Nash, really." With that, she strolled away. The cat jumped off the bed and followed.

"Yeah," Nash said to the now-snoozing Pan. "I guess she can take care of it."

Sitting back, he prepared to drink his coffee in solitary splendor. As he sipped, he studied the room. This was the first chance he'd taken to see what Morgana surrounded herself with in her most private place.

There was drama, of course. She walked with drama wherever she went. Here it was typified in the bold jewel colors she'd chosen. Turquoise for the walls. Emerald for the spread they had kicked aside during the night. Bleeding hues of both were in the curtains that fluttered at the windows. A daybed upholstered in sapphire stretched under one window. It was plumped with fat pillows of garnet, amethyst and amber. Arched over it was a slender brass lamp with a globe shaped like a lush purple morning glory. The bed itself was magnificent, a lake of tumbled sheets bordered by massive curved head and footboards.

Intrigued, Nash started to get up. Pan was still pinning his legs, but after a couple of friendly nudges, he rolled aside obligingly to snore in the center of the bed. Naked, mug in one hand, Nash began to wander the room.

A polished silver dragon stood on the nightstand, his head back, his tail flashing. The wick between his open jaws announced that he would breathe fire. She had one of those pretty mirrored vanities with a padded stool that Nash had always considered intensely feminine. He could imagine her sitting there, running the jewel-crusted, silver-backed brush through her hair, or anointing her skin with the creams or lotions from one of the colorful glass pots that stood on it, winking in the sunlight.

Unable to resist, he picked one up, removing the long crystal top and sniffing. At that moment she was so much in the room with him, he could almost see her. That was the complexity and power of a woman's magic.

Reluctantly he recapped the bottle and set it aside. Damn it, he didn't want to wait through the day for her. He didn't want to wait an hour.

Easy, Kirkland, he lectured himself. She'd only been gone five minutes. He was acting like a man besotted. Or bewitched. That thought set off a niggling little doubt that he frowned over for a moment, then shoved aside. He wasn't under any kind of spell. He knew exactly what he was doing, and he was in complete control of his actions. It was just that the room held so much of her, and being in it made him want.

Frowning, he ran his fingers through a pile of smooth colored stones she kept in a bowl. If he was obsessing about her, that, too, could be explained. She wasn't an ordinary woman. After what he'd seen, with what he knew, it was natural for him to think about her more often than he might about someone else. After all, the supernatural was his forte. Morgana was living proof that the extraordinary existed in an ordinary world.

She was an incredible lover. Generous, free, outrageously responsive. She had humor and wit and brains, as well as an agile body. That combination alone could make a man sit up and beg. When you added the fairy dust, she became downright irresistible.

Plus, she'd helped him with his story. The more Nash thought about it, the more he was certain the script was his best work to date.

But what if she hated it? The idea jumped into his mind like a warty toad and had him staring into space. Just because they had shared a bed, and something else too intangible for him to name, didn't mean she would understand or appreciate his work.

What the hell had he been thinking of, giving it to her to read before he'd polished it?

Terrific, he thought in disgust and bent to snatch up his jeans. Now he had that to worry about for the next several hours. As he strode off to shower, Nash wondered how he had gotten in so deep that a woman could drive him crazy in so many ways.

Chapter Eight

It was more than four hours later before Morgana had a chance for a cup of tea and a moment alone. Customers, phone calls, arriving shipments, had kept her busy enough that she'd had time enough only to glance at the first page or two of Nash's script.

What she saw intrigued her enough to have her resenting each interruption. Now she heated water and nibbled on tart green grapes. Mindy was in the shop, waiting on two college students. Since both students were male, Morgana knew Mindy wouldn't need any help.

With a sigh, she brewed the tea, set it to steep, then settled down with Nash's script.

An hour later, she'd forgotten the tea that grew cold in the pot. Fascinated, she flipped back to page one and began all over again. It was brilliant, she thought, and felt a surge of pride that the man she loved could create something so rich, so clever, so absorbing.

Talented, yes. She'd known he was talented. His movies had always entertained and impressed her. But she'd never read a screenplay before. Somehow she'd thought it would be no more than an outline, the bare bones that a director, actors, technicians, would flesh out for an audience. But this was so rich in texture, so full of life and spirit, that it didn't seem like words on paper at all. She could already see, and hear, and feel.

She imagined that, when those extra layers were added by the actors, the camera, the director, Nash might very well have the film of the decade on his hands.

It stunned her that the man she thought of as charming, a bit cocky and often full of himself had something like this inside him. Then again, it had rocked her the night before to discover that he had such deep wells of tenderness.

Setting the script aside, she leaned back in her chair. And she had always considered herself so astute, she thought with a little smile. Just how many more surprises did Nash Kirkland have up his sleeve?

He was working on the next one as hard as he could. Inspiration had struck, and Nash had never been one to let a good idea slip away.

He'd had a moment's twinge at the notion of leaving Morgana's back door unlocked. But he'd figured that with her reputation, and with the wolf-dog roaming the grounds, nobody would dare break in.

For all he knew, she'd cast some sort of protective spell over the house in any case.

It was going to be perfect, he told himself as he struggled to arrange an armload of flowers—purchased this time—in a vase. They seemed to take on a life of their own, stems jamming, heads drooping. After several tries, the arrangement still looked as though the flowers had been shoved into the container by a careless ten-year-old. By the time he'd finished, he'd filled three vases and was happy to admit he'd never be a set director.

But they smelled good.

A glance at his watch warned him that time was running short. Crouching in front of the hearth, he built a fire. It took him longer, and he imagined it took considerably more effort, than it would have taken Morgana, but at last the flames were licking cheerfully at the wood. A fire was hardly necessary, but he liked the effect.

Satisfied, he rose to check the scene he'd so carefully set. The table for two was laid with a white cloth he'd found in the drawer of the sideboard in Morgana's dining room. Though that room had had possibilities, with its soaring ceiling and its huge fireplace, he thought the drawing room more intimate.

The china was hers, too, and looked old and lovely, with little rosebuds hugging the edges of gleaming white plates. He'd arranged the heavy silverware and the crystal champagne glasses. All hers, as well. And folded the deep rose damask napkins into neat triangles.

Perfect, he decided. Then swore.

Music. How could he have forgotten the music? And the candlelight. He made a dash to the stereo and fumbled through a wide selection of CDs. Chopin, he decided, though he was more in tune with the Rolling Stones than with classical music. He switched it on and slipped the disc in, then nodded his approval after the first few bars. Then he went on a treasure hunt for candles.

Ten minutes later, he had over a dozen ranged throughout the room, glowing and wafting out the fragrances of vanilla, jasmine, sandalwood.

He'd barely had time to pat himself on the back when he heard her car. He beat Pan to the door by inches.

Outside, Morgana lifted a brow when she spotted Nash's car. But the fact that he was nearly a half hour early didn't annoy her. Not in the least. She was smiling as she crossed to the door, his script under one arm, a bottle of champagne in the other.

He opened the door and scooped her up into a long, luxurious kiss. Wanting his own greeting, Pan did his best to crowbar between them.

"Hi," Nash said when he freed her mouth.

"Hello." She handed Nash both bottle and envelope so that she could ruffle Pan's fur before closing the door. "You're early."

"I know." He glanced at the label on the bottle. "Well, well... Are we celebrating?"

"I thought we should." As she straightened, her braid slid over her shoulder. "Actually, it's a little congratulatory gift for you. But I'd hoped you'd share."

"Be glad to. What am I being congratulated for?"

She nodded toward the envelope in his hand. "For that. Your story."

He felt the little knot that had remained tight in his stomach all day loosen. "You liked it."

"No. I loved it. And once I sit down and take my shoes off I'll tell you why."

"Let's go in here." After shifting the bottle and envelope to one arm, he tucked the other around her. "How was business?"

"Oh, it's ticking right along. In fact, I may see if Mindy can squeak out another hour or two a day for me. We've been..." Her words trailed off as she stepped into the drawing room.

The candleglow was as mystic and romantic as moonbeams. It glinted on silver, tossed rainbows from crystal. Everywhere was the perfume of flowers and candle wax, and the haunting strains of violins. The fire smoldered gently.

It wasn't often she was thrown off balance so completely. Now she felt the sting of tears in the back of her throat, tears that sprang from an emotion so pure and bright she could hardly bear it.

She looked at him, and the flickering light tossed dozens of stars into her eyes. "Did you do this for me?"

A little off balance himself, he skimmed his knuckles over her cheek. "Must've been elves."

Her curving lips brushed his. "I'm very, very fond of elves."

He shifted until their bodies met. "How do you feel about screenwriters?"

Her arms slid comfortably around his waist. "I'm learning to like them."

"Good." As he settled into the kiss, Nash realized his arms were too encumbered to allow him to give it his best shot. "Why don't I get rid of this stuff, open the champagne?"

"That sounds like an excellent idea." With a long, contented sigh, she slipped out of her shoes while he walked over to pluck out a bottle already nestled in the ice bucket. He turned both hers and his around to show the identical labels.

"Telepathy?"

Moving toward him, she smiled. "Anything's possible."

He tossed the envelope aside, snuggled the second bottle in the ice, then opened the first with a cheerful pop and fizz. He poured, and then after handing her a glass, rang his against it. "To magic."

"Always," she murmured, and sipped. Taking his hand, she led him to the couch, where she could curl up close and watch the fire. "So, what did you do today besides call up some elves?"

"I wanted to show you my Cary Grant side."

With a chuckle, she brushed her lips over his cheek. "I like all of your sides."

Contented, he propped his feet on the coffee table. "Well, I spent a lot of time trying to get those flowers to look like they do in the movies."

She glanced over. "We'll concede that your talents don't run to floral arranging. I love them."

"I figured the effort was worth something." He entertained himself by toying with her earring. "I did a little fine-tuning on the script. Thought about you a lot. Took a call from my very excited agent. Thought about you some more."

She chuckled and laid her head on his shoulder. Home. She was home. Completely. "Sounds like a very productive day. What was your agent excited about?"

"Well, it seems he'd taken a call from a very interested producer."

Delight shimmered from her eyes as she sat up again. "Your
screenplay."

"Right the first time." It felt a little odd.... No, Nash
thought, it felt wonderfully odd to have someone so obviously
excited for him. "Actually, it's the treatment, but since my luck's
been running pretty well we've got a deal in the works. I'm
going to let the script cook a couple of days and take another
look. Then I'll ship it off to him."

"It's not luck." She tapped her glass to his again. "You've got
magic. Up there." She laid a finger on his temple. "And in here."
And on his heart. "Or wherever imagination comes from."

For the first time in his adult life, he thought he might
blush. So he kissed her instead. "Thanks. I couldn't have done
it without you."

With a light laugh, she settled back. "I'd hate to disagree
with you. So I won't."

He ran an idle hand down the braid on her shoulder. It felt
tremendously good, he realized, just to sit here like this at the
end of the day with someone who was important to him. "Why
don't you stroke my ego and tell me what you liked about it?"

She held out her glass so that he could top off her champagne.
"I doubt your ego needs stroking, but I'll tell you anyway."

"Take your time. I wouldn't want you to leave anything out."

"All of your movies have texture. Even when there's blood
splashing around or something awful scratching at the window,
there's a quality that goes beyond being spooked or shocked. In
this—though you're bound to set some hearts pumping with
that graveyard scene, and that business in the attic—you go a
step further." She shifted to face him. "It's not just a story of
witchcraft and power or of conjuring forces, good and bad. It's
about people, their basic humanity. Of believing in wonderful
things and trusting your heart. It's a kind of funny celebration

of being different, even when it's difficult. In the end, even though there's terror and pain and heartbreak, there is love. That's what we all want."

"You didn't mind that I had Cassandra casting spells with graveyard dirt or chanting over a cauldron?"

"Artistic license," Morgana said with a lifted brow. "I suppose I found it possible to overlook your creativity. Even when she was prepared to sell her soul to the devil to save Jonathan."

With a shrug, he drained his glass. "If Cassandra had the power of good, the story would hardly have enough punch if she didn't have at least one match with the power of evil. You see, there are some basic commandments of horror. Even though that's not exactly what this turned out to be, I think they still apply."

"Ultimate good against ultimate evil?" she suggested.

"That's one. The innocent must suffer," he added. "Then there's the rite of passage. That same innocent must spill blood."

"A manhood thing," Morgana said dryly.

"Or womanhood. I'm no sexist. And good must, through great sacrifice, triumph."

"Seems fair."

"There's one more. My personal favorite." He skimmed a fingertip up her neck. Chills chased it. "The audience should wonder, and keep wondering, if whatever evil that's been vanquished slinked free again after the final fade-out."

She pursed her lips. "We all know evil's always slinking free."

"Exactly." He grinned. "The same way we all wonder, from time to time, if there really is something drooling in the closet at night. After the lights go out. And we're alone." He nipped at her earlobe. "Or what's really rustling the bushes outside the cellar window or skulking in the shadows, ready, waiting, to ooze out and—"

When the doorbell rang, she jolted. Nash laughed. Morgana swore.

"Why don't I get it?" he suggested.

She made a stab at dignity and smoothed down her skirt. "Why don't you?"

When he walked out, she let go with a quick shudder. He was good, she admitted. So damn good that she, who knew better, had been sucked right in. She was still deciding whether to forgive him or not when Nash came back with a tall, gangly man hefting a huge tray. The man wore a white tux and a red bow tie. Stitched over his chest pocket was Chez Maurice.

"Set it right on the table, Maurice."

"It's George, sir," the man said in a sorrowful voice.

"Right." Nash winked at Morgana. "Just dish everything right on up."

"I'm afraid this will take me a moment or two."

"We've got time."

"The mocha mousse should remain chilled, sir," George pointed out. Nash realized that the poor man had a permanent apology stuck in his throat.

"I'll take it into the kitchen." Morgana rose to take the container. As she left them, she heard George murmuring sadly that the radicchio had been off today and they'd had to make do with endive.

"He lives for food," Nash explained when Morgana returned a few moments later. "It makes him weep to think how careless some of the new delivery boys are with the stuffed mushrooms. Bruising them heedlessly."

"Heathens."

"Exactly what I said. It seemed to put George in a better frame of mind. Or maybe it was the tip."

"So what has George brought us?" She wandered over to the table. "Endive salad."

"The radicchio—"

"Was off. I heard. Mmm. Lobster tails."

"À la Maurice."

"Naturally." She smiled over her shoulder as Nash pulled out her chair. "Is there a Maurice?"

"George was sorry to report that he's been dead for three years. But his spirit lives on."

She laughed and began to enjoy her food. "This is very inventive takeout."

"I'd considered a bucket of chicken, but I thought this would impress you more."

"It does." She dipped a bite of lobster in melted butter, watching him as she slipped it between her lips. "You set a very attractive stage." Her hand brushed lightly over his. "Thank you."

"Anytime." The fact was, he was hoping there'd be dozens of other times, dozens of other stages. With the two of them, just the two of them, as the only players.

He caught himself, annoyed that he was thinking such serious thoughts. Such permanent thoughts. To lighten the mood, he poured more champagne.

"Morgana?"

"Yes."

"There's something I've been wanting to ask you." He brought her hand to his lips, finding her skin much more alluring than the food. "Is Mrs. Littleton's niece going to the prom?"

She blinked first, then threw her head back with a rich laugh. "My God, Nash, you're a romantic."

"Just curious." Because he couldn't resist the way her eyes danced, he grinned. "Okay, okay. I like happily-ever-after as well as the next guy. Did she get her man?"

Morgana sampled another bite. "It seems Jessie worked up the courage to ask Matthew if he'd like to go to the prom with her."

"Good for her. And?"

"Well, I have this all secondhand from Mrs. Littleton, so it may not be precisely accurate."

Nash leaned forward to flick a finger down her nose. "Listen, babe, I'm the writer. You don't have to pause for dramatic effect. Spill it."

"My information is that he blushed, stuttered a bit, pushed up these cute horn-rim glasses he wears, and said he guessed so."

Solemnly Nash raised his glass. "To Jessie and Matthew."

Morgana lifted her own. "To first love. It's the sweetest."

He wasn't sure about that, since he'd been so successful in avoiding the experience. "What happened to your high school sweetheart?"

"What makes you think I had one?"

"Doesn't everyone?"

Morgana acknowledged that with a faint cock of her brow. "Actually, there was one boy. His name was Joe, and he played on the basketball team."

"A jock."

"I'm afraid Joe was second-string. But he was tall. Height was important to me in those days, as I loomed over half the boys in my class. We dated on and off through senior year." She sipped her wine. "And did a lot of necking in his '72 Pinto."

"Hatchback?" Nash asked between bites.

"I believe so."

"I like to get a clear visual." He grinned. "Don't stop now. I can see it. Exterior scene, night. The parked car on a dark, lonely road. The two sweethearts entwined, stealing desperate kisses as the radio sings out with the theme from *A Summer Place*."

"I believe it was 'Hotel California,'" she corrected.

"Okay. Then the last guitar riff fades...."

"I'm afraid that's about it. He went to Berkeley in the fall, and I went to Radcliffe. Height and a nice pair of lips just wasn't enough to keep my heart involved at a distance of three thousand miles."

Nash sighed for all men. "'Frailty, thy name is woman.'"

"I believe Joe recovered admirably. He married an economics

major and moved to St. Louis. At last count, they'd produced three-fifths of their own basketball team."

"Good old Joe."

This time Morgana refilled the glasses. "How about you?"

"I never played much ball."

"I was talking about high school sweethearts."

"Oh." He leaned back, enjoying the moment—the fire crackling at his back, the woman smiling at him through the candlelight, the good-natured fizz of champagne in his head. "She was Vicki—with an *i*. A cheerleader."

"What else?" Morgana agreed.

"I mooned over her for nearly two months before I worked up the courage to ask her out. I was shy."

Morgana smiled over the rim of her glass. "Tell me something I can believe."

"No, really. I'd transferred in the middle of junior year. By that time all the groups and cliques are so firmly established it took a crowbar to break them up. You're odd man out, so you spend a lot of time watching and imagining."

She felt a stirring of sympathy, but she wasn't sure he'd welcome it. "And you spent time watching Vicki with an *i*."

"I spent a whole lot of time watching Vicki. Felt like decades. The first time I saw her do a C jump, I was in love." He paused to study Morgana. "Were you a cheerleader?"

"No. Sorry."

"Too bad. I still get palpitations watching C jumps. Anyway, I finally sweated up the nerve to ask her to the movies. It was *Friday the 13th*. The movie, not the date. While Jason was hacking away at the very unhappy campers, I made a fumbling pass. Vicki received. We were an item for the rest of the school year. Then she dumped me for this hood with a motorcycle and a tattoo."

"The hussy."

Shrugging philosophically, he polished off his lobster. "I

heard she eloped with him and they went to live in a trailer park in El Paso. Which is no more than she deserved after breaking my heart."

Tilting her head, Morgana gave him a narrowed look. "I think you made it up."

"Only part of it." He didn't like to talk about his past, not with anyone. To distract her, he rose and changed the music. Now it was slow, dreamy Gershwin. Coming back to the table, he took her hand to draw her to her feet. "I want to hold you," he said simply.

Morgana moved easily into his arms and let him lead. At first they merely swayed to the music, his arms around her waist, hers around his neck, their eyes on each other's. Then he guided her into a dance so that their bodies flowed together to the low throb of the music.

He wondered if he would always think of her in candle-light. It suited her so well. That creamy Irish skin glowed as fragilely as the rose-tipped china. Her hair, black as the night that deepened beyond the windows, was showered with little stars of light. There were more stars in her eyes, sprinkled like moondust over the deep midnight blue.

The first kiss was quiet, a soft meeting of lips that promised more. That promised anything that could be wished. He felt the champagne spin in his head as he lowered his mouth to hers again, as her lips parted beneath his like the petals of a rose.

Her fingers glided silkily along his neck, teasing nerves to the surface. A low moan sounded in her throat, a moan that had his blood humming in response. Her body moved against his as she deepened the kiss. Her eyes remained open, drawing him in.

He slid his hands up her back, aroused by her quick shudder of response. Watching her, wanting her, he tugged the band from the end of her braid, combing tensed fingers through to loosen the intricate coils. He could hear her breath catch, see her eyes darken, as he dragged her head back and plundered that wide, unpainted mouth.

She tasted danger and delight and desperation. The combination swirled inside her, a headier brew than any wine. His muscles were wire taut under her hands, and she shivered with a mixture of fear and pleasure at the thought of what would happen when they sprang free.

Desire took many forms. Tonight, she knew, it would not come as the patient, reverent exploration they had known before. Tonight, there were fires raging.

Something snapped. He could all but hear the chains on his control break. He pulled away, his hands still gripping her arms, his body a mass of aches and needs. She said nothing, only stood, her lips soft and swollen from his, her hair tumbled like restless night around her shoulders. Her eyes full of smoke and secret promises.

He dragged her back again. Even as his mouth was devouring hers, he lifted her off her feet.

She'd never believed she would allow herself to be swept away. She'd been wrong. As he strode from the room and up the stairs, both her mind and her body went willingly with him. Reckless and ready, she let her lips race over his face, down his throat and back up to meet his avid mouth.

He didn't pause at the bedroom door, not even when he saw that she'd brought the candles and music with them. The bed was centered in their glow, beckoning. He tumbled onto it with her.

Impatient hands, hungry mouths, desperate words. He couldn't get enough. There couldn't be enough to fill this gnawing need. He knew she was with him, flame for flame, demand for demand, but he wanted to push her further and faster, until there was nothing but blazing heat and wild wind.

She couldn't get her breath. The air was too heavy. And hot, so hot she wondered that her skin didn't burst into flames. She reached for him, thinking she would ask, beg, for a moment to stop and catch her sanity. Then his mouth crushed hers again and even the wish for reason was lost.

In a mindless haze of greed, he yanked his hand down the front of her dress. Snaps burst open like tiny explosions to reveal flushed skin and seductive black lace. With a breathless oath, he ripped the flimsy cloth aside so that her breasts spilled into his restless hands.

She cried out—not in fear or in pain, but in wonder—as his greedy mouth scorched her skin.

He was ruthless, relentless, reckless. Need sliced through him, hot knives of desire that cut all ties to the civilized. His hands moved over her, leaving aches and trembles in their wake.

Her response was not submission, not surrender, but rather a greed that swelled as ripely as his own. She took, she tormented, she tantalized.

They went tumbling over the bed, caught up in a war of passion, wild hands tugging and tearing at clothes, seeking the pleasure of flesh slicked from the heat. He did as he chose, releasing every dark fantasy that had spun in his mind. Touching, tasting, devouring.

She crested hard, clinging to him as the wave shot her up and left her wrecked. His name was a mindless chant through her trembling lips, a chant that ended on a sob when he sent her soaring again.

Dazed, she rose above him. He could see the candlelight shivering over her skin, and her eyes, dark and glazed with what he had given her. He knew he would die if he didn't have her tonight, tomorrow, a thousand tomorrows.

He pressed her back into the mattress, clamping his hands on hers. Breath heaving, he held on long enough for their eyes to meet. Was it challenge he saw in hers? Was it triumph?

Then he plunged deep. Her hands fisted beneath his, and her body rose up to meet him.

Speed. Power. Glory. They raced together, stroke for stroke, with a strength born of shattering needs. His mouth sought hers again in a bruising kiss. Her arms vised around him, those short, neat nails raking desperately down his back.

He felt her agile body convulse, heard her broken gasp of stunned pleasure. Then his mind went dim as he leapt off the razor's edge to follow her.

A long time later, he clawed his way back to reason. He'd rolled off her, wanting to let her breathe. Now she lay on her stomach, sprawled across the bed. Catching his own breath, he stared into the shadows, flipping back through his mind what had passed between them. He wasn't sure whether to be appalled or delighted.

He'd...well, he supposed *plundered* would be an apt word. He certainly hadn't been worried about the niceties. However much pleasure he'd found in making love with a woman before, he'd never slipped over the edge into madness. It had its points, he realized. But he wasn't sure how Morgana might feel about having had her clothes ripped off her.

Nash laid a tentative hand on her shoulder. She shuddered. Wincing, he took it away again. "Morgana...are you all right?"

She made some sound, something between a whimper and a moan. He felt a quick stab of fear at the thought that she might be crying. Good going, Kirkland, he thought furiously, then tried again. He stroked a hand down her hair.

"Babe. Morgana. I'm sorry if I..."

He let his words trail off, not certain what to say. Slowly she turned her head, managed to lift up a limp hand far enough to rake the tangled hair out of her eyes. She blinked at him.

"Did you say something?"

"I was just... Are you okay?"

She sighed. It was a long, catlike sound that made his treacherous body twang. "Okay?" She seemed to roll the word around, testing it with her tongue. "I don't think so. Ask me again when I find the energy to move." She slid her hand over the tangled sheets to take his. "Are you?"

"Am I what?"

"Okay."

"I wasn't the one being plundered."

The word had a smile spreading lazily over her face. "No? I thought I did a pretty good job." She stretched and was pleased to see that her body was nearly in working order again. "Give me an hour and I'll try again."

Relief began to trickle through. "You're not upset?"

"Do I look upset?"

He thought it over. She looked like a cat who'd happily gorged on a gallon of cream. He didn't even realize he'd started to grin. "No, I guess not."

"Pleased with yourself, aren't you?"

"Maybe I am." He started to reach out to drag her closer and found his fingers tangled in what was left of her bra. "Are you?"

She wondered that the grin didn't split his face. He was watching her, all but whistling a tune as he spun the tattered lace on one finger. Morgana pushed up to her knees, noted his very satisfied eyes skimmed over her. "Do you know what, Nash?"

"No. What?"

"I'm going to have to wipe that grin off your face."

"Yeah? How?"

Tossing her hair back, she planted herself over him. Slowly, sinuously, she slid down. "Watch me."

Chapter Nine

As far as Nash was concerned, life was a pretty good deal. He spent his days doing something he loved, and he was paid very well to do it. He had his health, a new home, and an interesting deal in the works. Best of all, he was enjoying an incredible affair with a fascinating woman. A woman whom, he'd discovered in the past weeks, he was not only desperately attracted to, but considered a friend.

Nash had learned through trial and error that a lover you couldn't enjoy out of bed satisfied the body but left the spirit wanting. With Morgana, he'd found a woman he could laugh with, talk with, argue with and make love with, all with a sense of intimacy he'd never experienced before.

A sense of intimacy he hadn't realized he wanted before.

There were even times he forgot she was something more than a woman.

Now, as he finished the series of push-ups he forced himself to perform three times a week, he thought over their last few days together.

They'd taken a long, leisurely drive up to Big Sur to stand at an overlook, wind whipping their hair as they looked out over the staggering view of hills and water and cliffs. Like tourists, they'd taken snapshots with her camera, videos with his.

Though he'd felt a little foolish, he'd even scooped up a few pebbles—when she wasn't looking—to slip into his pocket as a souvenir of the day.

He'd tagged along while she'd poked around in the shops in Carmel—and had been good-naturedly resigned when she piled packages into his arms.

Lunch on the terrace of some pretty café, surrounded by flowers. Sunset picnics on the beach, sitting with his arm around her, her head on his shoulder, while the great red orb bled fire into the sky and then sank into the indigo sea.

Quiet kisses at dusk. Easy laughter. Intimate looks in crowded places.

It was almost as if he was courting her.

With a grunt, Nash let his arms relax. Courting? No, that wasn't what it was at all, he assured himself, rolling over on his back. They simply enjoyed each other's company, a great deal. But it wasn't courtship. Courtship had a sneaky habit of leading to marriage.

And marriage, Nash had decided long ago, was one experience he could do without.

A niggling doubt worked into his mind as he stood to flex the muscles he'd toned over the past half hour. Had he done anything to make her think that what they had together might lead to something...well, something legal and permanent? With DeeDee he had spelled out everything from the get-go, and still she'd been smugly certain she could change his mind.

But with Morgana he'd said nothing. He'd been too busy falling for her to be practical.

The last thing he wanted to do was hurt her. She was too important, she meant too much. She was...

Slow down, Kirkland, he warned himself uneasily. Sure, she was important. He cared about her. But that didn't mean he was going to start thinking about love. Love also had a nasty habit of leading to marriage.

Frowning, he stood in the middle of the room he'd set up with benches and weights. Sweat trickled unnoticed down his face as he cautiously took a peek at what was in his heart. Okay, yes, he cared about her. Maybe more than he'd ever cared about anyone. But that was a long way from orange blossoms, station wagons and a cozy cottage for two.

Rubbing a hand over his heart, he geared himself up for a closer look. Why did he think about her so often? He couldn't remember another woman intruding on his daily routine the way Morgana did. There were times when he stopped whatever he was doing just to wonder what she was doing. It had gotten so that he didn't sleep well unless she was with him. If he awakened in the morning and she wasn't there, he started the day with a nagging sense of disappointment.

It was a bad sign, he thought as he grabbed a towel to wipe his face. A sign he should have picked up on long before this. How come there'd been no warning bells? he wondered. No quiet little voice whispering in his ear that it was time to take a long, casual step in retreat.

Instead, he'd been moving forward in a headlong rush.

But he hadn't gone over the edge. Not Nash Kirkland. He took a deep breath and tossed the towel aside. It was just the novelty, he decided. Soon the immediacy of the feelings she brought out in him would fade.

As he walked off to shower, he assured himself, like any addict, that he was still in control. He could back off anytime.

But like fingers reaching for an itch, his mind kept worrying the problem. Maybe he was fine, maybe he was in control, but what about Morgana? Was she getting in too deep? If she was as tied up as he was, she could be imagining—what? A life in the burbs, monogrammed towels? A riding lawn mower.

The cool spray of water blasted his face. Nash found himself grinning.

And he'd said he wasn't sexist. Here he was worrying that Morgana was harboring delusions of marriage and family. Just because she was a woman. Ridiculous. She was no more interested in taking that deadly leap than he.

But as he let the water sluice over his head, he began to imagine.

Interior scene, day. The room is a jumbled heap of toys, clothes overflowing out of plastic hampers, dirty dishes. In a playpen dumped in the center of the room, a toddler squalls. Our hero walks in, a bulging briefcase in his hand. He wears a dark suit and a strangling tie. Wing tips. There is a weary cast to his face. A man who has faced problems all day and has come home to more.

"Honey," he says with an attempt at cheer, "I'm home."

The baby howls and rattles his cage. Resigned, our hero sets his briefcase aside and goes to pick up the screaming baby. The child's wet diaper sags.

"You're late again." The wife shuffles in. Her hair is a tangled mess around a face set in stern, angry lines. She wears a ratty bathrobe and a pair of fuzzy slippers. As our hero bounces the wet, screaming baby, the wife slaps her hands on her hips and begins to rattle off a list of all of his shortcomings, punctuated by announcements that the washing machine has overflowed, the sink is clogged, and she's pregnant—again.

Just as the scene he was creating began to ease both Nash's conscience and mind, it faded out, to be replaced by a new one.

Coming home with the scent of flowers and the sea in the air. Smiling because you were almost where you wanted to be. Needed to be. Starting up the walk, carrying a bouquet of tulips. The door opens, and she stands there, her hair pulled back in a sleek ponytail, her lips curved in welcome. She cradles a pretty, dark-haired child on her hip, a child who giggles and holds out its pudgy arms. He cuddles the child, smelling talc and baby and his wife's subtle perfume.

"We missed you," she says, and lifts her face for a kiss.

Nash blinked. With a wrench of his wrist, he shut off the water, then shook his head.

He had it bad, he admitted. But, since he knew that second scene was more of a fantasy than anything he'd ever written, he was still in control.

When he stepped out of the shower, he wondered how soon she would be there.

Morgana punched down on the accelerator and leaned the car into a curve. If felt good...no, it felt fabulous, to be buzzing along the tree-lined road with the windows down and the sea breeze blowing through her hair. What made it fabulous was that she was going somewhere to be with someone who had made a difference in her life.

She'd been content without him. Perhaps she would have gone on being content if she had never met him. But she had, and nothing was ever going to be the same again.

She wondered if he knew how much it meant that he accepted her for what she was. She doubted it. She hadn't known how much it could mean until it had happened. And, as for Nash, he had a habit of looking at things at a skewed angle and seeing the humor in them. She imagined he saw her...talents as some kind of great joke on science. And perhaps they were, in a way.

But the important thing, to her, was that he knew, and accepted. He didn't look at her as if he expected her to grow a second head at any moment. He looked at her as a woman.

It was easy to be in love with him. Though she had never considered herself a romantic, she had come to appreciate all the books, the songs, the poetry, written to celebrate the caprices of the heart. It was true that when you were in love, the air smelled clearer, the flowers sweeter.

On a whim, she wished a rose into her hand, smiling as she sniffed the delicate closed bloom. Her world felt like that, she realized. Like a rose that was just about to open.

It made her feel foolish to think like that. Giddy, light-headed. But her thoughts were her own, she reminded herself. Until she made them someone else's. It occurred to her that, sooner or later, she would have to share them with Nash.

She couldn't be sure how long it would be before complications set in, but for now it was glorious simply to enjoy the soft spread of emotion glowing inside her.

As she pulled into his driveway, she was smiling. She had a few surprises for Nash, starting with her plan for this balmy Saturday night. She reached for the bag on the seat beside her, and Pan stuck his head over her shoulder.

"Just give me a minute," she told him, "and you can get out and see what's what. Luna will show you around."

From her perch on the floor of the passenger seat, Luna glanced up, eyes slitted.

"If you don't behave, I'll dump you both back home. You'll have only yourselves for company until Monday."

As she stepped from the car, she felt a flicker, like a curtain fluttering over her mind. She stood, one hand resting on the door, absorbing a wash of wind, a whisper of sound. The air thickened, grayed. There was no dizziness. It was as if she had stepped from sunshine into shadows, shadows where mysteries waited to be solved. She strained to see beyond that mist, but it lay heavy, teasing her with hints and glimpses only.

Then the sun was back, and there was only the sound of water rushing against rock.

Though she hadn't Sebastian's gift for precognition, or Anastasia's empathetic tendencies, she understood.

Things were about to change. And soon. Morgana also understood that those changes might not be something she would have wished for.

Shaking off the mood, she started up the walk. Tomorrow could always be changed, she reminded herself. Especially if one concentrated on now. Since now equaled Nash, she was willing to fight to keep it.

He opened the door before she reached it and stood, hands tucked in his pockets, smiling at her. "Hi, babe."

"Hi." Dangling the bag from one hand, she linked an arm around his neck and curved her body to his for a kiss. "Do you know how I feel?"

"Yeah." He skimmed his hands down her sides to her hips. "I know exactly how you feel. Fantastic."

She chuckled and pushed the last lingering doubts aside. "As it happens, you're right." Riding on pure emotion, she handed him the rose.

"For me?" He wasn't exactly sure what a man's response should be when a woman gave him a rosebud.

"Absolutely for you." She kissed him again while Luna strolled territorially into the house. "How would you like to spend an evening—" she moved her mouth seductively to his ear "—an entire evening...doing something—" voice breathy, she walked her fingers up his chest "—decadent?"

His blood leapt in his veins and roared in the ear she was tormenting. "When do we get started?"

"Well." She rubbed against him, tilting her head back just enough to look into his eyes. "Why waste time?"

"God, I love an aggressive woman."

"Good. Because I've got big plans for you..." She caught his lower lip in her teeth, sucked gently. "Babe. And it's going to take hours."

He wondered if he'd ever breathe normally again. He hoped not. "Want to start here and work our way inside?"

"Uh-uh." She eased away, sliding her hand down and gripping his waistband to pull him inside with her. Pan padded in behind them, decided he wouldn't get much attention from either of them and moved along to check out the house. "We can't do what I have in mind outside. Follow me." Tossing him a sultry look over her shoulder, she started upstairs.

"You bet."

He made a grab for her at the top of the stairs. After a moment's debate, she let him catch her. Sliding into the kiss was like sliding into a hot tub. Full of heat and bubbles. But when he tugged on her zipper, she eased herself away.

"Morgana..."

She only shook her head and strolled into the bedroom.

"I've got a treat for you, Nash." Reaching into the bag, she pulled out a thin shimmer of black silk and tossed it carelessly on his bed. He glanced at it, back at her. He could imagine her wearing it.

He could imagine taking it off of her.

His fingertips began to tingle.

"I made a stop on the way over. Picked up a few...things."

Without taking his eyes off her, he laid the rose on the dresser. "So far, I like it."

"Oh, it gets better." She pulled something else out of the bag and handed it to him. Nash frowned at the plastic video case. A grin flickered on his mouth.

"Adult movies?"

"Read the title."

Amused, he turned the case over. And let out a whoop. *"The Crawling Eye?"* His grin flashed as he looked over at her.

"Approve?"

"Approve, hell—this is great! A classic. I haven't seen it in years."

"There's more where that came from." She upended the bag on the bed. Scattered among a handful of toiletries were three more tapes. Nash snatched them up like a kid grabbing for packages under the Christmas tree.

"An American Werewolf in London, Nightmare on Elm Street,

Dracula. This is great." Laughing, he scooped her against him. "What a woman. You want to spend the evening watching horror flicks?"

"With a few lengthy intermissions."

This time he unzipped her dress with one quick motion. "Tell you what—let's start the whole thing off with an overture."

She laughed as they tumbled onto the bed. "I love a good overture."

Nash couldn't imagine a more perfect weekend. They watched movies—among other things—until dawn. Slept late, then had a lazy, and sloppy, breakfast in bed.

He couldn't imagine a more perfect woman. Not only was she beautiful, smart and sexy, but she also appreciated the subtleties of a movie like *The Crawling Eye.*

He didn't even mind the fact that she'd put him to work Sunday afternoon. Puttering around the yard, mowing, weeding, planting, took on a whole new meaning when he could look over and see her kneeling in the grass wearing one of his T-shirts and a pair of his jeans hitched up at the waist with twine.

It made him wonder what it would be like, what it could be like, if she were always there. Within reach.

Nash lost track of the weeding he'd been assigned, and, nuzzling the dog, who had trotted over to butt his head against his chest, he just watched Morgana.

She was humming. He didn't recognize the tune, but it sounded exotic. Some witch's song, he supposed. Handed down through time. She was magic. Even without the talents she'd inherited, she would be magic.

She'd tucked her hair up under his battered Dodgers cap. There wasn't a touch of makeup on her face. His jeans bagged around her hips. Still, she looked erotic. Black lace or faded denim, her sensuality radiated like sunlight.

More, there was a purity to her face, a confidence, an awareness of self, that he found utterly irresistible.

He could imagine her kneeling there, in that very spot, a year from now. Ten years. And still setting off that stirring in his blood.

My God. His hand slid bonelessly from the dog's head. He was in love with her. Really in love. Totally caught in the big, scary L word.

And what the hell was he going to do about it?

In control? he thought, dazed. Able to back off anytime? What a crock.

He rose on unsteady legs. The clutching in his stomach was plain fear. And it was for both of them. She glanced over, tipping the cap down so that the brim shaded her eyes.

"Something wrong?"

"No. No, I... I was going to go in and get us something cold."

He all but ran into the house, leaving Morgana staring after him.

Coward. Wimp. Idiot. All the way into the kitchen, he cursed himself. After filling a glass with water, he gulped it down. Maybe it was a touch of sun. A lack of sleep. An overactive libido.

Slowly he set the glass aside. Like hell. It was love.

Step right up, ladies and gentlemen. Step right up and see an average man transformed into a puddle of nerves and terror by the love of a good woman.

He bent over the sink and splashed water on his face. He didn't know how it had happened, but he was going to have to deal with it. As far as he could see, there was no place to run. He was a grown man, Nash reminded himself. So he would do the adult thing and face it.

Maybe he should just tell her. Straight out.

Morgana, I'm crazy about you.

Blowing out a breath, he dashed more water onto his face. Too weak. Too ambivalent.

Morgana, I've come to realize that what I feel for you is more than attraction. Even more than affection.

This time his breath hissed out. Too wordy. Too damn stupid.

Morgana, I love you.

Simple. To the point. And scary as hell.

He majored in scary, he reminded himself. He ought to be able to pull this off. Straightening his shoulders, bracing his system, he started out of the kitchen.

The wall phone shrilled and nearly had him jumping out of his shoes.

"Easy, boy," he muttered.

"Nash?" Morgana stood in the kitchen doorway, eyes full of curiosity and concern. "Are you all right?"

"Me? Yeah, yeah, I'm great." He dragged a nervous hand through his hair. "How about you?"

"Fine," she said slowly. "Are you going to answer the phone?"

"The phone?" While his mind scattered in a thousand directions, he glanced at the ringing phone. "Sure."

"Good. I'll fix us that cold drink while you do." Still frowning at him, she walked to the refrigerator.

Nash didn't notice that his palms were wet until he picked up the receiver. Forcing a grin, he wiped his free hand on his jeans.

"Hello." The excuse for a smile faded instantly. Stunned, Morgana paused with one hand on a soft-drink bottle and the other on the refrigerator door.

She'd never seen him look like this. Cold. His eyes had frosted over. Ice over velvet. Even as he leaned back against the counter, there was tension in every line of his body.

Morgana felt a shudder rush down her spine. She'd known he could be dangerous, and the man she was staring at now had stripped off all the easygoing charm and good-natured humor. Like one of the characters Nash might have conjured out of his imagination, this man was capable of quick and bloodless violence.

Whoever was on the other end of the telephone should have been grateful for the distance between them.

"Leeanne." He said the name in a flat, gelid tone. The voice rattling brightly in his ear set his teeth on edge. Old memories, old wounds, swam to the surface. He let her ramble for a moment, until he was sure he had himself under control. "Just cut to the chase, Leeanne. How much?"

He listened to the wheedling, the whining, the recriminations. His responsibilities, he was reminded. His obligations. His family.

"No, I don't give a damn. It's not my fault you got hung up with another loser." His lips curved in a humorless smile. "Yeah, right. Bad luck. How much?" he repeated, barely lifting a brow at the requested amount. Resigned, he pulled open a drawer and rummaged until he found a tattered scrap of paper and the stub of an old pencil. "Where do I send it?" He scribbled. "Yes, I've got it. Tomorrow." He tossed the paper onto the counter. "I said I would, didn't I? Just drop it. I've got things to do. Sure. You bet."

He hung up and started to let loose with a stream of oaths. Then he focused on Morgana. He'd forgotten she was there. When she started to speak, he shook his head.

"I'm going for a walk," he said abruptly, and slammed out of the screen door.

Carefully Morgana set the bottle she still held on the counter. Whoever had called had done more than anger him, she realized. She had seen more than anger in his eyes. She had seen grief, too. One had been as vicious as the other.

Because of it, she blocked her first inclination, to go after him. She would give him a few minutes alone first.

His long strides ate up the ground quickly. He stalked over the grass that had given him so much pleasure when he had mowed it only an hour before, passed without noticing the flowers that were already lapping up the sun now that they were free of choking weeds. Automatically he headed for the tumble of rocks at the edge of his property that separated his land from the bay.

This was another reason he'd been drawn to this place. The combination of wildness and serenity.

It suited him, he supposed as he dug his hands deep in his pockets. On the surface he was a relaxed, contented man. Those qualities usually extended deeper. But often, maybe too often, there was a recklessness swarming inside him.

Now he dropped down on a rock and stared out over the water. He would watch the gulls, the waves, the boats. And he would wait until he felt that contentment again.

He drew a deep breath, cleansing. *Thank God* was all he could think. Thank God he hadn't spoken of his feelings to Morgana. All it had taken was one phone call from the past to remind him that there was no place for love in his life.

He would have told her, he realized. He would have gone with the impulse of the moment, and told her he loved her. Maybe—probably—he would have started to make plans.

Then he would have messed it up. No doubt he would have messed it up. Sabotaging relationships was in his blood.

His hands curled and uncurled as he struggled to level again. Leeanne, he thought with a short, bitter bark of laughter. Well, he would send her the money, and she would fade out of his life. Again. Until the money ran out.

And that pattern would repeat itself over and over again. For the rest of his life.

"It's beautiful here," Morgana said quietly from behind him.

He didn't jolt. He just sighed. Nash supposed he should have expected her to follow him. And he supposed she would expect some sort of explanation.

He wondered how creative he might be. Should he tell her

Leeanne was an old lover, someone he'd pushed aside who wouldn't stay aside? Or maybe he'd weave some amusing tale about being blackmailed by the wife of a Mafia don, with whom he'd had a brief, torrid affair. That had a nice ring.

Or he could work on her sympathies and tell her Leeanne was a destitute widow—his best friend's widow—who tapped him for cash now and again.

Hell, he could tell her it had been a call for the policemen's fund. Anything. Anything but the bitter truth.

Her hand brushed his shoulder as she settled on the rock beside him. And demanded nothing. Said nothing. She only looked out over the bay, as he did. Waiting. Smelling of night. Of smoke and roses.

He had a terrible urge to simply turn and bury his face at her breast. Just to hold her and be held until all this helpless anger faded away.

And he knew that, no matter how clever he was, how glib, she would believe nothing but the truth.

"I like it here," he said, as if several long, silent minutes hadn't passed between her observation and his response. "In L.A. I looked out of my condo and saw another condo. I guess I didn't realize I was feeling hemmed in until I moved here."

"Everyone feels hemmed in from time to time, no matter where they live." She laid a hand on his thigh. "When I'm feeling that way, I go to Ireland. Walk along an empty beach. When I do, I think of all the people who have walked there before, and will walk there again. Then it occurs to me that nothing is forever. No matter how bad, or how good, everything passes and moves on to another level."

"'All things change; nothing perishes,'" he mumbled.

She smiled. "Yes, I'd say that sums it up perfectly." Reaching over, she cupped his face in her hands. Her eyes were soft and clear, and her voice was full of comfort ready to be offered. "Talk to me, Nash. I may not be able to help, but I can listen."

"There's nothing to say."

Something else flicked into her eyes. Nash cursed himself when he recognized it as hurt. "So, I'm welcome in your bed, but not into your mind."

"Damn it, one has nothing to do with the other." He wouldn't be pushed, wouldn't be prodded or maneuvered into revealing parts of himself he chose to keep hidden.

"I see." Her hands dropped away from his face. For a moment she was tempted to help him, to spin a simple charm that would give him peace of mind. But it wasn't right; it wouldn't be real. And she knew using magic to change his feelings would only hurt them both. "All right, then. I'm going to go finish the marigolds."

She rose. No recriminations, no heated words. He would have preferred them to this cool acceptance. As she took a step away, he grabbed her hand. She saw the war on his face, but offered nothing but silence.

"Leeanne's my mother."

Chapter Ten

His mother.

It was the anguish in his eyes that had Morgana masking her shock. She remembered how cold his voice had been when he spoke to Leeanne, how his face had fallen into hard, rigid lines. Yet the woman on the other end of the telephone line had been his mother.

What could make a man feel such distaste and dislike for the woman he owed his life to?

But the man was Nash. Because of that, she worked past her own deeply ingrained loyalty to family as she studied him.

Hurt, she realized. There had been as much hurt as anger in his voice, in his face, then. And now. She could see it plainly now that all the layers of arrogance, confidence and ease had been stripped away. Her heart ached for him, but she knew that wouldn't lessen his hurt. She wished she had Anastasia's talent and could take on some of his pain.

Instead, she kept his hand in hers and sat beside him again. No, she was not an empath, but she could offer support, and love.

"Tell me."

Where did he begin? Nash wondered. How could he explain to her what he had never been able to explain to himself?

He looked down at their joined hands, at the way her strong fingers entwined with his. She was offering support, under-standing, when he hadn't thought he needed any.

The feelings he'd always been reluctant to voice, refused to share, flowed out.

"I guess you'd have to know my grandmother. She was—" he searched for a polite way of putting it "—a straight arrow. And she expected everyone to fly that same narrow course. If I had to choose one adjective, I'd go with intolerant. She'd been widowed when Leeanne was about ten. My grandfather'd had this insurance business, so she'd been left pretty well off. But she liked to scrape pennies. She was one of those people who didn't have it in her to enjoy life."

He fell silent, watching the gulls sweep over the water. When his hand moved restlessly in hers, Morgana said nothing, and waited.

"Anyway, it might sound kind of sad and poignant. The widow with two young girls to raise alone. Until you under-stand that she liked being in charge. Being the widow Kirkland and having no one to answer to but herself. I have to figure she was pretty rough on her daughters, holding holiness and sex over their heads like lightning bolts. It didn't work very well with Leeanne. At seventeen she was pregnant and didn't have a clue who the father might have been."

He said it with a shrug in his voice, but Morgana saw be-neath it. "You blame her for that?"

"For that?" He looked at her, his eyes dark. "No. Not for that. The old lady must have made her life hell for the best part of nine months. Depending on who you get it from, Leeanne was a poor, lonely girl punished ruthlessly for one little slip. Or my grandmother was this long-suffering saint who took her sinful daughter in. My own personal opinion is that we had two selfish women who didn't give a damn about anyone but themselves."

"She was only seventeen, Nash," Morgana said quietly.

Anger carved his face into hard, unyielding lines. "That's supposed to make it okay? She was only seventeen, so it's okay that she bounced around so many guys she didn't know who got her pregnant. She was only seventeen, so it's okay that two days after she had me she took off, left me with that bitter old woman without a word, without a call or even a thought, for twenty-six years."

The raw emotion in his voice squeezed her heart. She wanted to gather him close, hold him until the worst of it passed. But when she reached out, he jerked away, then stood.

"I need to walk."

She made her decision quickly. She could either leave him to work off his pain alone, or she could share it with him. Before he could take three strides, she was beside him, taking his hand again.

"I'm sorry, Nash."

He shook his head violently. The air he gulped in was as sweet as spring, and yet it burned like bile in his throat. "I'm sorry. No reason to take it out on you."

She touched his cheek. "I can handle it."

But he wasn't sure he could. He'd never talked the whole business through before, not with anyone. Saying it all out loud left an ugly taste in his mouth, one he was afraid he'd never be rid of. He took another careful breath and started again.

"I stayed with my grandmother until I was five. My aunt, Carolyn, had married. He was in the army, a lifer. For the next few years I moved around with them, from base to base. He was a hard-nosed bastard—only tolerated me because Carolyn would cry and carry on when he got drunk and threatened to send me back."

Morgana could imagine it all too clearly. The little boy in the empty middle, controlled by everyone, belonging to no one. "You hated it."

"Yeah, I guess that hits the center. I didn't know why, exactly, but I hated it. Looking back, I realize that Carolyn was as unstable as Leeanne, in her own way. One minute she'd fawn all over me, the next she'd ignore me. She wasn't having any luck getting pregnant herself. Then, when I was about eight or nine, she found out she was going to have a kid of her own. So I got shipped back to my grandmother. Carolyn didn't need a substitute anymore."

Morgana felt her eyes fill with angry tears at the image of the child, helpless, innocent, being shuffled back and forth between people who knew nothing of love.

"She never looked at me like a person, you know? I was a mistake. That was the worst of it," he said, as if to himself. "The way she drummed that point home. That every breath I took, every beat of my heart was only possible because some careless, rebellious girl had made a mistake."

"No," Morgana said, appalled. "She was wrong."

"Yeah, maybe. But things like that stick with you. I heard a lot about the sins of the father, the evils of the flesh. I was lazy, intractable and wicked—one of her favorite words." He sent Morgana a grim little smile. "But that was no more than she expected, seeing as how I'd been conceived."

"She was a horrible woman," Morgana bit out. "She didn't deserve you."

"Well, she'd have agreed with you on the second part. And she made me understand just how grateful I should be that she put food in my belly and a roof over my head. But I wasn't feeling very grateful, and I ran away a lot. By the time I was twelve, I got slipped into the system. Foster homes."

His shoulders moved restlessly, in a small outward showing of the turmoil within. He was pacing back and forth over the grounds, his stride lengthening as the memories worked on him.

"Some of them were okay. The ones that really wanted you. Others just wanted the check you brought in every month, but sometimes you got lucky and ended up in a real home. I spent one Christmas with this family, the Hendersons." His voice changed, took on a hint of wonder. "They were great—treated me just like they treated their own kids. You could always smell cookies baking. They had the tree, the presents under it. All that colored paper and ribbon. Stockings hanging from the mantel. It really blew me away to see one with my name on it.

"They gave me a bike," he said quietly. "Mr. Henderson bought it secondhand and took it down to the basement to fix it up. He painted it red. Bug-eyed, fire-engine red, and he'd polished all the chrome. He put a lot of time into making that bike something special. He showed me how to hook baseball cards on the spokes."

He sent her a sheepish look that had Morgana tilting her head. "What?"

"Well, it was a really great bike, but I didn't know how to ride. I'd never had a bike. Here I was, nearly twelve years old, and that bike might as well have been a Harley hog for all I knew."

Morgana came staunchly to his defense. "That's nothing to be ashamed of."

Nash sent her an arch look. "Obviously you've never been an eleven-year-old boy. It's pretty tough to handle the passage into manhood when you can't handle a two-wheeler. So, I mooned over it, made excuses not to ride it. I had homework, I'd twisted my ankle, it looked like rain. Thought I was pretty clever, but she—Mrs. Henderson—saw right through me. One day she got me up early, before anyone else was awake, and took me out. She taught me. Held the back of the seat, ran along beside me. Made me laugh when I took a spill. And when I managed to wobble down the sidewalk on my own, she cried. Nobody'd ever..." He let his words trail off, embarrassed by the scope of emotion that memory evoked.

Tears burned the back of her throat. "They must have been wonderful people."

"Yeah, they were. I had six months with them. Probably the best six months of my life." He shook off the memory and went on. "Anyway, whenever I'd get too comfortable, my grand-mother would yank the chain and pull me back. So I started counting the days until I was eighteen, when nobody could tell me where to live, or how. When I got free, I was damn well going to stay that way."

"What did you do?"

"I wanted to eat, so I tried a couple of regular jobs." He glanced at her, this time with a hint of humor in his eyes. "I sold insurance for a while."

For the first time since he'd begun, she smiled. "I can't pic-ture it."

"Neither could I. It didn't last. I guess when it comes right down to it, I've got the old lady to thank for trying writing as a career. She used to whack me good whenever she caught me scribbling."

"Excuse me." Morgana was certain she must have misun-derstood. "She hit you for writing?"

"She didn't exactly understand the moral scope of vampire hunters," he said dryly. "So, figuring it was the last thing she'd want me to do, I kept right on doing it. I moved to L.A., man-aged to finesse a low-level job with the special-effects guys. Then I worked as a script doctor, met the right people. Finally managed to sell *Shape Shifter*. My grandmother died while that was in production. I didn't go to the funeral."

"If you expect me to criticize you for that, I'll have to dis-appoint you."

"I don't know what I expect," he muttered. Stopping be-neath a cypress, he turned to her. "I was twenty-six when the movie hit. It was…well, we'll risk a bad pun and call it a howl-ing success. Suddenly I was riding the wave. My next script was picked up. I got myself nominated for a Golden Globe. Then I started getting calls. My aunt. She just needed a few bills to tide her over. Her husband had never risen above sergeant, and she had three kids she wanted to send to college. Then Leeanne."

He scrubbed his hands over his face, wishing he could scrub away the layers of resentment, of hurt, of memory.

"She called you," Morgana prompted.

"Nope. She popped up on my doorstep one day. It would have been ludicrous if it hadn't been so pathetic. This stranger, painted up like a Kewpie doll, standing at my front door telling me she was my mother. The worst part was that I could see me in her. The whole time she was standing there, pouring out the sad story of her life, I wanted to shut that door in her face. Bolt it. I could hear her telling me that I owed her, how having me had screwed up her life. How she was divorced for the second time and running on empty. So I wrote her out a check."

Tired, he slid down the tree and sat on the soft ground beneath. The sun was hanging low, the shadows stretching long. Morgana knelt beside him.

"Why did you give her money, Nash?"

"It was what she wanted. I didn't have anything else for her, anyway. The first payment lasted her almost a year. In between, I'd get calls from my aunt, or one of my cousins." He tapped a fisted hand on his thigh. "Months will go by, and you'll think you've got your life pretty well set. But they don't let you forget what you've come from. If the price for that's a few thousand now and again, it's not a bad bargain."

Morgana's eyes heated. "They have no right, no right to take pieces of you."

"I've got plenty of money."

"I'm not talking about dollars. I'm talking about you."

His gaze locked on hers. "They remind me who—what—I am."

"They don't even know you," she said furiously.

"No, and I don't know them. But that doesn't mean a hell of a lot. You know about legacies, Morgana. About what comes down in the blood. Your inheritance is magic. Mine's self-interest."

She shook her head. "Whatever we inherit, we have the choice of using it, or discarding it. You're nothing like the people you came from."

He took her by the shoulders then, his fingers tense. "More than you think. I've made my choices. Maybe I stopped running away because it never got me anywhere. But I know who I am. That's someone who does best alone. There's no Henderson family in my future, Morgana. Because I don't want it. Now and again, I write out a check. Then I can close that all off so it's just me again. That's the way I want it. No ties, no obligations, no commitments."

She wouldn't argue with him, not when the pain was so close to the surface. Another time she could show him how wrong he was. The man holding her now was capable of tenderness, of generosity, of sweetness—none of which had been given to him. All of which he'd found for himself.

But she could give him something. If only for a short time.

"You don't have to tell me who you are, Nash." Gently she brushed his hair from his face. "I know. There's nothing you can't give that I'll ask for. Nothing you don't want to give that I'll take." She lifted her amulet, closed his hand over it, and hers over his. Her eyes deepened as they stared into his. "That's an oath."

He felt the metal grow warm in his hand. Baffled, he looked down to see it pulsing with light. "I don't—"

"An oath," she repeated. "One I can't break. There's something I want you to take, that I can give. Will you trust me?"

Something was stealing over him. Like a shadow cast by a cloud, it was cool and soft and weightless. His tensed muscles relaxed; his eyes grew pleasantly heavy. As from a great distance, he heard himself speak her name. Then he glided into sleep.

When he awakened, the sun was warm and bright. He could

hear birdsong, and the babbling music of water running over rock. Disoriented, he sat up.

He was in a wide, rolling meadow of wildflowers and dancing butterflies. A few feet away, a gentle-eyed deer stopped her peaceful walk to study him. There was the lazy drone of bees and the whisper of wind through the high, green grass.

With a half laugh, he rubbed a hand over his chin, half expecting to find a beard like Rip Van Winkle's. But there was no beard, and he didn't feel like an old man. He felt incredible. Standing, he looked out over the acres of flowers and waving grass. Above, the sky was a rich blue bowl, the deep blue of high spring.

Something stirred in him, as gently as the wind stirred the grass. After a moment, he recognized it. Serenity. He was utterly at peace with himself.

He heard the music. The heartbreaking beauty of harp song. The smile was already curving his lips as he followed it, wading through the meadow grass and flowers, startling butterflies.

He found her on the bank of the brook. Sun flashed off the water as it tumbled over smooth, jewel-colored rocks. The full white skirts of her dress pooled over the grass. Her face was shaded by a wide-brimmed hat, tipped flirtatiously over one eye. In her lap was a small golden harp. Her fingers caressed the strings, coaxing out music that floated over the air.

She turned her head, smiled at him, continued to play.

"What are you doing?" he asked her.

"Waiting for you. Did you rest well?"

He crouched beside her, then lifted a hesitant hand to her shoulder. She was real. He could feel the warmth of her skin through the silk. "Morgana?"

Her eyes laughed up at his. "Nash?"

"Where are we?"

She stroked the harp again. Music soared, spreading like the wings of a bird. "In dreams," she told him. "Yours and mine."

After setting the harp aside, she took his hands. "If you want to be here, we can stay a while. If you want to be somewhere else, we can go there."

She made it sound so easy, so natural. "Why?"

"Because you need it." She brought his hand to her lips. "Because I love you."

He didn't feel the scrabble of panic. Her words slid easily into his heart, making him smile. "Is it real?"

She rubbed her cheek over his hand, then kissed it again. "It can be. If you want it." Her teeth grazed lightly over his skin, sparking desire. "If you want me."

He drew the hat from her head, tossing it aside as her hair rained down over her shoulders and back. "Am I spellbound, Morgana?"

"No more than I." She cupped his face in her hands to bring his lips to hers. "I want you," she murmured against his mouth. "Love me here, Nash, as though it were the first time, the last time, the only time."

How could he resist? If it was a dream, so be it. All that mattered was that her arms welcomed him, her mouth tempted him.

She was everything a man could want, all silk and honey, melting against him. Her body seemed boneless as he laid her back on the soft green grass.

There was no time here, and he found himself pleased to linger over little things. The velvet flow of her hair under his hands, the teasing flavors at the corners of her mouth, the scent of her skin along her jaw. She yielded to him, a malleable fantasy of silks and scents and seduction. Her quiet sigh sweetened the air.

He couldn't know how easy it had been, Morgana thought as his mouth drank from hers. As different as they were, their dreams were the same. For this hour, or two, they could share each other, and the peace she had wrapped them in.

When he lifted his head, she smiled at him. His eyes darkened as he traced the shape of her face with a fingertip. "I want it to be real," he said.

"It can be. Whatever you take from here, whatever you want for us, can be."

Testing, he brought his lips to hers again. It was real, as was the feeling that flooded him when those lips parted for his. He sank deep into that long, luxurious melding of lips and tongues. Beneath his, her heart beat fast and true. When his hand covered it, he felt its rhythm leap.

Slowly, wanting to spin out the moment, he unfastened the tiny pearls that ranged down her bodice. Beneath, she was all warm, soft skin. In fascination, he explored the textures as her breath quickened.

Satin and silk. The color of rich cream.

His eyes flicked back to hers as his fingertips skimmed. Through the fringe of dark lashes, her irises had deepened, hazed. Lightly he brushed his lips over the soft slopes of her breasts.

Honey and rose petals.

With a murmur of approval, he teased her flesh with lazy, openmouthed kisses, circling in until he could roll his tongue over the aching peaks. He nipped, knowing by her gasp that he was holding her at that dazzling point between pleasure and pain.

He drew her in, driving them both quietly mad with teeth and tongue. Her hands were in his hair, gripping hard. And he felt her body arch, go taut, then shudder into pliancy. When he lifted his head to look at her, her eyes were glazed with shock and delight.

"How—?" She shivered again, throbbing with the aftermath of that fast, unexpected crest.

"Magic," he said, pressing his lips to her heated flesh again. "Let me show you."

He took her places she'd never seen. As she gloried in each dizzying journey, her hands and lips moved freely over him. When she trembled, so did he.

A mixing of sighs, a melding of bodies. A murmured request, a breathless answer. Fired by need, she pulled his shirt away to taste the hot, damp flesh of his heaving chest.

Where there was fire, there was joy—in feeling his blood leap for her, his pulse quicken.

Within the small slice of paradise she had conjured, they made their own. Each time his mouth came to hers, the spell grew stronger. Possessive, persuasive, her hands streaked over him, and she rejoiced in the way his muscles bunched and quivered at her touch.

He wanted—needed—her to be as desperate as he. With his heart pounding in his ears, he began a torturous journey down her torso, streaking toward the center of her heat. His teeth scraped the sensitive skin of her thigh, dragging a broken moan from her.

Her hands fisted in the grass as his tongue pleasured and plundered. Blind with need, she cried out as he drove her from peak to shattering peak. As her body writhed and arched, he steeped himself in her.

Damp flesh slid over damp flesh as he began the return journey. When his mouth crushed down on hers, he sheathed himself in her. And his vision dimmed as he felt her open for him, surround him, welcome him.

Fighting back the grinding need, he moved slowly, savoring, watching the flickers of pleasure on her face, feeling her pulse throb as she rose to meet him.

The breath sighed out between her lips. Her eyes fluttered open. They stayed on his while her hands slid down his arms. With their fingers locked, they tumbled past reason together.

When she felt his body shatter, when his muscles went to water, he rested his head between her breasts. Lulled by the beat of her heart, he let his eyes close. He began to sense the world beyond Morgana. The warm sun on his back, the call of birds, the scent of flowers growing wild on the banks of the rushing brook.

Beneath him, she sighed and lifted a hand to stroke his hair. She had given him peace, and she had found pleasure. And she had broken one of her firmest rules by manipulating his emotions.

Perhaps it had been a mistake, but she wouldn't regret it.

"Morgana."

She smiled at the husky murmur. "Sleep now," she told him.

In the dark, he reached for her. And found the bed empty. Groggy, he forced his heavy eyes open. He was in bed, his own bed, and the house held the heavy hush of predawn.

"Morgana?" He didn't know why he said her name when he knew she wasn't there.

Dreaming? Fumbling with the sheets, he pushed himself out of bed. Had he been dreaming? If it had been only a dream, nothing in the waking world had ever seemed more real, more vivid, more important.

To clear his head, he walked to the window and breathed deeply of the cool air.

They'd made love—incredible love—in a meadow beside a stream.

No, that was impossible. Leaning on the sill, he gulped in air like water. The last thing he remembered clearly, they had been sitting under the tree in the side yard, talking about—

He jolted back. He'd told her everything. The whole ugly business about his family had come pouring out of him. Why the hell had he done that? Dragging a hand through his hair, he paced the room.

That damned phone call, he thought. But then he recalled abruptly that the phone call had stopped him from making an even bigger mistake.

It would have been worse if he'd told Morgana he loved her—a lot worse than telling her about his parentage and upbringing. At least now she wouldn't get any ideas about where their relationship was headed.

In any case, it was done, and it couldn't be taken back. He'd just have to live with the fact that it embarrassed the hell out of him.

But after that, after they had been sitting in the yard. Had he fallen asleep?

The dream. Or had it been a dream? It was so clear in his mind. He could almost smell the flowers. And he could certainly remember the way her body had flowed like water under his hands. More, much more, he could remember feeling as though everything he had done up to that point in his life had been leading to that moment. To the moment when he could lie on the grass with the woman he loved, and feel the peace of belonging.

Illusions. Just illusions, he assured himself as panic began to set in. He'd just fallen asleep under the tree. That was all.

But what the hell was he doing back in his room, in the middle of the night—alone?

She'd done it. Giving in to unsteady legs, he lowered to the bed. All of it. Then she'd left him.

She wasn't getting away with it. He started to rise, then dropped down again.

He could remember the peace, the utter serenity, of waking with the sun on his face. Of walking through the grass and seeing her playing the harp and smiling at him.

And when he'd asked her why, she'd said...

She'd said she loved him.

Because his head was reeling, Nash clamped it between his hands. Maybe he'd imagined it. All of it. Morgana included. Maybe he was back in his condo in L.A., and he'd just awakened from the granddaddy of all dreams.

After all, he didn't really believe in witches and spells. Gingerly he lowered one hand and closed it around the stone that hung from a chain around his neck.

The hell he didn't.

Morgana was real, and she loved him. The worst part was, he loved her right back.

He didn't want to. It was crazy. But he was in love with her, so wildly in love that he couldn't get through an hour without thinking about her. Without wishing for her. Without imagining that maybe, just maybe, it could work.

And that was the most irrational thought in the whole irrational business.

He needed to think it all through, step by step. Giving in to fatigue, he lay back to stare at the dark.

Infatuated. That was what he was. Infatuation was a long way from love. A long, safe way. She was, after all, a captivating woman. A man could live a long, happy life being infatuated by a captivating woman. He'd wake up every morning with a smile on his face, knowing she belonged to him.

Nash began to weave a pretty fantasy. And brought himself up short.

What the hell was he thinking of?

Her, he thought grimly. He was always thinking of her.

Maybe the best thing to do would be to take a little vacation, a quick trip to anywhere to shake her out of his system.

If he could.

The niggling doubt lay in his gut like a stone.

How did he know, even before he began, that he wouldn't be able to shake her out?

Because it wasn't infatuation, he admitted slowly. It wasn't even close to infatuation. It was the big four-letter word. He wasn't in lust. He'd taken the big leap. He was in love.

She'd made him fall in love with her.

That thought had him sitting straight up. She'd made him.

She was a witch. Why hadn't it ever occurred to him that she could cast her spells, snap her fingers and have him groveling at her feet?

Part of him rejected the notion as absurd. But another part, the part that had grown out of fear and self-doubt, plucked at the idea. The longer he considered it, the darker his thoughts became.

In the morning, he told himself, he was going to face off with a witch. When he was done, he'd clear the decks, and Nash Kirkland would be exactly where he wanted to be.

In control.

Chapter Eleven

It felt odd not going in to open the shop Monday morning. It also felt necessary, not just for her weary body, but also for her mind. A call to Mindy eased Morgana's conscience. Mindy would pick up the slack and open the shop at noon.

It didn't bother her too much to take a day off. But she would have preferred to steal a day when she felt better. Now she walked downstairs wrapped in her robe, feeling light-headed and queasy, with the restless night weighing heavily on her.

The die had been cast. Matters had been taken out of her hands. With a weary sigh, Morgana wandered into the kitchen to brew some tea. It had never really been in her hands. The awkward thing about power, she mused, was that you could never let yourself become so used to wielding it that you forgot there were bigger, more vital powers than your own.

Pressing a gentle hand to her stomach, she walked to the window while the kettle heated. She wondered if she sensed a storm in the air, or if it was merely her own unsettled thoughts. Luna curled in and out of her legs for a moment, then sensed her mistress's mood and padded off.

She hadn't chosen to be in love. She certainly hadn't chosen to have this avalanche of emotion barrel down on her and sweep her away. To have her life changed. It was nothing less than that now.

There was always a choice, of course. And she had made hers. It wouldn't be easy. The most important things rarely were.

Heavy-limbed, she turned to the stove to make the tea. It had barely had time to cool in her cup before she heard the front door open.

"Morgana!"

Resigned, Morgana poured two more cups just as her cousins came into the kitchen. "There." Anastasia shot Sebastian a look as she hurried to Morgana. "I told you she wasn't feeling well."

Morgana kissed her cheek. "I'm fine."

"I said you were fine," Sebastian put in, digging a cookie out of the jar on the counter. "Just grumpy. You were sending out signals loud enough and cranky enough to drag me out of bed."

"Sorry." She offered him a cup. "I guess I didn't want to be alone."

"You're not well," Ana insisted. Before she could probe deeper, Morgana stepped away.

"I had a restless night, and I'm paying for it this morning."

Sebastian sipped his tea. He'd already taken in the pale cheeks and shadowed eyes. And he was getting a flicker of something else, something Morgana was working hard to block. Patient, and always willing to match his will against hers, he settled back.

"Trouble in paradise," he said, just dryly enough to make her eyes flash.

"I can handle my own problems, thanks."

"Don't tease her, Sebastian." Anastasia set a warning hand on his shoulder. "Have you argued with Nash, Morgana?"

"No." She sat. She was too tired not to. "No," she said again. "But it is Nash who worries me. I learned a few things about him yesterday. About his family."

Because she trusted them as much as she loved them, Morgana told them everything, from the call from Leeanne to the moment beneath the cypress. What had happened after that, because it belonged only to her and to Nash, she kept to herself.

"Poor little boy," Anastasia murmured. "How awful to feel unwanted and unloved."

"And unable to love," Morgana added. "Who could blame him for being afraid to trust his feelings?"

"You do."

Her gaze shot up to meet Sebastian's. It was no use cursing him for being so perceptive. Or so right. "Not really blame. It hurts, and it saddens, but I don't blame him for it. I'm just not sure how to love someone who can't, or won't, love me back."

"He needs time," Ana told her.

"I know. I'm trying to figure out how much time I can give him. I made a vow. Not to take more than he wanted to give." Her voice thickened, and she swallowed to clear it. "I won't break it."

Her defenses slipped. Quick as a whip, Sebastian snatched her hand. He looked deep, and then his fingers went lax on hers. "My God, Morgana. You're pregnant."

Furious at the intrusion, and at her own wavering emotions for permitting it, she sprang to her feet. But even as she started to spew at him, she saw the concern and the worry in his eyes.

"Damn it, Sebastian. That's an announcement a woman particularly likes to make for herself."

"Sit down," he ordered, and he would have carried her to a chair himself if Anastasia hadn't waved him off.

"How long?" Ana demanded.

Morgana only sighed. "Since the spring equinox. I've only been sure for a few days."

"Are you well?" Before Morgana could answer, Ana spread a hand over Morgana's belly. "Let me." With her eyes on Morgana's, Anastasia searched. She felt the warm flesh beneath the robe, the throb of pulse, the flow of blood. And the life, not yet formed, sleeping. Her lips curved. "You're fine," she said. "Both of you."

"Just a little sluggish this morning." Morgana laid a hand over hers. "I don't want you to worry."

"I still say she should sit down, or lie down, until her color's back." Sebastian scowled at both of them. The idea of his cousin, his favorite sparring partner, being fragile and with child made him uneasy. With a light laugh, Morgana bent over to kiss him.

"Are you going to fuss over me, Cousin?" Pleased, she kissed him again, then sat. "I hope so."

"With the rest of the family in Ireland, it's up to Ana and me to take care of you."

Morgana murmured an absentminded thank-you as Ana re-filled her cup. "And what makes you think I need to be taken care of?"

Sebastian shrugged the question away. "I'm the eldest here," he reminded her. "And, as such, I want to know what Kirk-land's intentions are."

Ana grinned over her cup. "Lord, Sebastian, how medieval. Do you intend to run him through for trifling with your cousin?"

"I don't find this whole situation quite the hoot you do." His eyes darkened when his cousins rolled theirs. "Let's clear it up, shall we? Morgana, do you want to be pregnant?"

"I am pregnant."

He pressed a hand on hers until she looked at him again. "You know very well what I mean."

Of course she did. She let out another sigh. "I've only had a day or two to think of it, but I have thought of it, carefully. I realize that I can undo what's been done. Without shame. I know the idea upsets you, Ana."

Ana shook her head. "The choice has to be yours."

"Yes, it does. I took precautions against conception. And fate chose to ignore them. I've searched my heart, and I believe I was meant to have the child. This child," she said with a faint curve of the lips. "At this time, and with this man. However unsettled I feel, however afraid I am, I can't shake that belief. So, yes, I want to be pregnant."

Satisfied, Sebastian nodded. "And Nash? How does he feel about it?" He didn't wait for her to speak. It only took a heartbeat for him to know. His voice thundered to the roof. "What in the name of Finn do you mean, you haven't told him?"

Her glare was sharp enough to cut ten men off at the knees. "Keep out of my head, or I swear I'll turn you into a slug."

He merely lifted a brow. "Just answer the question."

"I've only just come to be certain myself." Tossing back her hair, she rose. "And, after yesterday, I couldn't simply drop the news on him."

"He has a right to know," Ana said quietly.

"All right." Her temper bubbled until she clenched her hands into fists. "I'm going to tell him. When I'm ready to tell him. Do you think I want to bind him this way?" It shocked her to feel a tear slip down her cheek. She brushed it away impatiently.

"That's a choice he has to make for himself." Sebastian had already decided that, if Nash chose incorrectly, he would take great pleasure in breaking several vital bones—the conventional way.

"Sebastian's right, Morgana." Concerned but firm, Ana rose again to wrap her arms around her cousin. "It's his choice to make, as it was yours. He can't make it if he doesn't know the choice exists."

"I know." To comfort herself, Morgana laid her head on Ana's shoulder. "I'll go this morning and tell him."

Sebastian rose to stroke a hand down Morgana's hair. "We'll be close."

She was able to smile with a trace of her usual verve. "Not too close."

Nash rolled over in bed and muttered into his pillow. Dreams. He was having so many dreams. They were flitting in and out of his head like movie scenes.

Morgana. Always Morgana, smiling at him, beckoning to him, promising him the incredible, and the wonderful. Making him feel whole and strong and hopeful.

His grandmother, her eyes bright with anger, whacking him with her ubiquitous wooden spoon, telling him over and over again that he was worthless.

Riding a bright red bike down a suburban sidewalk, the wind in his hair and the sound of flipping, flapping baseball cards thrumming in the spokes.

Leeanne, standing close, too close, with her hand out, reminding him that they were blood. That he owed her, owed her, owed her.

Morgana, laughing that wild, wicked laugh, her hair billowing back like a cloud while she streaked over the dark waters of the bay on her broomstick.

Himself, plunged into a steaming cauldron with his grandmother stirring the stew with that damned spoon. And Morgana's voice—his mother's voice?—cackling like one of the Weird Sisters from Shakespeare.

"Double, double, toil and trouble."

He sat up with a jolt, breathing fast and blinking against the streaming sunlight. He lifted shaking hands to his face and rubbed hard.

Great. Just dandy. In addition to everything else, he was losing his mind.

Had she done that to him, as well? he wondered. Had she insinuated herself into his mind to make him think what she wanted him to think? Well, she wasn't going to get away with it.

Nash stumbled out of bed and tripped over his own shoes. Swearing, he kicked them aside and headed blindly for the shower. As soon as he'd pulled himself together, he and the Gorgeous Witch of the West were going to have a little chat.

While Nash was holding his head under the shower, Morgana pulled up in his driveway. She'd come alone. When she'd refused to let Luna accompany her, the cat had stalked off, tail twitching in indignation. Sighing, Morgana promised herself she'd make it up to her. Maybe she'd run by Fisherman's Wharf and pick up a seafood feast to soften the cat's heart.

In the meantime, she had her own heart to worry about.

Tilting down the rearview mirror, she took a careful study of her face. With a sound of disgust, she leaned back. What had made her think she could cover the signs of strain and worry with simple cosmetics?

She pressed her lips together and looked toward his house. She wasn't going to let him see her like this. She wasn't going to go to him with this kind of news when she appeared vulnerable and needy.

He had enough people pulling his strings.

She remembered that she'd once thought he was a completely carefree man. Perhaps, for long periods of time, he was. He'd certainly made himself believe so. If Nash was entitled to his front, then so was she.

After taking a long, soothing breath, Morgana crooned a quiet chant. The shadows vanished from under her eyes, the color crept back into her cheeks. As she stepped out of the car, all signs of a restless night had been erased. If her heart was beating too quickly, she would deal with it. But she would not let him see that she was miserably in love and terrified.

There was an easy smile on her face as she rapped on his door. A slick, sweaty fist was lodged in her gut.

Cursing, Nash jammed one leg then the other into jeans. "Just a damn minute," he mumbled as he yanked them up. He stalked down the steps barefoot and bare chested, all but growling at the thought of a visitor before coffee. "What?" he demanded as he flung open the door. Then he stopped dead, staring.

She looked as fresh and beautiful as the morning. As sultry and sexy as midnight. Nash wondered how it was that the damp still clinging to his skin didn't turn to steam.

"Hi." She leaned in to brush his lips with hers. "Did I get you out of the shower?"

"Just about." Off balance, he slicked his fingers through his dripping hair. "Why aren't you at the shop?"

"I'm taking the day off." She sauntered in, willing herself to keep her voice natural and her muscles relaxed. "Did you sleep well?"

"You should know." At the mild surprise in her eyes, his temper strained. "What did you do to me, Morgana?"

"Do to you? I did nothing *to* you." She made the effort to smile again. "If I'm not mistaken, you're in dire need of coffee. Why don't I fix some?"

He grabbed her arm before she could turn toward the kitchen. "I'll fix it myself."

She measured the anger in his eyes and nodded slowly. "All right. Would you rather I came back later?"

"No. We'll settle this now." When he strode down the hallway, Morgana squeezed her eyes tight.

Settle it, she thought with a vivid premonition of disaster. Why did that phrase sound so much like "end it"? Bracing, she started to follow him into the kitchen, but found her courage fading. Instead, she turned into the living room and sat on the edge of a chair.

He needed his coffee, she told herself. And she needed a moment to regroup.

She hadn't expected to find him so angry, so cold. The way he'd looked when he'd spoken to Leeanne the day before. Nor had she had any idea how much it would hurt to have him look at her with that ice-edged and somehow aloof fury.

She rose to wander the room, one hand placed protectively over the life beginning in her womb. She *would* protect that life, she promised herself. At all costs.

When he came back, a steaming cup in his hand, she was standing by the window. Her eyes looked wistful. If he hadn't known better, he would have said she looked hurt, even vulnerable.

But he did know better. Surely being a witch was the next thing to being invulnerable.

"Your flowers need water," she said to him. "It isn't enough just to plant them." Again her hand lay quietly over her stomach. "They need care."

He gulped down coffee and scalded his tongue. The pain helped block the sudden need to go to her and take her into his arms, to whisk away the sadness he heard in her voice. "I'm not much in the mood to talk about flowers."

"No." She turned, and the traces of vulnerability were gone. "I can see that. What are you in the mood to talk about, Nash?"

"I want the truth. All of it."

She gave him a small, amused smile, turning her palms up questioningly. "Where would you like me to begin?"

"Don't play games with me, Morgana. I'm tired of it." He began to pace the room, his muscles taut enough to snap. His head came up. If she had been fainter of heart, the look in his eyes would have had her stumbling back in defense. "This whole business has been one long lark for you, hasn't it? Right from the beginning, from the minute I walked into your shop, you decided I was a likely candidate." God, it hurt, he realized. It hurt to think of everything he'd felt, everything he'd begun to wish for. "My attitude toward your...talents irritated you, so you just had to strut your stuff."

Her heart quivered in her breast, but her voice was strong. "Why don't you tell me what you mean? If you're saying I showed you what I am, I can't deny it. I can't be ashamed of it."

He slapped the mug down so that coffee sloshed over the sides and onto the table. The sense of betrayal was so huge, it overwhelmed everything. Damn it, he loved her. She'd made him love her. Now that he was calling her on it, she just stood there, looking calm and lovely.

"I want to know what you did to me," he said again. "Then I want you to undo it."

"I told you, I didn't—"

"I want you to look me in the eye." On a wave of panic and fury, he grabbed her arms. "Look me in the eye, Morgana, and tell me you didn't wave your wand or chant your charm and make me feel this way."

"What way?"

"Damn you, I'm in love with you. I can't get through an hour without wanting you. I can't think about a year from now, ten years from now, without seeing you with me."

Her heart melted. "Nash—"

He jerked back from the hand she lifted to his cheek. Stunned, Morgana let it fall back to her side. "How did you do it?" he demanded. "How did you get inside me like this, to make me start thinking of marriage and family? What was the point? To play around with the mortal until you got tired of him?"

"I'm as mortal as you," she said steadily. "I eat and sleep, I bleed when I'm cut. I grow old. I feel."

"You're not like me." He bit off the words. Morgana felt her charm slipping, the color washing out of her cheeks.

"No. You're right. I'm different, and there's nothing I can do to change it. Nothing I would do. If you're finding that too difficult to accept, then let me go."

"You're not going to walk out of here and leave me like this. Fix it." He gave her a brisk shake. "Undo the spell."

The illusion fell away so that she stared at him with shadowed eyes. "What spell?"

"Whatever one you used. You got me to tell you things I've never told anyone. You stripped me bare, Morgana. Didn't you think I'd figure out that I'd never have told you about my family, my background, if I'd been in my right mind? That was mine." He released her, and turned away to keep from doing something drastic. "You tricked it out of me, just like you tricked all the rest. You used my feelings."

"I never used your feelings," she began furiously, then stopped, paling even more.

When he noted the look, his lips thinned. "Really?"

"All right, I used them yesterday. After your mother called, after you'd told me all those things, I wanted to give you some peace of mind."

"So it was a spell."

Though her chin came up, he wavered. She looked so damn fragile just then. Like glass that would shatter at his touch. "I let my emotions rule my judgment. If I was wrong, as it's obvious now I was, I apologize."

"Oh, fine. Sorry I took you for a ride, Nash." He jammed his hands into his pockets. "What about the rest?"

She lifted a shaky hand to her hair. "The rest of what?"

"Are you going to stand there and tell me you didn't cause all of this, manipulate my feelings? Make me think I was in love with you, that I wanted to start a life with you? God, have children with you?" Because he still wanted it, still, his anger grew. "I know damn well it wasn't my idea. No way in hell."

The hurt sliced deep. But, as it cut, it freed something. His anger, his sense of betrayal and confusion, was nothing compared to what bubbled inside her. She reined it in with a light hand as she studied him.

"Are you saying that I bound you to me with magic? That I used my gifts for my own gain, charmed you into loving me?"

"That's just what I'm saying."

Morgana released the reins. Color flooded back into her face, had her eyes gleaming like suns. Power, and the strength it brought, filled her. "You brainless ass."

Indignant, he started to snap back. His words came out like the bray of a donkey. Eyes wide, he tried again while she swooped around the room.

"So you think you're under a spell," she muttered, her fury making books fly through the room like literary missiles. Nash ducked and scrambled, but he didn't manage to avoid all of them. As one rapped the bridge of his nose, he swore. He felt a moment's dizzy relief when he realized he had his own voice back.

"Look, babe—"

"No, you look. *Babe.*" On a roll now, she had a gust of wind tossing his furniture into a heap. "Do you think I'd waste my gifts captivating someone like you? You conceited, arrogant jerk. Give me one reason I shouldn't turn you into the snake you are."

Eyes narrowed, he started toward her. "I'm not going to play along with this."

"Then watch." With a flick of her hand she had him shooting back across the room, two feet above the floor, to land hard in a chair. He thought about getting up, but decided it was wiser to get his breath back first.

To satisfy herself, she sent the dishes soaring in the kitchen. Nash listened to the crashing with a resigned sigh.

"You should know better than to anger a witch," she told him. The logs in his fireplace began to spit and crackle with flame. "Don't you know what someone like me, someone without integrity, without scruples, might do?"

"All right, Morgana." He started to rise. She slapped him back in the chair so hard his teeth rattled.

"Don't come near me, not now, not ever again." Her breath was heaving, though she was struggling to even it. "I swear, if you do, I'll turn you into something that runs on four legs and howls at the moon."

He let out an uneasy breath. He didn't think she'd do it. Not really. And it was better to take a stand than to whimper. His living room was a shambles. Hell, his life was a shambles. They were going to have to deal with it.

"Cut it out, Morgana." His voice was admirably calm and firm. "This isn't proving anything."

The fury drained out of her, leaving her empty and aching and miserable. "You're quite right. It isn't. My temper, like my feelings, sometimes clouds my judgment. No." She waved a hand before he could rise. "Stay where you are. I can't trust myself yet."

As she turned away, the fire guttered out. The wind died. Quietly Nash breathed a sigh of relief. The storm, it appeared, was over.

He was very wrong.

"So you don't want to be in love with me."

Something in her voice had his brows drawing together. He wanted her to turn around so that he could see her face, but she stood with her back to him, looking out the window.

"I don't want to be in love with anyone," he said carefully, willing himself to believe it. "Nothing personal."

"Nothing personal," she repeated.

"Look, Morgana, I'm a bad bet. I like my life the way it was."

"The way it was before you met me."

When she said it like that, he felt like something slimy that slithered through the grass. He checked his hands to make certain he wasn't. "It's not you, it's me. And I... Damn it, I'm not going to sit here and apologize because I don't like being spellbound." He got to his feet gingerly. "You're a beautiful woman, and—"

"Oh, please. Don't strain yourself with a clever brush-off." The words choked out of her as she turned.

Nash felt as though she'd stuck a lance in his heart. She was crying. Tears were streaming out of her brimming eyes and flowing down her pale cheeks. There was nothing, nothing, he wanted more at that moment than to take her in his arms and kiss them away.

"Morgana, don't. I never meant to—" His words were cut

off as he rapped into a wall. He couldn't see it, but she'd thrown it up between them, and it was as solid as bricks and mortar. "Stop it." His voice rose on a combination of panic and self-disgust as he rammed a hand against the shield that separated them. "This isn't the answer."

Her heart was bleeding. She could feel it. "It'll do until I find the right one." She wanted to hate him, desperately wanted to hate him for making her humiliate herself. As the tears continued to fall, she laid both hands on her stomach. She had more than herself to protect.

He spread his own impotent hands against the wall. Odd, he thought, he felt as though it was he who had been closed off, not her. "I can't stand to see you cry."

"You'll have to for a moment. Don't worry, a witch's tears are like any woman's. Weak and useless." She steadied herself, blinking them away until she could see clearly. "You want your freedom, Nash?"

If he could have, he'd have clawed and kicked his way through to her. "Damn it, can't you see I don't know what I want?"

"Whatever it is, it isn't me. Or what we've made together. I promised I wouldn't take more than you wanted to give me. And I never go back on my word."

He felt a new kind of fear, a rippling panic at the thought that what he did want was about to slip through his fingers. "Let me touch you."

"If you thought of me as a woman first, I would." For herself, she laid a hand on the wall opposite his. "Do you think, because of what I am, that I don't need to be loved as any man loves any woman?"

He shoved and strained against the wall. "Take this damn thing down."

It was all she had—a poor defense. "We crossed purposes somewhere along the line, Nash. No one's fault, I suppose, that I came to love you so much."

"Morgana, please."

She shook her head, studying him, drawing his image inside her head, her heart, where she could keep it. "Maybe, because I did, I somehow drew you in. I've never been in love before, so I can't be sure. But I swear to you, it wasn't intentional, it wasn't done to harm."

Furious that the tears were threatening again, she backed away. For a moment she stood—straight, proud, powerful.

"I'll give you this, and you can trust what I say. Whatever hold I have on you is broken, as of this instant. Whatever feelings I've caused in you through my art, I cast away. You're free of me, and of all we made."

She closed her eyes, lifted her hands. "Love conjured is love false. I will not take, nor will I make. Such cast away is nothing lost. Your heart and mind be free of me. As I will, so mote it be."

Her eyes opened, glittered with fresh tears. "You are more than you think," she said quietly. "Less than you could be."

His heart was thudding in his throat. "Morgana, don't go like this."

She smiled. "Oh, I think I'm entitled to at least a dramatic exit, don't you?" Though she was several feet away, he would have sworn he felt her lips touch him. "Blessed be, Nash," she said. And then she was gone.

Chapter Twelve

He had no doubt he was going out of his mind. Day after day he prowled the house and the grounds. Night after night he tossed restlessly in bed.

She'd said he was free of her, hadn't she? Then why wasn't he?

Why hadn't he stopped thinking about her, wishing for her? Why could he still see the way she had looked at him that last time, with hurt in her eyes and tears on her cheeks?

He tried to tell himself she'd left him charmed. But he knew it was a lie.

After a week, he gave up and drove by her house. It was empty. He went to the shop and was told by a very cool and unfriendly Mindy that Morgana was away. But she wouldn't tell him where, or when she would be back.

He should have felt relief. That was what he told himself. Doggedly he pushed thoughts of her aside and picked up the life he'd led before her.

But when he walked the beach, he imagined what it would be like to stroll there with her, a toddler scampering between them.

That image sent him driving down to L.A. for a few days.

He wanted to think he felt better there, with the rush and the crowds and the noise. He took a lunch with his agent at the Polo Lounge and discussed the casting for his screenplay. He went alone to clubs and fed himself on music and laughter. And he wondered if he'd made a mistake in moving north. Maybe he belonged in the heart of the city, surrounded by strangers and distractions.

But, after three days, his heart yearned for home, for the rustle of wind and the whoosh of water. And for her.

He went back to the shop, interrogating Mindy ruthlessly enough to have customers backing off and murmuring. She wouldn't budge.

At his wits' end, he took to parking in her driveway and brooding at her house. It had been nearly a month, and he comforted himself with the thought that she had to come back sometime. Her home was here, her business.

Damn it, he was here, waiting for her.

As the sun set, he braced his elbows on the steering wheel and rested his head in his hands. That was just what he was doing, he admitted. Waiting for her. And he wasn't waiting to have a rational conversation, as he'd tried to convince himself he was over the past weeks.

He was waiting to beg, to promise, to fight, to do whatever it took to put things right again. To put Morgana back in his life again.

He closed his hand over the stones he still wore around his neck and wondered if he could will her back. It was worth a shot. A better idea than putting an ad in the personals, he thought grimly. Shutting his eyes, he focused all his concentration on her.

"Damn it, I know you can hear me if you want to. You're not going to shut me out this way. You're not. Just because I was an idiot is no reason to…"

He felt a presence, actually felt it. He opened his eyes cautiously, turned his head and looked up into Sebastian's amused face.

"What is this?" Sebastian mused. "Amateur night?"

Before he could think, Nash was shoving the car door open. "Where is she?" he demanded, taking Sebastian's shirt in his fists. "You know, and one way or the other you're going to tell me."

Sebastian's eyes darkened dangerously. "Careful, friend. I've been wanting to go one-on-one with you for weeks."

The notion of a good, nasty fight appealed to Nash enormously. "Then we'll just—"

"Behave," Anastasia commanded. "Both of you." With delicate hands, she pushed the men apart. "I'm sure you'd enjoy giving each other bloody noses and black eyes, but I'm not going to tolerate it."

Nash fisted his frustrated hands at his sides. "I want to know where she is."

With a shrug, Sebastian leaned on the hood of the car. "Your wants don't carry much weight around here." He crossed his feet at the ankles when Anastasia stepped between them again. "You're looking a little ragged around the edges, Nash, old boy." And it pleased him no end. "Conscience stabbing at you?"

"Sebastian." Ana's quiet voice held both censure and compassion. "Don't snipe. Can't you see he's unhappy?"

"My heart bleeds."

Ana laid a hand on Nash's arm. "And that he's in love with her?"

Sebastian's response was a short laugh. "Don't let the hangdog look twist your feelings, Ana."

She shot Sebastian an impatient glare. "For heaven's sake, you only have to look."

Reluctantly, he did. As his eyes darkened, he clamped a hand on Nash's shoulder. Before Nash could shrug it angrily away, Sebastian laughed again. "By all that's holy, he is." He shook his head at Nash. "Why the devil did you make such a mess of it?"

"I don't have to explain myself to you," Nash muttered. Absently he rubbed a hand over his shoulder. It felt as though it had been sunburned. "What I have to say, I'll say to Morgana."

Sebastian was softening, but he didn't see any reason to make it easy. "I believe she's under the impression that you've already had your say. I don't know that she's in any condition to listen to your outrageous accusations again."

"Condition?" Nash's heart froze. "Is she sick?" He grabbed Sebastian by the shirtfront again, but the strength had left his hands. "What's wrong with her?"

A look passed between the cousins, so brief, so subtle, that it went unnoticed. "She's not ill," Ana said, and tried not to be furious with Morgana for not telling Nash about the child. "In fact, she's quite well. Sebastian meant that she was upset by what happened between you the last time."

Nash's fingers loosened. When he had his breath back, he nodded. "All right, you want me to beg. I'll beg. I have to see her. If after I've finished crawling she boots me out of her life, I'll live with it."

"She's in Ireland," Ana told him. "With our family." Her smile curved beautifully. "Do you have a passport?"

Morgana was glad she'd come. The air in Ireland was soothing, whether it was the balmy breeze that rolled down from the hills or the wild wind that whipped across the channel.

Though she knew it would soon be time to go back and pick up her life again, she was grateful for the weeks she'd had to heal.

And for her family.

Stretched out on the window seat in her mother's sitting room, she was as much at home, and at peace, as she could be anywhere in the world. She felt the sun on her face, that luminous sun that seemed to belong only to Ireland. If she looked through the diamond panes of glass, she could see the cliffs that hacked their way down to the rugged beach. And the beach, narrow and rough, stretching out to the waves. By changing the angle, she could see the terraced lawn, the green, green grass scattered with a profusion of flowers that stirred in the wind.

Across the room, her mother sat sketching. It was a cozy moment, one that reminded Morgana sweetly of childhood. And her mother had changed so little in the years between.

Her hair was as dark and thick as her daughter's, though she wore it short and sleek around her face. Her skin was smooth, with the beautiful luster of her Irish heritage. The cobalt eyes were often dreamier than Morgana's, but they saw as clearly.

When Morgana looked at her, she was washed by an intense flood of love. "You're so beautiful, Mother."

Bryna glanced up, smiled. "I won't argue, since it feels so good to hear that from a grown daughter." Her voice carried the charming lilt of her homeland. "Do you know how wonderful it is to have you here, darling, for all of us?"

Morgana raised a knee and linked her hands around it. "I know how good it's been for me. And how grateful I am you haven't asked me all the questions I know you want to."

"And so you should be. I've all but had to strike your father mute to keep him from badgering you." Her eyes softened. "He adores you so."

"I know." Morgana felt weak tears fill her eyes again, and she tried to blink them away. "I'm sorry. My moods." With a shake of her head, she rose. "I don't seem to be able to control them."

"Darling." Bryna held out both hands, waiting until Morgana had crossed the room to link hers with them. "You know you can tell me anything, anything at all. When you're ready."

"Mother." Seeking comfort, Morgana knelt down to rest her head in Bryna's lap. She gave a watery smile as her hair was stroked. "I've come to realize recently how very lucky I am to have had you, all of you. To love me, to want me, to care about what happens to me. I haven't told you before how grateful I am for you."

Puzzled, Bryna cradled her daughter. "Families are meant to love and want and care."

"But all families don't." Morgana lifted her head, her eyes dry now and intense. "Do they?"

"The loss is theirs. What's hurting you, Morgana?"

She gripped her mother's hands again. "I've thought about how it must feel not to be wanted or loved. To be taught from childhood that you were a mistake, a burden, something only to be tolerated through duty. Can anything be colder than that?"

"No. Nothing's colder than living without love." Her tone gentled. "Are you in love?"

She didn't have to answer. "He's been hurt so, you see. He never had what you, what all of you, gave me, what I took for granted. And, despite it all, he's made himself into a wonderful man. Oh, you'd like him." She rested her cheek on her mother's palm. "He's funny and sweet. His mind is so, well, fluid. So ready to test new ideas. But there's a part of him that's closed off. He didn't do it, it was done to him. And, no matter what my powers, I can't break that lock." She sat back on her heels. "He doesn't want to love me, and I can't—won't—take what he doesn't want to give."

"No." Bryna's heart broke a little as she looked at her daughter. "You're too strong, too proud, and too wise for that. But people change, Morgana. In time…"

"There isn't time. I'll have his child by Christmas."

All the soothing words Bryna had prepared slipped away down her throat. All she could think was that her baby was carrying a baby. "Are you well?" she managed.

Morgana smiled, pleased that this should be the first question. "Yes."

"And certain?"

"Very certain."

"Oh, love." Bryna rose to her feet to rock Morgana against her. "My little girl."

"I won't be little much longer."

They laughed together as they broke apart. "I'm happy for you. And sad."

"I know. I want the child. Believe me, no child has ever been wanted so much. Not only because it's all I might ever have of the father, but for itself."

"And you feel?"

"Odd," Morgana said. "Strong one moment, terrifyingly fragile the next. Not ill, but sometimes light-headed."

Understanding, Bryna nodded. "And you say the father is a good man."

"Yes, he's a good man."

"Then, when you told him, he was just surprised, unprepared…" She noted the way Morgana glanced away. "Morgana, even when you were a child you would stare past my shoulder when you were preparing to evade."

Wincing at the tone, Morgana met her mother's eyes again. "I didn't tell him. Don't," she pleaded before Bryna could launch into a lecture. "I had intended to, but it all fell apart. I know it was wrong not to tell him, but it was just as wrong to hold him to me by the telling. I made a choice."

"The wrong choice."

Morgana's chin angled as her mother's had. "My choice, right or wrong. I won't ask you to approve, but I will ask you to respect. And I'll also ask you not to tell anyone else just yet. Including Father."

"Including Father what?" Matthew demanded as he strode into the room, the wolf that was Pan's sire close at his heels.

"Girl talk," Morgana said smoothly and moved over to kiss his cheeks. "Hello, handsome."

He tweaked her nose. "I know when my women are keeping secrets."

"No peeking," Morgana said, knowing Matthew was nearly

as skilled at reading thoughts as Sebastian. "Now, where's everyone else?"

He wasn't satisfied, but he was patient. If she didn't tell him soon, he would look for himself. He was, after all, her father.

"Douglas and Maureen are in the kitchen, arguing over who's fixing what for lunch. Camilla's rousting Padrick at gin." Matthew grinned, wickedly. "And he's not taking it well. Accused her of charming the cards."

Bryna managed a smile of her own. "And did she?"

"Of course." Matthew stroked the wolf's silver fur. "Your sister's a born cheat."

Bryna sent him a mild look. "Your brother's a poor loser."

Morgana laughed and linked arms with them both. "And how the six of you managed to live in this place together and not be struck by lightning is a mystery to me. Let's go down and make some more trouble."

There was nothing like a group meal with the Donovans to lift her mood. And a mood lift was precisely what Morgana needed. Watching with affection the squabbling, the interplay between siblings and spouses, was better than front-row seats at a three-ring circus.

She was well aware that they didn't always get along. Just as she was aware that, whatever the friction, they would merge together like sun and light in the face of a family crisis.

She didn't intend to be a crisis. She only wanted to spend some time being with them.

They might have been two sets of triplets, but there was little physical resemblance between the siblings. Her father was tall and lean, with a shock of steel-gray hair and a dignified bearing. Padrick, Anastasia's father, stood no higher than Morgana, with the husky build of a boxer and the heart of a prankster. Douglas was nearly six-four, with a receding hairline that swept back dramatically into a widow's peak. Eccentricity was his hobby.

At the moment, he was sporting a magnifying glass around his neck that he peered through when the whim took him.

He'd only removed his deerstalker hat and cape because his wife, Camilla, had refused to eat with him otherwise.

Camilla, often thought of as the baby of the brood, was pretty and plump as a pigeon, and she had a will of iron. She matched her husband's eccentricities with her own. This morning, she was trying out a new hairstyle of blazing orange curls that corkscrewed around her head. A long eagle feather dangled from one ear.

Maureen, as skilled a medium as Morgana had ever known, was tall and stately and had an infectious, bawdy laugh that could rattle the rafters.

Together with Morgana's serene mother and dignified father, they made a motley crew. Witches all. As she listened to them bicker around her, Morgana was nearly swamped with love.

"Your cat's been climbing the curtains in my room again," Camilla told Maureen with a wave of her fork.

"Pooh." Maureen shrugged her sturdy shoulders. "Just hunting mice, that's all."

Camilla's massive curls jiggled. "You know very well there's not a mouse in this house. Douglas cast them out."

"And did a half-baked job," Matthew muttered.

"Half-baked." Camilla huffed in her husband's defense. "The only thing half-baked is this pie."

"Aye, and Doug made that, as well," Padrick interjected and grinned. "But I like my apples crunchy."

"It's a new recipe." Douglas peered owlishly through his magnifying glass. "Healthy."

"The cat," Camilla insisted, knowing very well she'd lose control of the conversation.

"Cat's healthy as a horse," Padrick said cheerfully. "Isn't that right, lamb chop?" He sent his wife a lusty wink. Maureen responded with an equally lusty giggle.

"I don't give a tinker's damn about the cat's health," Camilla began.

"Oh, now, now..." Douglas patted her chubby hand. "We don't want a sick cat around, do we? Reenie will brew him up a nice remedy."

"The cat's not sick," Camilla said in a strangled voice. "Douglas, for heaven's sake, keep up."

"Keep up with what?" he demanded, indignant. "If the cat's not sick, what in Finn's name is the problem? Morgana, lass, you're not eating your pie."

She was too busy grinning. "It's wonderful, Douglas. I'm saving it." She sprang up, dancing around the table to smack kisses on every cheek. "I love you, all of you."

"Morgana," Bryna called as her daughter spun out of the room. "Where are you going?"

"For a walk on the beach. For a long, long walk on the beach."

Douglas scowled through his glass. "Girl's acting odd," he pronounced. Since the meal was nearly over, he plucked up his hat and dropped it on his head. "Don't you think?"

Nash was feeling odd. Perhaps it had something to do with the fact that he hadn't slept in two days. Traveling steadily for approximately twenty hours in planes, trains, cabs and shuttle buses might have contributed to the dazed, dreamlike state he was currently enjoying. Still, he'd managed to get from the West Coast to the East, to catch another plane in New York and snatch a little twilight sleep crossing the Atlantic. Then there'd been the train south from Dublin and a frantic search for a car he could buy, rent or steal to carry him the last jarring miles from Waterford to Castle Donovan.

He knew it was important to stay on the right side of the road. Or rather the wrong side. He wondered why the devil it should matter, when the rutted, ditch-lined dirt track he was currently bouncing along couldn't remotely be considered a road of any kind.

And the car, which he'd managed to procure for the equivalent of twelve hundred American dollars—nobody could say the Irish weren't shrewd bargainers—was threatening to break apart on him at every bump. He'd already lost the poor excuse for a muffler, and was making enough noise to wake the sleeping dead.

It wasn't that the land didn't have style and grace, with its towering cliffs and its lush green fields. It was that he was afraid he'd end up staggering up the final hill with nothing but a steering wheel in his hands.

Those were the Knockmealdown Mountains to the west. He knew because the same slippery horse trader who'd sold him the car had been expansive enough to offer directions. The mountains to the west, St. George's Channel to the east, and you'll trip right over the Donovans before teatime.

Nash was beginning to believe he'd find himself buried in a peat bog before teatime.

"If I live," Nash mumbled. "If I find her and I live, I'm going to kill her. Slowly," he said with relish, "so she knows I mean it."

Then he was going to carry her off to some dark, quiet place and make love with her for a week. Then he was going to sleep for a week, wake up and start all over again.

If, he reminded himself, he lived.

The car sputtered and bucked and jolted his bones. He wondered how many of his internal organs had been shifted. Gritting his teeth, Nash cursed and cajoled and threatened the stuttering car up a rise. When his mouth fell open, he slammed on the brakes. The act managed to slow his descent. As he slid down the hill, he didn't notice the smell of rubber burning, or see the smoke beginning to pour out of the hood.

His eyes were all for the castle.

He hadn't really expected a castle, despite the name. But this was the real McCoy, perched high on the cliffs, facing the arrogant sea. Gray stone glittered in the sun, with flashing chips of quartz and mica. Towers lanced into the pearly sky. From the topmost, a white flag flew. Nash saw with awe and amazement that it was a pentagram.

He blinked his eyes, but the structure remained, as fanciful as something from one of his movies. If a mounted knight had burst across the drawbridge—by God, there *was* a drawbridge—Nash wouldn't have turned a hair.

He started to laugh, as delighted as he had been stunned. Recklessly, he punched the gas, and when the steering locked, drove straight into a ditch.

Calling up every oath he knew, Nash climbed out of what was left of the car. Then he kicked it and watched the rusted fender clatter off.

He squinted against the sun and judged that he was about to add a good three-mile hike to his travel arrangements. Resigned, he snagged his duffel bag out of the rear seat and started to walk.

When he saw the white horse gallop across the bridge, he set himself to the task of deciding whether he was hallucinating or whether it was real. Though the horseman wasn't wearing armor, he was striking—lean and masculine with a waving silver mane. And Nash was not surprised to note the hawk clamped to the leather glove of his left arm.

Matthew took one look at the man staggering up the road and shook his head. "Pitiful. Aye, Ulysses, pitiful. Wouldn't even make you a decent meal." The hawk merely blinked in agreement.

At first glimpse, Matthew saw a disheveled, unshaven, bleary-eyed man with a knot forming on his forehead and a line of blood trickling down his temple.

Since he'd seen the fool drive into the ditch, he felt honor-bound to set him right again. He pulled up his mount and stared haughtily down at Nash.

"Lost, are you, lad?"

"No. I know just where I'm going. There." He lifted a hand and gestured.

Matthew lifted a brow. "Castle Donovan? Don't you know the place is lousy with witches?"

"Yeah. That's just why I'm going."

Matthew shifted in the saddle to reassess the man. He might be disheveled, but he wasn't a vagrant. His eyes might be bleary with fatigue, but there was a steely glint of determination behind them.

"If you'll pardon my saying so," Matthew continued, "you don't look to be in any shape to battle witches at the moment."

"Just one," Nash said between his teeth. "Just one particular witch."

"Hmm. Did you know you're bleeding?"

"Where?" Nash lifted a hand gingerly, looked at his smeared fingers in disgust. "Figures. She probably cursed the car."

"And who might you be speaking of?"

"Morgana. Morgana Donovan." Nash wiped his fingers on his grimy jeans. "I've come a long way to get my hands on her."

"Mind your step," Matthew said mildly. "It's my daughter you're speaking of."

Tired, aching, and at the end of his tether, Nash stared back into the slate-gray eyes. Maybe he'd find himself turned into a squashed beetle, but he was taking his stand.

"My name's Kirkland, Mr. Donovan. I've come for your daughter. And that's that."

"Is it?" Amused, Matthew tilted his head. "Well, then, climb up and we'll go see about that." He sent the hawk soaring, then offered his gloved hand. "It's pleased I am to meet you, Kirkland."

"Yeah." Nash winced as he hauled himself onto the horse. "Likewise."

The journey took less time on horseback than it would have on foot—particularly since Matthew shot off at a gallop. The moment they were across the drawbridge and into the court-yard, a tall, dark-haired woman rushed out of a doorway.

Grinding his teeth, Nash jumped down and started toward her. "You've got a lot to answer for, babe. You cut your hair. What the hell do you—" He skidded to a halt as the woman stood her ground, watching him with bemused eyes. "I thought you were... I'm sorry."

"I'm flattered," Bryna countered. With a laugh, she looked toward her husband. "Matthew, what have you brought me?"

"A young man who drove into a ditch and seems to want Morgana."

Bryna's eyes sharpened as she took another step toward Nash. "And do you? Want my daughter?"

"I... Yes, ma'am."

A smile flirted around her lips. "And did she make you un-happy?"

"Yes— No." He let out a heavy sigh. "I did that all by my-self. Please, is she here?"

"Come inside." Bryna gently took his arm. "I'll fix your head, then send you to her."

"If you could just—" He broke off when he saw a huge eye peering at him from the doorway. Douglas dropped his mag-nifying glass and stepped out of the shadows.

"Who the devil is this?"

"A friend of Morgana's," Bryna told him, nudging Nash in-side.

"Ah. The girl's acting odd," Douglas said, giving Nash a hearty clap on the back. "Let me tell you."

Morgana let the brisk, chill wind slap her face and sneak through the heavy knit of her sweater. It was so cleansing, so healing. In a few more days, she would be ready to go back and face reality again.

With a small, helpless sound, she sat on a rock. Here, alone, she could admit it. Had to admit it. She would never be healed. She would never be whole. She would go on and make a good life for herself and the child, because she was strong, because she was proud. But something would always be missing.

But she was through with tears, through with self-pity. Ireland had done that for her. She'd needed to come here, to walk this beach and remember that nothing, no matter how painful, lasts forever.

Except love.

Rising, she started back, watching the water spray on rocks. She would brew some tea, perhaps read Camilla's tarot cards or listen to one of Padrick's long, involved stories. Then she would tell them, as she should have told them all along, about the baby.

And, being her family, they would stand behind her.

How sorry she was that Nash would never experience that kind of union.

She sensed him before she saw him. But she thought her mind was playing tricks on her, teasing her because she was pretending to be so fearless. Very slowly, her pulse hammering in a hundred places, she turned.

He was coming down the beach, in long, hurried strides. The spray had showered his hair, and droplets of water were gleaming on it. His face was shadowed with a two-day beard, and there was a neat white bandage at his temple. And a look in his eyes that had her heart screaming into her throat.

In defense, she took a step back. The action stopped him cold.

She looked... The way she looked at him. Oh, her eyes were dry. There were no tears to tear up his gut. But there was a glint in them. As if—as if she was afraid of him. How much easier it would have been if she'd leapt at him, clawing and scratching and cursing.

"Morgana."

Giddy, she pressed a hand over the secret she held inside. "What happened to you? You're hurt?"

"It's…" He touched his fingers to the bandage. "Nothing. Really. I had a car fall apart on me. Your mother put something on it. On my head, I mean."

"My mother?" Her gaze flickered over his shoulder, toward the towers of the castle. "You've seen my mother?"

"And the rest of them." He managed a quick smile. "They're…something. Actually, I ditched the car a couple of miles from the castle. Literally. That's how I met your father." He knew he was babbling, but he couldn't stop. "Then they were taking me in the kitchen and pouring tea into me and… Hell, Morgana, I didn't know where you were. I should have. You told me you came to Ireland to walk the beach. I should have known. I should have known a lot of things."

She braced a hand on the rock for balance. She was deathly afraid she was about to have a new experience and faint at his feet. "You've come a long way," she said dully.

"I would have been here sooner, but— Hey." He jumped forward as she swayed. The shock came first, that she felt so frighteningly fragile in his arms.

But her arms were strong enough as she pushed at him. "Don't."

Ignoring her, Nash pulled her close and buried his face in her hair. He drew in her scent like breath. "God, Morgana, just give me a minute. Let me hold you."

She shook her head, but her arms, her treacherous arms, were already wrapping hard around him. Her moan was not of protest, but of need, when his mouth rushed to hers and took. He sank into her like a parched man into a clear, cool lake.

"Don't say anything," he murmured as he rained kisses over her face. "Don't say anything until I've told you what I have to tell you."

Remembering what he had told her before, she struggled against him. "I can't go through this again, Nash. I won't."

"No." He caught her hands by the wrists, his eyes burning into hers. "No walls this time, Morgana. On either side. Your word."

She opened her mouth to refuse, but there was something in his eyes she was powerless against. "You have it," she said briefly. "I want to sit down."

"Okay." He let her go, thinking it might be best if he wasn't touching her while he was struggling to fight his way clear of the morass he'd made of things. When she sat on the rock, folded her hands in her lap and lifted her chin, he remembered he'd given serious thought to murdering her.

"No matter how bad things were, you shouldn't have run away."

Her eyes widened and gleamed. "I?"

"Yes, you," he shot back. "Maybe I was an idiot, but that's no reason for making me suffer the way you did when you weren't there when I came to my senses."

"So, it's my fault."

"That I've been going out of my mind for the last month? Yeah, it is." He blew out a breath between his teeth. "Everything else, all the rest of it's on my head." He took a chance and touched a hand to her cheek. "I'm sorry."

She had to look away or weep. "I can't accept your apology until I know what it's for."

"I knew you'd make me crawl," he said in disgust. "Fine, then, I'm sorry for all the stupid things I said."

Her lips curved a little. "All of them?"

Out of patience now, he hauled her back to her feet. "Look at me, damn it, I want you to look at me when I tell you I love you. That I know it has nothing to do with charms or spells, that it never did. That all it has to do with is you, and me."

When she closed her eyes, he felt panic skitter up his spine.

"Don't shut me out, Morgana. I know that's what I did to you. I know it was stupid. I was scared. Hell, I was terrified. Please." He cupped her face in his hands. "Open your eyes and look at me." When she did, he let out a shudder of relief. He could see it wasn't too late. "This is a first for me," he said carefully. "First I have to ask you to forgive me for the things I said. I can tell you that I didn't mean them, that I was just using them to push you away, but that's not the point. I did say them."

"I understand being afraid." She touched her hand to his wrist. "If it's forgiveness you want, you have it. There's no need to hold it back from you."

"Just like that?" He pressed his lips to her brow, her cheeks. "You don't want to maybe turn me into a flounder for three or four years?"

"Not for a first offense." She drew back, praying they could find some light and friendly plane to walk on for a little while. "You've had a long trip, and you're tired. Why don't we go back in? The wind's picking up, and it's nearly teatime."

"Morgana." He held her still. "I said I loved you. I've never said that to anyone before. Not to anyone in my life before you. It was hard the first time, but I think it might get easier as we go."

She looked away again. Her mother would have recognized it as evasion. Nash saw it as dismissal. "You said you loved me." His voice tightened, and so did his grip.

"Yes, I did." She met his eyes again. "And I do."

He gathered her close again to rest his brow on hers. "It feels good," he said in a wondering voice. "I didn't know how damn good it would feel to love someone, to have her love me back. We can go from here, Morgana. I know I'm not a prize, and I'll probably mess up. I'm not used to having someone there for me. Or for being there for someone else. But I'll give it all I've got. That's a promise."

She went very still. "What are you saying?"

He stepped back, nervous all over again, and stuck his hands in his pockets. "I'm asking you to marry me. Sort of."

"Sort of?"

He swore. "Look, I want you to marry me. I'm not doing a good job of asking. If you want to wait until I've set the stage, gotten down on one knee with a ring in my pocket, okay. It's just… I love you so much, and I didn't know I could feel this way, be this way. I want a chance to show you."

"I don't need a stage, Nash. And I wish it could be simple."

His fingers clenched. "You don't want to marry me."

"I want a life with you. Oh, yes, I want that very much. But it isn't only myself you'd be taking."

For a moment, he was baffled. Then his face cleared with a smile. "You mean your family, and the, ah, Donovan legacy. Babe, you're everything I want, and more. The fact that the woman I love is a witch just adds some interest to the situation."

Touched, she lifted a hand to his cheek. "Nash, you're perfect. Absolutely perfect for me. But it's not only that you'd be taking on." Her eyes stayed level on his. "I'm carrying your child."

His face went utterly blank. "What?"

She didn't need to repeat it. She watched as he staggered back and dropped onto the rock where she had sat earlier.

He gulped in air before he managed to speak again. "A baby? You're pregnant? You're having a child?"

Outwardly calm, she nodded. "That about sums it up." She gave him a moment to speak. When he didn't, she forced herself to go on. "You were very clear about not wanting a family, so I realize this changes things, and…"

"You knew." He had to swallow to make his voice rise above the sound of wind and sea. "That day, the last day, you knew. You'd come to tell me."

"Yes, I knew. I'd come to tell you."

On unsteady legs, he got up to walk to the verge of the

water. He remembered the way she'd looked, the things he'd said. He'd remember for a long time. Was it any wonder she'd left him that way, keeping the secret inside her?

"You think I don't want the baby?"

Morgana moistened her lips. "I understand you'd have doubts. This wasn't planned by either of us." She stopped, appalled. "I didn't plan it."

Eyes fierce, he whipped back to her. "I don't often make the same mistake twice, and certainly not with you. When?"

She folded her hands over her belly. "Before Christmas. The child was conceived that first night, on the spring equinox."

"Christmas," he repeated. And thought of a red bike, of cookies baking, of laughter and a family that had nearly been his. A family that could be his. She was offering something he'd never had, something he'd wished for only in secret.

"You said I was free," he said carefully. "Free of you, and everything we'd made together. You meant the baby."

Her eyes darkened, and her voice was strong and beautiful. "This child is loved, is wanted. This child is not a mistake, but a gift. I would rather it be mine alone than to risk that for one instant of its life it would not feel cherished."

He wasn't sure he could speak at all, but when he did, the words came straight from the heart. "I want the baby, and you, and everything we made together."

Through a mist of tears she studied him. "Then you have only to ask."

He walked back to her, laid his hand over where hers rested. "Give me a chance" was all he said.

Her lips curved when his moved to meet them. "We've been waiting for you a long time."

"I'm going to be a father." He said it slowly, testingly, then let out a whoop and scooped her off her feet. "We made a baby."

She threw her arms around his neck and laughed. "Yes."

"We're a family."

"Yes."

He kissed her long and hard before he began to walk. "If we do a good job with the first, we can have more, right?"

"Absolutely. Where are we going?"

"I'm taking you back and putting you to bed. With me."

"Sounds like a delightful idea, but you don't have to carry me."

"Every bloody step. You're having a baby. My baby. I can see it. Interior scene, day. A sunny room with pale blue walls."

"Yellow."

"Okay. With bright yellow walls. Under the window stands a gleaming antique crib, with one of those funny mobiles hanging over it. There's a sound of gurgling, and a tiny, pudgy hand lifts up to grab at one of the circling…" He stopped, his face whipping around to Morgana's. "Oh, boy."

"What? What is it?"

"It just hit me. What are the chances? I mean how likely is it that the baby will, you know, inherit your talent?"

Smiling, she curled a lock of his hair around her finger. "You mean, what are the chances of the baby being a witch? Very high. The Donovan genes are very strong." Chuckling, she nuzzled his neck. "But I bet she has your eyes."

"Yeah." He took another step and found himself grinning. "I bet she does."

★ ★ ★ ★ ★